A PYRAMID LAKE STORY
BELOW THE SURFACE

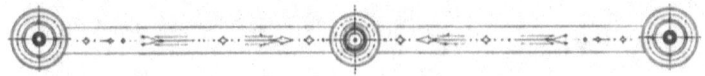

A PYRAMID LAKE STORY
BELOW THE SURFACE

There is a secret hidden deep underneath Pyramid Lake

RICARDO L. OGDON

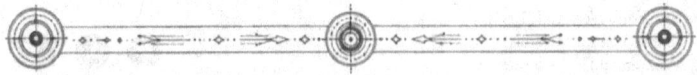

A Pyramid Lake Story:
Below the Surface

By Ricardo L. Ogdon
Edited by Roch De Silva and Taylor Hale
Published by Piramide Dorada Publications

First published July 2022
Revised printing June 2026

ISBN 13 (Hardcover): 979-8-9859637-0-0
ISBN 13 (Paperback): 979-8-9859637-1-7
ISBN 13 (Kindle): 979-8-9859637-2-4

Library of Congress Control Number:
2022905339

Piramide Dorada Publications:
240 E 28th St, Suite 10
New York, New York 10016
United States of America
www.piramidedorada.com

Printed on 100% recycled paper.
Printed on acid-free paper.
Printed in the United States of America

Scan the QR code to download additional content from the book and learn more about the author.

DEDICATION

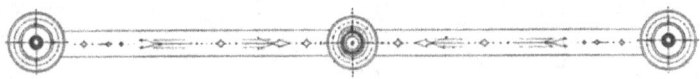

To all who journey into the unknown with calm and courage: may your bravery light the way to a life fully lived.

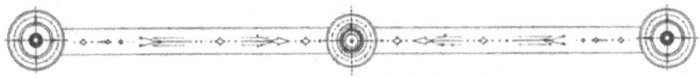

TABLE OF CONTENTS

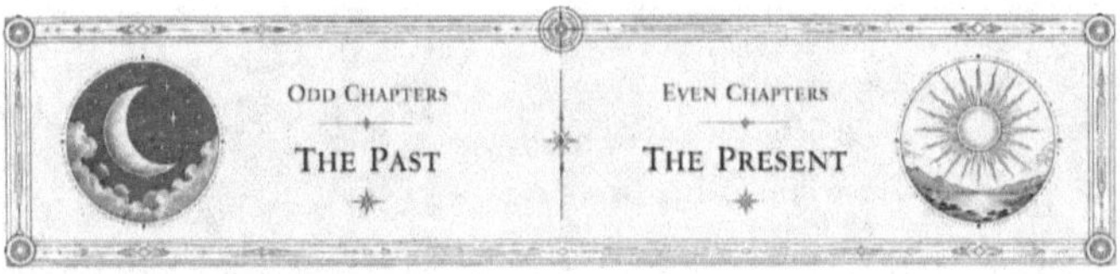

INTRODUCTION

Some places seem larger than themselves. They occupy a point on a map, yet their presence extends beyond geography. Long after a person leaves them behind, something remains. A memory. A feeling. A question.

Pyramid Lake is one of those places.

Resting within the desert of northern Nevada, surrounded by mountains, wind, and silence, it has inspired stories for generations. Some belong to history. Others belong to memory. Many continue to live somewhere between the two.

The story you are about to read was born from a deep admiration for that landscape and the people whose connection to it extends across countless generations. While this novel draws inspiration from real places, cultures, and traditions, it remains a work of fiction shaped by imagination, mythology, and a fascination with the mysteries that have accompanied humanity since the beginning of time.

At its heart, this is a story about remembrance.

About the unseen forces that influence our lives.

About the choices that shape our destinies.

And about the possibility that the world may be far deeper, stranger, and more interconnected than it first appears.

Perhaps the greatest mysteries are not hidden in distant places, but quietly waiting within the landscapes we think we already know.

The journey begins at the water's edge.

The rest belongs to you.

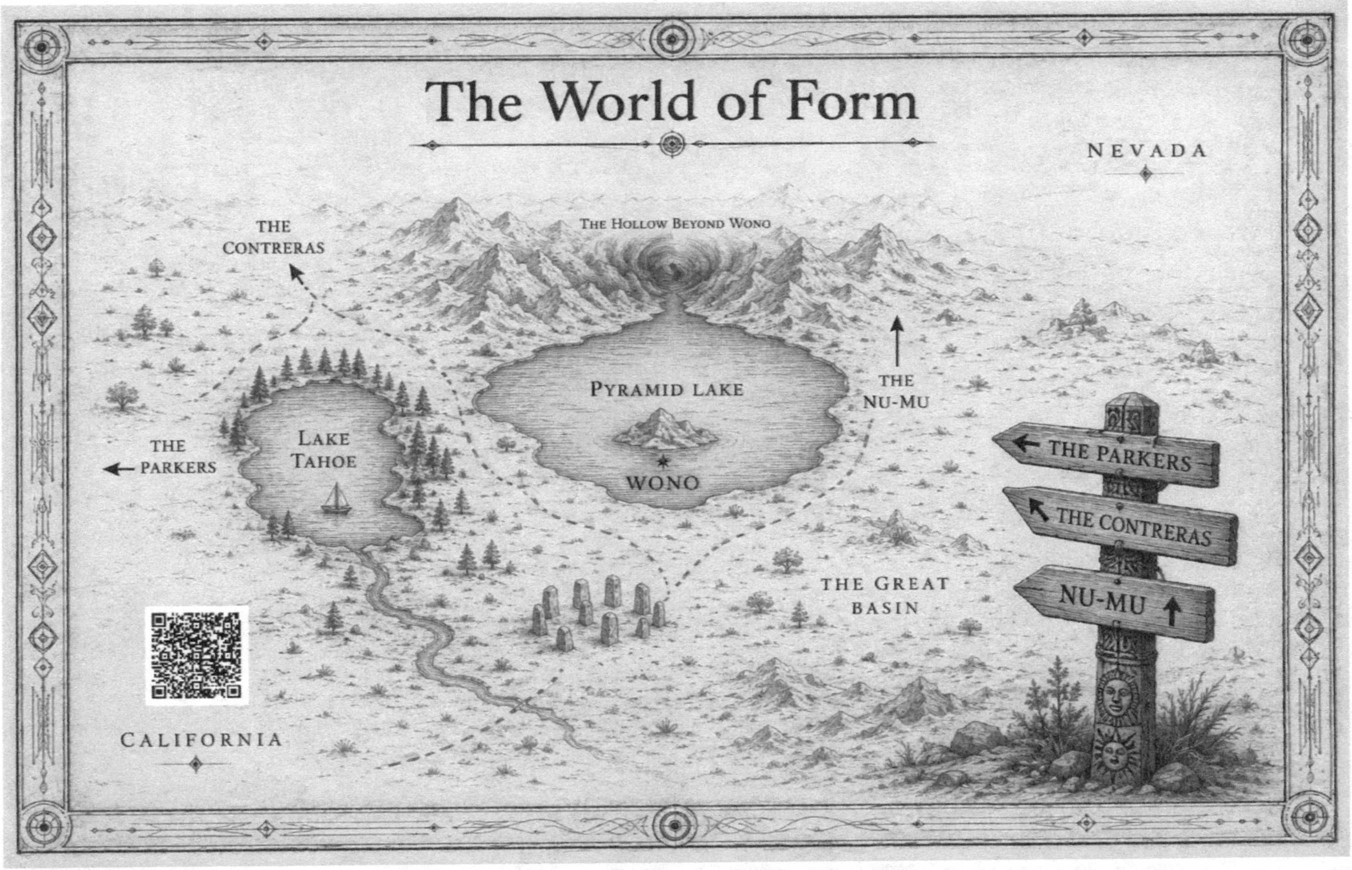
The World of Form
NEVADA
THE CONTRERAS
THE HOLLOW BEYOND WONO
PYRAMID LAKE
WONO
THE NU-MU
LAKE TAHOE
THE PARKERS
THE PARKERS
THE CONTRERAS
NU-MU
THE GREAT BASIN
CALIFORNIA

CHAPTER I
Ancient Waters

We are more than flesh. Within us flows a fragment of Puha, a current of the immeasurable that crosses between worlds.

The rustic drape pulled inward, drawing desert dust with it. Moonlight cut across the hut, silver and sharp. Galilhai fumbled with her moccasins, nearly losing her balance as she forced her feet inside.

"Quick," Wovoka called from the dark, his voice low and urgent, barely rising above the wind.

"Is my spirit leaving my body tonight?" Galilhai asked, hurrying to catch up with her father, who had already stepped into the wilderness.

He did not slow. A coyote's howl rose in the distance. His words broke apart in the wind.

"It will return to you."

Along the northern side of the lake, where the canyons tightened the sky and the desert stretched beyond sight, Wovoka walked at the center of a people hardened by both.

The land did not forgive carelessness. The words passed down to him had settled bone deep, though there were nights he wished they had not.

That night, Galilhai turned nine.

The procession had already begun descending from the ridge. Behind them, the woven huts thinned into shadow, their branch frames barely distinguishable from the darkening slope. Ahead, the earth opened into desert brushed with sage and needlegrass, their pale leaves catching what little moonlight slipped through drifting clouds.

The wind moved differently beyond the huts, traveling unobstructed now, carrying the dry scent of juniper and distant water. Crickets pulsed in the grass. Somewhere farther off, a nightbird called once, then fell silent.

Ten young men walked at the front, their strides measured, their shoulders squared beneath the weight of woven reed baskets. Inside lay suckerfish from the lake, alongside dried fruit and harvest roots bound in careful bundles. The baskets creaked faintly with each step.

Behind them, the women moved as one shifting current. Their bulrush garments bore tight, patient stitching, trimmed with bands of rabbit fur. Layered skirts, dyed in muted earth tones, trembled with the breeze.

Paint marked their faces, not as ornaments, but as language. Ochre and charcoal traced deliberate lines along cheekbones and temples. Deep blue curved beneath the eyes, lengthening their gaze into something almost otherworldly. On some foreheads, white mineral dust had been pressed into small pale discs that reflected even the faintest light. No two designs were identical, yet each carried the same meticulous intent.

Galilhai walked among them, aware of the air shifting as the ground began to slope. The desert thinned. Vegetation gave way to stone and sand. With every step, the horizon widened. Below them, unseen, something vast held its breath. She had the sense that it was aware of her.

She nearly missed her footing on a patch of loose sand and caught herself quickly, glancing at either side to see if anyone had noticed. No one had. Still, she straightened, forcing her steps into the same steady rhythm as the others.

Where her feet touched the earth, the sand seemed to soften, holding the shape of her step a moment longer before releasing it. The breeze curved gently around her, lifting a loose strand of hair as though testing its weight. Sage brushed her calves as she passed, its narrow leaves grazing her skin with a faint resinous warmth. Even the night insects altered their rhythm near her, their pulse rising briefly before settling again.

She felt the difference, though she could not have said why. The air lingered. The ground seemed to wait. A quiet pressure gathered in her chest. She swallowed and kept walking.

Through the thinning brush, Wovoka moved steadily, guiding the procession with a certainty that reached beyond his sight.

He walked as though listening. The wind did not simply move. It altered. The desert did not endure. It answered. When others debated, he listened for what shifted beneath their voices, what pressed at the edges of thought.

There were nights when he walked beyond the settlement alone, stopping where stone met open sky. He would stand long enough for the stars to shift in subtle patterns. He did not feel separate from what lay beyond sight. He knew when something without boundary moved through the dark. And yet, on rare occasions, something in that vastness did not align.

And then there was Puha.

Puha was the axis of all that lived and moved beyond sight. It stirred in the turning of seasons and in the hush before rain. It settled behind Wovoka's ribs, immense and unyielding, older than the mountains and deeper than the lake.

It did not answer. It did not favor. It did not alter its course. The world unfolded within its design.

Wovoka had long ago learned that alignment required attention, not pleading. To him, the world of flesh and the unseen were not divided by distance, but by attention. When he attended, the air altered. The desert stilled. The night continued its vast and indifferent turning, whether he understood it or not.

At last, they reached the lake's edge. A short distance from the shore, a pyramid-shaped rock rose from the depths, dark and unwavering. The tribe called it Wono. No one spoke of how long the name had existed. Nearby, a reed boat rested on the sand, its hull scuffed and weathered.

A cold breeze drifted across Pyramid Lake, brushing their faces and tugging at hair and fabric. Offerings had been arranged with deliberate care along the shore facing Wono. Nothing lay casually placed. Each object bore the intention of its making. The tribe kindled a fire at the center of the beach. Flames rose and took the logs as the people leaned into its warmth.

They drew inward until the circle was unbroken, each body angled toward the lake. Their bodies and faces glowed in a deep amber by the firelight. No one spoke.

Only then did an elderly woman step forward. Her silver hair caught the firelight, strands glinting like molten metal. From a worn cloth satchel, she withdrew a copper pot, its base darkened from years of flame. Along its sides, concentric engravings spiraled inward, as if tracing a pattern older than memory.

She knelt at the water's edge. The surface gave beneath her touch. When she rose, droplets clung briefly to the hammered copper before slipping back into the depths.

She returned to the circle, carrying the pot with care, water sloshing in rhythm with her steps. She set it atop the burning logs. Reaching deep into her pocket, she crushed desert herbs into the simmering water. Their scent rose sharp and bitter, cutting through the juniper smoke, as if they carried something that did not belong to this hour. With a willow stick, she stirred it sunwise in a steady, hypnotic motion. As a shooting star arced across the now cloudless night, the water began to boil.

Galilhai crept closer. She leaned forward, watching over the woman's shoulder as the tea darkened to caramel, the steam curling through the cold air.

"What are you making?" she whispered.

"A tea," the woman replied, her voice raspy but gentle, shaped by years of smoke and wind. "My mother taught me, as hers taught her, and hers before that, long before I drew breath in this world."

Galilhai pointed to a trumpet-shaped white flower floating in the pot.

"I like that flower," she said.

"This is datura," the woman replied, lifting her gaze to meet the girl's. "It has the power to carry you to worlds beyond your imagining."

A shiver ran through Galilhai. "What if my spirit wanders too far? What if it cannot find its way back?"

The woman laid a hand lightly on her shoulder. "Do not fear, child. The herbs hold you; the lake enfolds you; the waters carry you."

The ceremony began with a dance. Around the fire, men and women moved in deliberate unison, their voices low and resonant, rising and falling with the night air. Feet pressed into the sand. Arms carved arcs through the air. Shadows lengthened across the ground, shifting with each turn.

Wovoka crouched, eyes tracing the shifting shadows. Where a shape lingered, he marked the sand with stone. Where darkness gathered into shape, he did not disturb it. To others, it was only firelight breaking against uneven ground. To him, it was pattern.

He felt the past move beneath the surface of the night, not as memory, but as something still unfinished.

"It cannot be."

The pattern sharpened. Wovoka's breath shortened.

He crossed to the elderly woman as she poured the steaming tea into a clay cup, her hands steady.

"The stones speak of what was left unfinished," he said quietly. "It has not faded."

A shadow passed across her gaze, but it did not unsettle her.

"I know," she tilted her head, her eyes finding his. "What was begun must reach its end."

He stood motionless.

Galilhai stepped forward, breaking the circle, and knelt before the elderly woman. She stretched her small arms, slowed her breath, and steadied her hands, though her fingers trembled once before she stilled them. Wovoka caught it. In that moment, he glimpsed both fear and courage intertwined.

Her lips touched the hot liquid. She drank without hesitation. The cup was returned, and she rose with quiet grace. She fixed on the distant boat, and without thinking, moved toward it.

Wovoka followed close. They reached the boat. He draped a fur blanket over her shoulders. His hands lingered there, uncertain, before withdrawing. He pressed a soft kiss on her forehead, lingering longer than he intended.

Nine springs had passed since Puha marked her. The signs had been undeniable.

There would be no second child.

As Wovoka pushed the boat into the lake, the water lapped softly against its hull. Galilhai's small figure moved slowly away, framed by the firelight on the shore.

He almost called her name. But he did not.

The boat drifted farther from the shore, its dark silhouette swallowed by the breadth of the lake. Firelight thinned behind her. Voices faded. Only water remained.

A tremor moved through Galilhai, not of fear, but of unfastening. Her limbs grew distant, as though they belonged to another child, resting somewhere far below her awareness. The surface of the lake shimmered, no longer flat but breathing, rising and falling in slow, deliberate rhythm.

Wono stood before her.

The great pyramid of stone towered from the depths, immense and silent. Its edges cut clean against the night, yet its presence felt older than the landscape surrounding it. The boat glided toward it, as if guided by a hidden current. Its shadow stretched long and angular across the rippling surface until it overtook the boat.

Sound thinned. The moon dimmed, receding, as though yielding the night to something greater.

Galilhai's breath slowed until it no longer belonged to her. For one suspended instant, everything stilled. The wind, the water, the sky.

Then the stone opened, revealing depth within its darkness. The lake beneath her ceased to be surface. It became passage.

Only her body remained in the boat, wrapped in fur, eyes half-lidded. But Galilhai, the essence within her, stepped forward. She did not fall. She did not sink.

She crossed through the unseen threshold guarded by Wono.

The Other World had been waiting.

CHAPTER II
Blurry Borders

We learn more about ourselves through others than we ever could alone, for they are mirrors of the soul.

The GPS signal disappeared just outside Sparks. Noah Parker glanced toward the dashboard as the glowing route line dissolved into gray static before reappearing again a few seconds later. Beyond the windshield, the empty road stretched between scattered pines and dry desert brush beneath the pale light of early morning. Farther north, the basin surrounding Pyramid Lake remained hidden behind the mountains, though the thought of it already pressed quietly at the edge of his attention.

He slowed the car.

"Did I miss the turn?" he muttered quietly.

The town behind him had already fallen away into silence. Sunday mornings in that part of Nevada always felt unfinished somehow, as though the desert itself discouraged unnecessary movement before the sun climbed fully into the sky.

Noah checked the rearview mirror and made a slow U-turn along the roadside gravel.

Almost immediately, the GPS restored itself.

A narrow dirt road appeared behind him, half concealed between the trees.

"Signal restored," the device announced mechanically.

Noah exhaled through his nose and pulled onto the sandy shoulder. The trailhead waited just beyond a rusted fence where dry grass pushed through the stones. He grabbed his backpack from the trunk and began climbing.

The air still carried traces of mountain cold left behind by the night.

Above him, the ridges stretched northward in uneven layers toward Pyramid Lake while the trail twisted through scattered boulders and brittle sagebrush silvered faintly by the morning light. Some paths narrowed into little more than disturbances between the rocks before widening again farther uphill.

Noah had learned long ago that the desert rewarded early arrivals.

By midday, the heat stripped softness from everything.

As he climbed, the basin gradually opened behind him. Pines gave way to exposed stone, and beyond the descending ridges the distant waters of Pyramid Lake finally emerged beneath the widening horizon, pale and almost colorless beneath the early sun.

A weathered sign stood beside the trail.

SCENIC VIEW – 200 FEET.

Noah continued upward until the path leveled near the overlook.

The desert spread endlessly beneath him.

Far beyond the ridges, Pyramid Lake stretched across the basin like a sheet of faded silver suspended between the Nevada desert and the reservation, its distant shoreline dissolving so softly into the surrounding land that the border became nearly impossible to follow with the eye. People drew lines across maps and called them permanent, but out there, beneath enough distance and light, the world ignored them completely.

Blurry borders.

The phrase drifted through his mind unexpectedly.

Patches of stubborn snow still clung to the shaded rock near the overlook where winter refused to surrender completely to spring. Noah lowered himself onto a flat boulder and pulled his phone from his jacket pocket.

The lake shimmered faintly across the screen.

He framed the shot carefully before taking the picture.

For a moment, he studied it without moving.

"Sam would like this one," he murmured.

Even after all these years, he still associated the lake with her before anything else.

Pyramid Lake was the first place he had ever seen her.

They had been children then, part of a school field trip descending from the cold alpine waters of Lake Tahoe into the desert silence surrounding Pyramid Lake. Noah remembered the heat more than anything at first. The endless dust. The restless noise of students spilling from the buses and racing toward the shoreline while teachers shouted instructions nobody intended to follow.

And in the middle of all of it, Sam had remained still.

He remembered noticing her immediately, though he never fully understood why.

While the other children threw rocks into the water and chased one another across the sand, she stood several yards away from everyone else staring toward the lake with unusual concentration, as though listening to something too distant for anyone else to hear.

Noah had walked toward her mostly out of curiosity.

"Why aren't you going with them?" he had asked.

She barely looked at him before returning her attention to the water.

"Doesn't this place feel strange to you?"

At the time, he had laughed awkwardly because he did not know how to answer.

Now, years later, he still didn't.

The memory lingered while the morning wind moved softly across the overlook.

Noah took a sip from his water flask and looked toward the lake again. Even from miles away, something about it resisted familiarity. Tahoe invited admiration. Pyramid Lake demanded attention. The difference was difficult to explain to people who had never stood beside both waters.

He slipped the phone back into his pocket.

In a few days, Sam would finally return to Nevada.

The thought tightened something quietly inside him.

Nearly a year had passed since she moved back east after financial problems forced her to leave school. At first, Noah believed the distance would loosen naturally over time. Instead, her absence settled deeper into his life with each passing month, revealing itself unexpectedly through ordinary things: empty seats beside him during lectures, songs he almost sent her before remembering she lived across the country, conversations that still continued in his head long after he was alone again.

He had known Sam long enough that silence between them never felt uncomfortable. That alone made her different from almost everyone else he knew.

And somewhere along the way, without permission or announcement, friendship had become something more dangerous.

Not sudden. Not dramatic. Just impossible to ignore anymore.

Noah lowered his gaze toward the distant basin.

He was no longer sure what separated friendship from love.

Maybe it was this.

The thought stayed with him longer than he wanted it to.

Noah checked the time.

He still had over an hour before meeting her in Reno.

Excitement and unease tightened together inside him until he could no longer separate one from the other.

He rose from the overlook and began descending the trail.

The drive south toward Reno carried him gradually away from the silence of the mountains and back into the movement of ordinary life. Gas stations appeared beside the highway. Traffic thickened near the city limits. Billboards rose from the desert advertising casinos, injury lawyers, and new housing developments spreading farther into the basin each year.

Modern life always seemed loudest to Noah immediately after leaving the mountains.

By the time he reached the café downtown, the morning had already deepened into late sunlight.

He parked across the street and looked toward the outdoor seating area.

Then he saw her.

Sam sat alone beside a small dark green table near the sidewalk, one hand wrapped loosely around a coffee cup while a weathered suitcase rested beside her chair. For a moment Noah remained inside the car simply watching her through the windshield.

A year had passed.

Yet something inside him recognized her instantly before thought could intervene.

The same long brown curls falling loosely around her shoulders. The same thoughtful stillness that made crowded places seem quieter around her somehow. Even from a distance, she carried the faint impression of someone whose attention remained divided between the visible world and something farther away.

Then she looked up.

Their eyes met through the glass.

A slow smile appeared across her face.

Noah stepped out of the car and crossed the street.

"I hope that coffee is mine," he called out as he approached.

Sam laughed softly.

"I remembered the cinnamon."

The sound of her voice loosened something inside him immediately.

When he reached the table, they embraced without hesitation.

For a brief instant, the year between them disappeared.

Noah felt the familiar narrowness of her shoulders beneath his arms, the warmth of her body against the cold morning air still clinging faintly to his jacket.

Then they separated.

"Happy birthday," Sam said quietly.

Noah smiled.

"You flew across the country just to insult my age?"

"You were already old when I left."

He laughed, though his attention lingered upon her face.

Something about her seemed thinner now. Not physically alone. Tired in a deeper way. The kind of exhaustion sleep rarely touched.

"How was the flight?" he asked.

"Long."

"That bad?"

"I sat next to a man who spent four hours explaining cryptocurrency to me."

Noah groaned sympathetically.

"That's psychological warfare."

Another small laugh escaped her.

Cars moved slowly through downtown Reno behind them while sunlight reflected across nearby windows in fractured flashes. Somewhere farther down the street, music drifted faintly from an open storefront before dissolving into traffic noise.

Yet beneath the ordinary rhythm of the city, Noah sensed the same strange distance that had always existed around Sam, subtle but unmistakable, as though some hidden part of her remained elsewhere no matter where she stood.

"You okay?" he asked gently.

Sam looked toward him, briefly caught off guard by the question.

"Yeah," she said after a moment. "Just tired."

The answer arrived too quickly.

Noah recognized it anyway and chose not to press further.

Some people protected themselves with anger. Others with noise. Sam protected herself through disappearance.

He sat down across from her.

For a few moments neither of them spoke. Strangely, the silence felt easier than conversation.

Then Sam glanced toward the mountains visible beyond the city skyline.

"I missed Nevada," she admitted quietly.

Noah followed her gaze.

"The desert?"

"The space," she said. "Back east everything feels crowded. Here it still feels like the world leaves room for silence."

Her words lingered between them.

Noah studied her carefully.

"You're thinking about the lake again."

Sam smiled faintly without denying it.

"That obvious?"

"You always get that look."

"What look?"

"The one you get whenever Pyramid Lake enters your head."

Her fingers tightened slightly around the coffee cup.

For a moment she said nothing.

Then, quietly:

"Sometimes I think part of me never really left that place."

Noah studied her carefully. Slowly, he extended his hand across the table until his fingers rested lightly against hers.

"If you want to talk about it—"

Sam pulled her hand back almost immediately.

The movement was gentle, but instinctive.

"It's nothing," she said too quickly.

Noah remained still.

Sam lowered her gaze toward the coffee between her hands. For a brief instant, something unsettled passed across her expression, not fear exactly, but the discomfort of someone standing too close to a memory they no longer trusted themselves to touch.

Then she smiled again, smaller this time.

"I think I'm better not thinking about it too much."

The city noise continued around them while somewhere far beyond Reno, beyond the highways, mountains, and invisible borders drawn across the land, Pyramid Lake rested beneath the afternoon sun, silent and waiting.

CHAPTER III
Sacred Land

Every aspect of life is sacred. Failing to recognize this, even in the smallest things, represents a fundamental misunderstanding of life.

Galilhai opened her eyes and remained still, not out of hesitation, but because something within her understood, before thought could fully take shape, that her body no longer belonged to her in the way it once had. The surface beneath her held her with a softness unlike sand or earth, carrying the strange impression of awareness, as if the world beneath her had recognized her and chosen not to let her fall.

She waited for her breath to follow. The instinct rose naturally, familiar and unquestioned, yet nothing answered it. Her chest did not lift. No air entered her lungs. No sound marked the passage of life through her body. The absence did not bring panic, only the slow recognition that the rules governing her had changed.

Turning her head, she found herself suspended in a hammock woven from slender reeds, each strand faintly luminous and carrying its own quiet source of light. Beyond it stretched the shoreline of the lake, unchanged in form yet altered in essence. The water shimmered beneath a pale radiance that did not fall from the sky, but seemed to rise from within the world itself, uniting land and lake in a single hidden glow.

When she pushed herself upright, the motion came too easily. Her body rose with a lightness that nearly carried her forward before she steadied herself, as if the weight that had always anchored her had been gently removed. The lake remained before her, its reach unbroken and its edges familiar, yet something essential within it had changed in a way she could not name.

Her gaze lifted, and she saw that Wono had risen.

No longer bound to the depths, the great stone hovered above the lake, transformed into a vast pyramid of gold whose scale dwarfed the horizon. Its presence did not merely occupy space. It pressed against it, forcing the world to yield and rearrange itself around its form. The structure turned with immense force, each face catching the light and bending it from gold into deep crimson before returning again, like pressure sealed beneath a living surface.

Below it, the lake remained undisturbed. No ripple formed. No movement acknowledged the impossible weight above it. The water accepted what should not have been.

At the apex, the structure separated. The tip hovered just above the body of the pyramid, held apart by a narrow and perfect distance, while a smaller form, identical in precision, rotated in the opposite direction like a crown suspended above the whole. Between them, a single stream of water descended in an unbroken line, so narrow and flawless that it appeared carved rather than flowing, vanishing into the lake without leaving a trace.

There was no sound.

Galilhai could not look away. The longer her gaze remained fixed upon the pyramid, the less certain its distance became. At one moment it seemed far across the lake; at another, near enough to touch, its edges too deliberate to belong to anything natural. It did not reflect the world around it. The world adjusted itself in quiet obedience.

When she finally rose to her feet, the ground softened beneath her, responding not to her weight but to her presence. She stepped forward without fully deciding to do so, drawn by a quiet force that moved through her without asking.

Something along the shoreline broke her focus.

A white horse moved in the distance, its motion smooth and unnervingly precise as it crossed the shore without producing the slightest sound. Pale dust drifted lazily through the air around it, descending in slow currents toward the earth, yet within the space surrounding the animal the particles remained suspended, fixed motionless in the air. Nothing bent around it. Nothing yielded to its passage.

As it drew nearer, Galilhai noticed another detail that unsettled her even more. At the center of the horse's forehead rested a third eye, larger than the other two and sealed shut beneath a pale lid that never twitched or moved. The closed eye gave the creature a disturbing sense of restraint, like a force held dormant rather than asleep. The horse moved through the landscape untouched by the laws governing everything around it.

A rider sat upon its back, and even before Galilhai could distinguish her features, the difference was unmistakable. Where the world softened and adapted, this figure remained contained within her own boundaries, untouched by the fluid nature of the space around her.

The distance between them collapsed without warning. One moment the rider remained far along the shoreline, and the next she stood directly before her. The woman rose tall upon the horse, her form elongated yet clear, every line defined without distortion. Her skin carried a steady warmth, and her long red hair followed her motion without dispersing into the surrounding light, remaining whole and contained under a different order of being.

Her garments did not shimmer or shift. They held their glow in a constant state, light resting within them without pulse or variation. When she reached down and grasped Galilhai's arm, the contact felt immediate and sharply bounded, existing only where her fingers touched her skin.

Before Galilhai could react, her body lifted and settled behind the rider with effortless precision.

"Hold," the woman said.

Galilhai obeyed, tightening her arms around her as the horse surged forward, carrying them along the shoreline while the golden pyramid continued its silent rotation behind them. Ahead, the land rose into forest, and as they crossed beneath its branches, the stillness gave way to sound. Leaves brushed together in slow, deliberate layers, not like ordinary wind, but like a rhythm belonging to the forest itself.

"Where are you taking me?" Galilhai asked, her voice steady despite the unease gathering within her.

"You are not being taken," the woman replied.

The answer offered no comfort. It followed Galilhai as they rode deeper into the forest, where the trees grew taller and their branches folded over one another in intricate patterns that caught and held the light. The path beneath them did not appear worn or traveled, yet it opened before the horse and closed behind it without disturbance.

After some time, the forest parted, and a clearing opened before them.

A settlement stood within it.

The structures rose in layered forms, curved and precise, their surfaces shifting subtly between stone and something smoother, almost fluid. Light circulated beneath them in controlled patterns, giving the impression that they had not been built so much as arranged into being. Each stood in perfect relation to the others, held together by an order Galilhai could sense but not understand.

Figures moved through the open space. They were human in shape, yet refined beyond ordinary proportion, their bodies balanced with an intentional grace that made every gesture appear purposeful. Their garments clung close in fine layers that carried light within them. Brightness gathered along one edge, receded along another, and formed patterns that changed without repeating. Some held deep gold that darkened toward red, while others carried pale hues that thinned near the edges until they nearly dissolved into the air.

They did not speak, yet nothing about them felt silent. Their awareness of one another passed through the space without gesture or word, each figure moving in harmony with the rest. A few turned as Galilhai passed, not in surprise, but in recognition. Their gaze lingered only briefly before returning to their work.

Unease rose within her, but it did not push her away. Instead, it sharpened her attention, drawing her toward the smallest details: the rhythm of their steps, the flow of light beneath their garments, the quiet precision with which everything held together.

One figure passed close enough for the trailing edge of its garment to drift within reach. Without thinking, Galilhai lifted her hand and brushed it with her fingers. The surface yielded immediately, neither fabric nor light, but something that carried the qualities of both. Warmth spread through her hand, soft at first, then deeper, moving past the place of contact before slowly receding.

She withdrew her hand and watched the figure continue forward without pause.

At the center of the settlement, one structure rose above the rest, not through size alone, but through authority. Its form drew inward rather than outward, its surfaces marked by spiraling lines that shifted as light moved across them, creating the impression of motion within stillness.

The horse slowed and came to a stop.

There was no visible entrance. No door. Only the uninterrupted surface of the structure, alive with quiet rotation.

The woman dismounted and turned, extending her hand. Galilhai hesitated only briefly before taking it and stepping down, feeling the ground soften beneath her feet once more.

"I am Pamahas," the woman said.

Galilhai steadied herself. "Galilhai. Wovoka's daughter."

Pamahas regarded her without movement, her gaze calm and exacting. "It has been some time since one so young has crossed."

"My father said I should come."

"Fathers speak as if they know," Pamahas replied. "That does not make it so."

She turned toward the structure. The spiraling lines along its surface slowed, then parted along a narrow seam, the material softening just enough to allow passage. Pamahas entered first, and Galilhai followed.

Inside, the space expanded beyond what the exterior suggested. The walls emitted a low, steady glow, while pale mist drifted across the floor and blurred the boundary between ground and air. The curvature shifted continuously, preventing the eye from settling on any fixed form.

Two narrow seats rose from the floor as they approached, forming seamlessly from the surface beneath them.

"Sit," Pamahas said.

Galilhai climbed onto the seat, her body still lighter than she expected. Pamahas took her place beside her, and for a moment neither spoke. The silence held around them, attentive and deliberate.

Pamahas reached for Galilhai's hand. Her touch was warm but contained, never spreading beyond the point where their skin met.

"Some things cross that were never meant to," she said.

Galilhai turned toward her. "Here?"

"Closer than they have ever been."

The words darkened the space between them.

Pamahas did not release her hand. "Once, one crossed and did not return."

Galilhai remained still.

Pamahas's gaze shifted slightly, not away from her, but beyond her. "You will see what came of it."

The light in the room began to change. It did not dim. It rearranged itself, shifting the shape of the chamber until the walls could no longer be followed. The mist thickened, dissolving the floor, the seats, and the distance between them into a single pale uncertainty.

A pressure gathered behind Galilhai's eyes, steady and insistent, drawing her inward. She tried to remain present, but her focus loosened, slipping away from the room by degrees.

"Hold your attention," Pamahas said.

Her voice reached Galilhai from farther away now.

The pressure deepened.

The present released her.

And she was no longer there.

The fire had burned low.

The circle had loosened, its rhythm fading into scattered movement and quiet voices. Some still lingered near the flames, their bodies slow and unstructured, while others sat beyond the reach of the light, half lost in shadow.

Wovoka remained near the shore.

The lake stretched before him, dark and unbroken. The boat had long since disappeared into it, leaving no trace behind, yet he had not moved.

The older woman approached and lowered herself beside him. The sand shifted beneath her weight, but she did not look at him. For a while, neither spoke. Behind them, the fire crackled softly.

"It should have ended," Wovoka said at last.

"Nothing ends where you think it does," she replied.

"I saw it. It has not faded."

"No," she said quietly. "It has not."

A faint wind crossed the lake, disturbing the surface just enough to catch the reflection of the firelight.

"He chose it," Wovoka said. "Over his people."

"He chose what he could not turn away from."

"That is not the same."

"No."

Silence settled again.

"If Puha moves through all things," Wovoka said, "why allow it?"

She opened her eyes. "You are asking for a boundary. There is none."

Wovoka turned toward her. "Then what separates us from it?"

She met his gaze. "Attention."

The word remained between them.

"That is not enough," he said.

"It is the only thing that has ever been enough."

Wovoka looked back toward the lake. "And if it happens again?"

"It already has."

His breath caught.

"She is not ready."

"No one is."

His hands tightened. "I almost called her back."

"But you did not."

He said nothing.

The wind moved again, colder now. After a moment, the woman rose.

"The path has opened," she said. "It will not close for you."

Wovoka remained seated, his gaze fixed on the dark water, as if it might yet return what had been taken from him.

CHAPTER IV

The Tale of a Crying Mother

Bravery comes from the unshakable certainty that love is above all. Remarkable deeds will come from us in this state.

Noah smiled faintly across the café table. "Technically," he said, "it's not my birthday yet. I was born a few minutes before midnight."

Samantha Reyes laughed softly into her coffee.

"You're correcting birthday technicalities now? That's how I know you're getting old."

Outside, late afternoon sunlight drifted across downtown Reno in fractured reflections, bouncing between windows and passing cars before dissolving against the sidewalks. The city moved around them in restless noise, but beneath it Sam still felt strangely detached, as though part of her attention had remained somewhere farther north near the lake.

Nearly a year had passed since she left Nevada.

Sitting across from Noah again felt both familiar and unreal.

"You've changed," Noah said quietly.

Sam raised an eyebrow. "That sounds dangerous."

"You got a tattoo."

His eyes shifted briefly toward her shoulder where dark lines disappeared beneath the strap of her shirt.

Sam glanced down instinctively.

"A juniper tree," she said. "Or at least that's what the artist claimed it looked like."

Noah smiled faintly. "Very Nevada of you."

"I still blame tequila for the decision."

The corner of his mouth lifted slightly.

"The roots are nice."

Sam looked at him suspiciously. "You're analyzing it now?"

"You disappeared for a year and came back with desert symbolism carved into your body. I'm trying to keep up."

A quiet laugh escaped her before she lowered her eyes toward the coffee again.

"It felt important that night," she admitted. "I just couldn't explain why."

The tattoo had happened during one of the stranger months after leaving Nevada, when loneliness blurred together with exhaustion and too many late shifts at the diner near her father's apartment. One night after work, surrounded by loud music, tired coworkers, and enough alcohol to quiet her thoughts temporarily, she wandered into a tattoo shop a few blocks from the bar and pointed toward a sketch of a twisted desert juniper pinned carelessly along the wall.

Later, she would not remember exactly why that particular image unsettled her enough to choose it.

At the time, it felt less like self-expression and more like an attempt to leave proof behind that some part of her still belonged somewhere.

"How's your dad?" Noah asked.

"Still convinced I'm incapable of surviving adulthood alone."

"That sounds accurate."

She smiled despite herself.

"He means well."

"I know."

Sam looked past Noah toward the movement of traffic outside.

Her father had called almost every night since she arrived in Reno. Sometimes she answered. Sometimes she watched the phone vibrate until the screen went dark again. Concern exhausted her lately, even when it came from love.

Noah studied her carefully.

"I didn't think you'd come back," he admitted.

The honesty in his voice made her chest tighten slightly.

Neither had she.

"I know I disappeared," Sam said quietly. "I just..." She searched briefly for language that felt true enough. "Everything after my mom became difficult to sit still inside."

Noah lowered his gaze.

He understood grief differently than most people their age. His mother had died when he was young enough that many of his memories of her survived only through fragments: perfume lingering in hallways, unfinished songs, photographs whose emotional weight exceeded their detail.

But Sam's loss had unfolded differently.

Her mother had been everywhere inside her life.

Friends used to joke that the two of them looked less like parent and daughter and more like sisters who accidentally shared the same soul. Sam carried pieces of her mother constantly: gestures, expressions, the way she tilted her head while listening.

Her absence had not created emptiness.

It had created echo.

Noah reached across the table slowly, resting his hand over hers.

This time she did not pull away.

The warmth remained there quietly between them.

Before either of them spoke again, a loud car horn echoed through the parking lot outside.

Both turned instinctively toward the sound.

A black Mercedes-Benz curved sharply into an empty parking space beside Noah's truck.

Noah exhaled.

"Of course."

Alejandra Contreras stepped out wearing oversized sunglasses and a fitted blue dress that moved elegantly against the wind. Her short blonde hair framed a face that carried equal parts beauty and mischief, while bold red lipstick completed the carefully composed image she seemed to maintain effortlessly at all times.

She removed the sunglasses slowly.

"The reunion feels underwhelming," she announced.

Sam laughed immediately.

Ale crossed the sidewalk toward them and wrapped both of them into an exaggerated embrace before either could protest.

"Look at you two," she said. "Still pretending silence counts as emotional stability."

"You drive like a Bond villain," Noah muttered.

Ale ignored him completely.

Unlike the noise surrounding her family's casinos and luxury resorts spread across Nevada, Ale herself preferred smaller spaces: bookstores, desert roads, antique shops, ghost towns buried beneath dust and silence. Beneath the expensive clothes and theatrical confidence existed someone deeply fascinated by hidden things: old symbols, forgotten stories, strange coincidences she refused to call coincidences.

Most people mistook her curiosity for performance.

Sam knew better. Beneath all the teasing, Ale possessed an unsettling habit of noticing things other people overlooked.

"You look exhausted," Ale said bluntly to Sam.

"Good to see you too."

"I'm serious."

"She just got off a plane," Noah interrupted.

Something in Sam's expression kept Ale quiet for a moment before the feeling disappeared beneath her usual confidence.

"Anyway," Ale said, dropping into the chair beside them, "I assume Noah already convinced you to spend his birthday sleeping on dirt."

"It's called camping," Noah replied.

"It's called poor decision-making with scenery."

Sam laughed softly into her coffee.

"You're still going?"

Ale looked horrified.

"Absolutely not."

Then she paused.

"Unless you are going."

Noah pointed accusingly toward her. "That's emotional manipulation."

"Correct."

Sam watched them bicker while something quieter moved beneath her attention again.

Pyramid Lake.

Ever since returning to Reno, thoughts of the lake had begun surfacing constantly inside her mind without invitation. Sometimes through memory. Sometimes through dreams she could no longer fully recall after waking. Sometimes through nothing more than silence.

The feeling unsettled her.

She had spent nearly a year trying not to think about that place.

"And before you ask," Ale continued, "yes, you're staying at my house."

Sam sighed. "You already decided that before picking us up, didn't you?"

"Obviously."

Noah stood and grabbed Sam's suitcase before she could object.

The late afternoon gradually softened toward evening while they crossed the parking lot together beneath drifting city noise and fading sunlight. Traffic lights blinked against nearby windows. Music spilled faintly from an open storefront farther down the street.

For a brief stretch of ordinary conversation, things almost felt simple again.

But the feeling never lasted long around Pyramid Lake.

The Contreras estate stood along the quieter edge of Reno where the city began loosening into larger properties and older trees. Stone fountains lined the circular driveway while carefully trimmed hedges curved around flower beds glowing beneath warm exterior lights.

Sam remembered the house well.

During high school, she and Ale spent countless nights sneaking through those hallways after parties, climbing through windows to avoid waking Ale's parents, laughing quietly while carrying shoes through the dark.

The memories returned with unsettling clarity the moment they stepped inside.

Warm light spilled downward from an enormous chandelier suspended above the foyer. Marble floors reflected gold across the walls while long windows overlooked the illuminated pool behind the house.

"You still live like a movie villain," Sam said.

Ale smiled proudly. "Thank you."

Later that night they sat cross-legged across Ale's bed eating pizza directly from the box while music played softly somewhere deeper inside the house.

Outside the windows, clouds moved slowly above the city.

"So," Ale said carefully, "how weird has it been seeing Noah again?"

Sam narrowed her eyes immediately.

"Don't start."

"That wasn't denial."

Sam laughed despite herself.

"It's complicated."

"It's always complicated when people are in love."

"We are not—"

Ale raised one hand dramatically.

"Please. I survived high school with both of you. I deserve compensation."

Sam shook her head and reached for another slice of pizza.

Yet Noah's face kept returning to her thoughts unexpectedly: the way he looked at her across the café table, the warmth of his hand over hers, the quiet patience in him that had somehow survived the distance between them.

Ale watched her carefully.

"You missed him too."

Sam remained silent long enough to answer the question anyway.

Outside, wind brushed softly against the windows.

Then Ale's expression shifted.

"Actually," she said more quietly, "something strange happened while you were gone."

Sam looked up.

Ale stood from the bed and crossed toward a wooden desk beside the far wall where several books rested in uneven stacks. She picked up one with a faded garnet cover before returning.

Sam recognized it immediately.

"Maia gave you another folklore book?"

Ale ignored the tone.

"Mock me all you want. I'm serious."

The cover read:

NEVADA FOLKLORE: LOST LEGENDS OF THE NU-MU

Ale opened carefully toward a folded section near the center.

"The water level at Pyramid Lake rose again last month," she said quietly. "Almost ten inches."

"So?"

Ale looked directly at her.

"Some of the Nu-Mu still believe it means Stone Mother is crying."

The room grew strangely still after she said it.

Sam frowned faintly.

She had heard the name before.

Ale lowered her voice slightly before continuing.

"Long ago, there was a woman trapped in a terrible marriage to a bear who ruled through cruelty and fear. She eventually escaped and crossed the desert searching for another life beside a man who lived alone near the mountains. They fell in love and had children together, but one day the father sent some of those children far away toward the west."

The soft music continued faintly somewhere downstairs.

"The mother never recovered from losing them," Ale said. "She waited for their return until grief rooted her to the mountain itself. She cried for so long that her tears formed Pyramid Lake, and eventually she became stone."

Sam felt an unexpected chill move through her arms.

Outside, wind brushed harder against the glass.

"The Nu-Mu call her Stone Mother," Ale whispered. "Some people believe the lake rises whenever she mourns again."

Silence lingered between them afterward.

Not uncomfortable.

Heavy.

Sam stared toward the darkened windows.

Something about the story unsettled her more deeply than she wanted to admit. Not because it sounded impossible, but because part of it felt strangely familiar, as though the memory of hearing it existed somewhere just beyond reach.

"We can't even visit the formation anymore," Ale continued more quietly. "Some idiots vandalized it last year, and the Nu-Mu closed off that part of the reservation."

Sam shook her head.

"I don't understand why people destroy things they don't understand."

Ale closed the book slowly.

"Maybe because understanding requires attention."

The sentence lingered unexpectedly between them.

Then Sam smiled faintly.

"Noah's still going to try finding a way there."

Ale laughed.

"Obviously."

That night Sam dreamed of horses.

At first, there was only wind moving violently through black trees while dust spiraled upward from the forest floor in suffocating waves. The branches above her twisted against one another like enormous skeletal hands while the darkness beyond the woods seemed to deepen endlessly in every direction.

She could not tell whether she was running toward something or away from it.

The dream carried the weight of pursuit without revealing what pursued her.

Then the wind stopped.

Silence collapsed across the forest so completely that even her breathing sounded distant.

A low vibration emerged somewhere beyond the trees.

Not thunder.

Movement.

The horses appeared gradually through the darkness ahead of her, enormous black forms advancing between the trees with impossible stillness. Their riders wore armor darker than obsidian, yet the shapes beneath the armor never fully resolved into human form. The surrounding darkness bent strangely around them, swallowing detail before her eyes could fully grasp it.

Sam hid behind the massive trunk of a tree.

Every instinct inside her screamed not to be seen.

The riders continued forward slowly.

At the center of their formation moved something worse than a figure: an absence.

A shifting distortion where the forest itself seemed to collapse inward unnaturally, consuming light, shape, and distance around it.

Sam felt terror rise through her body with such force that waking should have followed immediately.

But the dream held her there.

Then a hand touched her shoulder gently.

Warm. Human.

She turned sharply.

Pamahas stood behind her beneath the darkened trees, her red hair moving softly against the stillness while silver light gathered faintly around her skin.

Unlike the riders, she felt entirely real.

Entirely present.

And somehow familiar.

Pamahas looked toward her with deep sadness and recognition intertwined within her gaze.

Then she leaned close enough for Sam to hear her whisper.

"It is time to come home."

CHAPTER V
Cursed Wedding

Sometimes, a curse can be a blessing in disguise. What we perceive as evil may carry the seed of good. Nothing exists as purely negative or positive. Everything is as it should be. Accept this.

Galilhai awakened once more upon the shores of Pyramid Lake, where the gentle movement of water against the sand greeted her like a memory returning from far away. For a brief moment she believed herself back within the ordinary world, among the familiar sounds of the lake and the quiet breath of the land.

Then she looked down.

A vanilla-colored dress flowed softly around her body, its fabric lighter than anything she had ever worn. Delicate white embroidery wound across its surface in intricate patterns that shimmered beneath the pale light, resembling constellations stitched into cloth. The garment felt ceremonial, though not chosen by her. It belonged to the moment she had entered.

Ahead of her, a procession moved toward Wono.

Dozens of figures crossed the shoreline in garments of ivory, gold, and muted crimson, their voices rising in laughter and song. Music drifted through the air in warm waves, carrying the unmistakable feeling of celebration. Beyond them, Wono hovered above the lake in silent majesty, its enormous golden body fixed in place rather than rotating as it had before.

A translucent bridge arched across the water, connecting the shore to the pyramid's entrance. Its surface glowed beneath the feet of the guests, refracting light through its structure like frozen crystal.

Drawn forward by the music, Galilhai hurried after them, though excitement soon gave way to confusion. No one acknowledged her presence. A woman passed directly through her shoulder without reacting, and another figure crossed through her body as if she were made of mist.

Pamahas had spoken the truth.

Here, Galilhai was only a witness.

The moment she stepped inside Wono, the scale of the structure overwhelmed her. Golden pillars rose toward immense arches that emitted a soft amber glow, while the trapezoidal walls shifted beneath embossed carvings of birds and trees moving in slow, fluid motion. Above her, streams of water coursed endlessly through engraved channels in the ceiling, circling through the chamber in unbroken currents that made the entire structure feel alive.

Benches hovered slightly above the floor in a circular arrangement surrounding the center of the chamber. When

Galilhai settled onto one of them, the surface responded immediately, lifting gently from the ground before rocking with a slow and almost comforting motion.

At the center of the room floated the altar.

Upon it knelt the bride.

Her gown shimmered with embedded stones that caught the surrounding light and scattered it in delicate fragments across the chamber. She was young, though the composure in her posture made her seem older in that moment, as if she had already accepted the weight of what her marriage represented. Her hands rested over one another in her lap, but her fingers moved slightly, betraying the anticipation she struggled to contain.

More than once, she turned toward the entrance.

Each time, hope returned to her face.

The atmosphere surrounding the ceremony held a sacred stillness beneath the music and celebration. This was not merely a marriage. Galilhai could feel that much. It was a union meant to bind two lineages, perhaps even two worlds. The scent of blossoms drifted through the air, mingling with soft whispers from the guests, and for a while everything inside Wono seemed ordered toward joy.

Then the entrance doors closed.

The sound echoed through the chamber with such force that every conversation ceased at once.

All eyes turned toward the entrance.

At first, Galilhai noticed only the groom.

He stood beneath the towering doorway in ceremonial garments adorned with intricate patterns woven in gold thread. He carried himself with the calm confidence of a warrior accustomed to standing between worlds, one of the Paiute guardians capable of entering the Other World to confront the Dark Shadows that threatened his people.

Yet something in his face disturbed the solemn dignity of his appearance.

His eyes were bright, almost fevered, and he did not look first at the bride.

He looked at the hand he was holding.

A murmur spread through the chamber.

The creature beside him glided into view with unnerving grace, her lower body moving in smooth serpentine motions across the polished floor. Vibrant magenta scales reflected the amber light in shifting shades of crimson and rose, while a long caudal fin swayed behind her in slow, fluid movements.

Above the waist, she resembled a woman.

Long golden hair flowed across pale skin and satin-covered breasts, framing a face so strikingly beautiful that several guests seemed unable to look away.

Galilhai felt the atmosphere inside the chamber change.

The water flowing through the ceiling slowed.

Not completely.

Just enough to feel wrong.

The groom stepped forward, holding the mermaid's hand as if the pressure of the room might otherwise pull her away from him. The bride rose slowly to meet him, relief still forming in her expression.

Then she saw Kewa.

Everything inside her seemed to stop.

Even before the groom spoke, the bride appeared to understand something was wrong. He had not looked at her once since entering the chamber, and the hand that once reached for hers without thought now remained tightly wrapped around the creature beside him.

The groom came to a halt before the altar.

For a moment, no one spoke.

The warrior looked at the bride, then away again, and that small failure of courage revealed more than any confession could have done.

"Say my name," the bride whispered.

The warrior closed his eyes.

"Do not ask that of me."

A tremor passed through her lips, but she forced herself to remain standing.

"You were able to say it yesterday."

The chamber remained silent. Even those who had begun whispering fell still.

"I did not come here to shame you," he said quietly.

"Then why did you come?"

He looked at Kewa, and when he answered, his voice carried both guilt and conviction.

"Because I cannot stand before Puha and bind myself to one soul while another already holds mine."

The bride absorbed the words slowly.

"And mine?" she asked. "What became of mine?"

The warrior finally looked at her then, and Galilhai saw the pain crossing his face. Countless evenings beside the lake seemed to pass silently between them in that single glance: shared meals beside the fire, laughter carried through summer nights, promises spoken with the certainty only young love could believe permanent.

Kewa turned toward the bride for the first time. Her expression held neither cruelty nor pity, only a calm certainty that made her seem untouched by the pain gathering around her.

"A soul cannot be kept by a promise it has already outgrown," she said softly.

The bride's eyes shifted to her.

"You speak of his soul as if you found it abandoned."

"I found it calling."

The warrior's grip tightened around the mermaid's hand, and Galilhai saw how desperately he wanted those words to be true. He looked like a man standing at the edge of a cliff and convincing himself the sky had invited him forward.

"When I was with her," he said, now addressing the chamber, "it was the first time in my life I did not feel divided against myself."

The words unsettled the room more than anger would have.

The bride stared at him in disbelief.

"You used to reach for my hand before you slept," she whispered. "You told me the sound of my voice made the world quieter inside your head."

Pain crossed the warrior's face.

"That was true."

"Then do not make me smaller so you can leave without guilt."

He swallowed hard, unable to answer.

A sharp crack suddenly echoed through Wono.

The bride's father had risen from his seat.

Though age had silvered parts of his thick copper beard, his broad frame still carried immense strength, and the authority in his eyes silenced the entire gathering before he spoke. Yet when he looked at the warrior, Galilhai sensed not only anger, but disappointment.

"I watched you become a man," Tate said quietly. "Do not stand before me now and call this wisdom."

The warrior straightened.

"I have fought for this tribe since I was old enough to cross into the Other World. I have bled for people who only know me as a blade placed in their hands."

"And she taught you to resent that sacrifice," Tate replied.

Kewa's eyes turned toward him.

"She taught me nothing," the warrior said. "She saw me."

Kewa lifted a hand gently toward his face.

"They taught you how to fight," she whispered. "How to endure. How to bury your fear beneath duty. But no one ever asked what you wanted your life to become."

The warrior looked at her with aching devotion.

For the first time, Galilhai understood why he had followed her.

Tate remained unmoved.

"Hunger often disguises itself as revelation," he said. "A starving man will kneel before poison if it promises to fill him."

Kewa's calm smile did not falter.

"And fear will call anything dangerous if it threatens the order it built."

The tension inside Wono tightened.

The warrior stepped forward.

"I have found my true union during my journey to Lake Tahoe. Before Puha, I ask to bind my soul to Kewa's."

Murmurs spread among the guests.

The bride lowered her gaze briefly, gathering what remained of herself before speaking again.

"I would have followed you into any world," she said softly. "You knew that."

His face twisted with grief.

"That is why I could not tell you."

"No," she replied. "That is why you should have."

For the first time, Kewa's expression shifted. The calm beauty thinned slightly, revealing something colder beneath it.

"She speaks only to bind you again."

The bride looked directly at her.

"No. I speak because he is still standing close enough to hear me."

The warrior's hand loosened around Kewa's.

Only slightly.

But the movement carried the terrible weight of hesitation. For the first time since entering the chamber, he looked fully at the bride standing before him, and something inside his expression began to fracture.

Kewa felt it immediately.

The amber glow inside the arches flickered.

Tate saw the hesitation as well.

"Release her," he said. "If there is truth between you, it will survive the light. If there is not, let Puha reveal what you have mistaken for love."

The warrior looked from Tate to the bride, then finally toward Kewa.

"Kewa," he whispered.

Her eyes fixed upon him.

"Do not make me return to darkness."

The plea was soft, almost childlike, and for one brief moment Galilhai felt the strange pull of it. Not evil. Not rage.

Fear.

"I gave you warmth," the warrior said quietly.

"You gave me form," Kewa answered.

The words changed the room.

The bride stepped backward.

The warrior stared at Kewa as understanding finally reached him.

"What did you say?"

Kewa's hand tightened around his with sudden force.

The water flowing through the ceiling stopped completely.

"I loved what you opened inside me," she said.

The arches darkened.

A violent tremor surged through Wono.

The floating altar cracked apart behind the bride, and screams erupted as fragments of stone and crystal scattered across the chamber. Guests rushed toward the exits while the enormous structure groaned around them.

Galilhai tried to stand, but her body remained fixed to the bench, held there by the vision and forced to witness what came next.

Kewa's transformation had already begun.

Her golden hair drained of color until it became white. Wrinkles spread rapidly across her pale skin, while near the center of her chest a dark void appeared, consuming the light around it. The beauty that had held the chamber in silence did not disappear all at once. It failed in pieces, like a mask cracking under pressure.

The warrior staggered backward, horror overtaking the certainty that had carried him into the room.

"No," he whispered.

Kewa turned toward him, and now her voice seemed to emerge from somewhere deeper than her mouth.

"You wanted truth."

He reached for his sword.

One of Kewa's scales extended outward like a sharpened spear and pierced directly through his chest.

He did not bleed.

His body shuddered, lost its shape, and dissolved instantly into water, collapsing into a lifeless pool at the entrance of Wono.

The bride screamed his name.

Then she fell beside the water spreading across the floor, reaching toward it with trembling hands as though she still believed she could gather him back together.

Chaos consumed the chamber.

Kewa moved toward the edge of the pyramid while dark mist spread behind her, clinging to every surface it touched. Above Wono, the once breathtaking watery sky had transformed into an enormous whirlpool, unleashing a devastating force upon the world below.

The guests fled in terror as cracks spread through the walls, but the bride remained where she had fallen, unable to pull herself away from the place where the warrior had vanished.

Tate reached her just before a section of the ceiling collapsed and dragged her back against him.

When Kewa reached the edge of the structure, she looked once over her shoulder. For a moment her eyes found the broken altar, the fleeing guests, the father holding his daughter against him.

Then she threw herself into the lake below.

A dark trail spread across the water behind her.

Galilhai finally tore herself free from the bench and ran, but after only a few steps the same overwhelming heaviness she had felt inside the boat returned to her body.

Her legs stopped moving.

A deep exhaustion spread through her mind.

The dream within the dream had come to an end.

Galilhai awoke beneath the night sky.

Though her vision remained blurred at first, she slowly became aware of thousands of stars stretching across a pale band of light overhead. The Milky Way shone brighter than the moon itself, flowing endlessly from east to west. The boat rocked gently beneath her, and cold water splashed across her face.

She had returned to the World of Form.

The difference struck her immediately. She could hear her own breathing again, the movement of water against the wood, and the distant sounds of insects hidden along the shore. Every detail carried a weight absent from the Other World.

Reaching beside her, she struck two stones together above the oil lantern resting near her feet. Sparks dropped into the liquid, and a reddish flame slowly illuminated the darkness around her.

She took hold of the oar and began rowing toward the faint red light burning upon the shoreline.

By the time she returned, the tribe had gathered waiting for her.

Music and laughter returned to the shore, but the instant Wovoka looked into his daughter's eyes, every trace of joy vanished from his face.

Something inside her had changed.

"Did you see her?" he asked quietly.

Galilhai nodded.

"The lake woman," she whispered.

For a moment, Wovoka said nothing. The fire beside them cracked softly while the wind carried smoke toward the dark water.

"She killed every fish in this lake," he said at last. "Your grandfather used to say the shore smelled like death for weeks after she disappeared."

Galilhai lowered her gaze.

"She killed the warrior too," she said quietly. "But before that… he loved her."

Wovoka lowered himself beside the fire and rested his forearms on his knees.

"Yes," he said.

"I don't understand why."

"That is why such things are dangerous."

Galilhai frowned slightly.

"Because she was beautiful?"

A faint sadness touched Wovoka's face.

"No. Beauty is not evil." He picked up a small stone and turned it slowly between his fingers. "A flower can be beautiful. The lake can be beautiful. Even the stars above us are beautiful."

He tossed the stone gently into the darkness.

"But when a man has wandered the dunes too long, even a mirage begins to look like water."

Galilhai watched the ripples vanish into the black surface of the lake.

"She told him he was more than a weapon."

Wovoka looked at her carefully then.

"And maybe part of him needed to hear that."

"Was it a lie?"

Wovoka remained silent for a moment, listening to the wind moving through the reeds.

"The hardest lies to escape," he said softly, "are the ones wrapped around something true."

Galilhai pulled her knees closer against her chest.

"She sounded afraid at the end."

Wovoka stared toward the lake, his expression growing distant.

"Even wolves fear death," he said. "That does not make their teeth harmless."

The fire settled lower between them.

After a while, Galilhai spoke again.

"Why do the Dark Shadows want to come here?"

Wovoka watched her for a long moment before answering.

"When winter comes, animals search for warmth. When a storm breaks branches from a tree, insects gather inside the wound. Darkness behaves the same way. It searches for places where the world has cracked open."

Galilhai thought about the warrior standing inside Wono, holding Kewa's hand as though nothing else existed.

"And people can crack too?"

Wovoka's eyes softened.

"Yes."

The answer frightened her more than the story itself.

They sat quietly for a time while the waves rolled against the shore in slow, repeating rhythms.

"What would have happened if they had married?" Galilhai finally asked.

Wovoka rested his palm gently against the center of her chest.

"Her spirit would have entered this world completely," he said. "No one knows the shape it would have taken. That is the danger. Some poisons arrive in beautiful colors."

Galilhai looked down at his hand.

"So how do you know when something beautiful is bad?"

Wovoka smiled faintly, though exhaustion remained in his eyes.

“You listen carefully to what it asks you to become.”

The words lingered within her.

For the remainder of the night, Galilhai sat beside her father speaking softly about Pamahas, Wono, and the vision she had witnessed inside the Other World. Wovoka did not seem surprised by what she described. Through the movement of leaves and the whispering of wind, he often sensed events long before they arrived.

As the fire surrendered itself to ashes, father and daughter remained beside the darkened shore beneath the endless sky, listening to the slow breathing of the lake.

For one fleeting moment, it felt as though Puha flowed through them both as a single spirit.

CHAPTER VI
The Meaning Beyond Words

Pay attention to the energy within your words. Do they reveal light and life or promote hindrance and disease? Do they honor and respect your fellowmen or diminish and insult them? Do they victimize you or empower you? Stay alert when you speak.

For the second time that month, Maia Hackett's car refused to start. She sat in the driver's seat with both hands resting on the wheel while the engine struggled beneath the hood, turning over again and again without catching. The sound filled the garage with a dry mechanical insistence that made the morning feel more fragile than it should have. Maia closed her eyes, counted silently to five, then turned the key once more.

Nothing.

"Please," she whispered.

The word sounded too small in the closed space.

She tried again.

This time the engine caught reluctantly, shuddering before settling into a rough idle while the dashboard lights steadied one by one. Maia exhaled and leaned back against the seat. She had already received one written notice from the bookstore owner for arriving late, and although the warning had been phrased politely, politeness did not make it less serious.

Outside, Sparks rested beneath the pale heat of late morning. The neighborhood of Las Vistas sat high enough on the hill that parts of Reno and the desert basin could be glimpsed between rooftops, roads, and scattered trees. Maia reversed carefully from the garage and guided the car downhill.

Unlike Ale, Maia did not move through the world as though it were a stage prepared for her entrance. She preferred narrow rooms, quiet shelves, and conversations that did not require performance. Her dark hair fell in loose waves around her face, often escaping whatever clip she used to hold it back, and her green eyes carried the alert patience of someone accustomed to noticing small changes in old things: brittle pages, misremembered stories, names copied incorrectly from one source to another.

She distrusted easy explanations.

That was one reason Ale loved her.

It was also one reason Sam had come looking for her.

The bookstore stood on a modest street not far from the older edge of Sparks, a narrow two-story building painted cream, with wooden shutters over the second-floor windows and a weathered sign swinging slightly above the entrance. By the time Maia arrived, the sun had already warmed the sidewalk. She unlocked the front door with a small bronze key and stepped inside.

The air smelled of paper, dust, and old glue.

She turned on the lamps first. One green desk lamp near the counter, then the softer overhead lights filling the front room with a muted glow. The OPEN sign lit up in the window. Behind the counter, the computer monitor woke to a spreadsheet of orders, inventory numbers, late shipments, and unpaid invoices.

Maia set her bag down and began sorting returned books.

The front of the store carried what people asked for most often: romance novels, thrillers, celebrity memoirs, glossy cookbooks, and the kind of inspirational books customers bought after difficult Mondays. The back aisles held the stranger subjects that rarely sold but kept the store from becoming ordinary: folklore, regional history, tribal studies, mythology, occult symbolism, forgotten religions, old maps, and several shelves of ghost stories whose covers had faded from too many years beneath fluorescent light.

Maia always took longer returning those books to their places.

She liked the silence in the back of the store.

It felt less empty there.

She had just climbed the small rolling ladder to return a book on nineteenth-century burial customs when the front door opened. The bell above it gave a thin metallic chime, followed by the heavier sound of the door closing.

"I'll be right there," Maia called.

She tucked the book into place and descended carefully. When she reached the end of the aisle, she stopped.

Sam stood near the front counter, one arm folded across her stomach, the other lifted in a small wave.

"Hi," Sam said. "I didn't mean to scare you."

For a moment Maia did not answer. Then warmth broke through her surprise.

"You didn't scare me." She crossed the room quickly and hugged her. "I work alone with ghost books. My standards for fear are higher than that."

Sam laughed softly into her shoulder.

"When did you get back?" Maia asked, pulling away.

"Yesterday."

Maia looked at her face more carefully than most people would have.

"You look tired."

"That seems to be the official greeting now."

"It's accurate."

Sam smiled, though the expression did not fully settle.

Maia did not push. She had never possessed Ale's talent for prying open a silence and making it sound like affection. Maia preferred to wait near the edge of things until people came closer on their own.

"You're coming this weekend?" Sam asked. "To the lake?"

"Noah told me last week." Maia walked back toward the counter and lifted a stack of invoices from the desk. "I believed that part. I had more trouble believing Ale would voluntarily sleep outside."

"She says she's doing it for me."

"She is. Ale performs inconvenience loudly, but she doesn't usually endure it unless she loves someone."

Sam looked down.

The words passed through the room quietly.

Maia saw the change and softened her voice.

"It's good you're here."

Sam nodded once. "It feels good. Strange, but good."

For a moment, neither of them spoke.

Both knew where the silence wanted to go. Toward Sam's mother. Toward the accident. Toward everything Sam had left behind too quickly because staying had become unbearable.

Maia let the silence remain.

Sam looked toward the back shelves.

"I actually came because I wanted to ask you something."

"That sounds serious."

"It might not be." Sam hesitated. "You wrote your senior project on the Paiute, right?"

"Not the whole tribe," Maia corrected automatically. "Mostly oral tradition around Pyramid Lake and how outside writers kept flattening it into folklore."

Sam smiled faintly. "That sounds like you."

"What do you want to know?"

Sam glanced toward the window, then back at her.

"Do you think those stories can mean something even if they aren't literally true?"

Maia was quiet for a moment.

She liked questions that revealed more about the person asking than the subject itself.

"Yes," she said. "But I'd phrase it differently."

Sam followed her toward the back of the store.

"Stories like that aren't trying to behave like newspaper articles. They are not less true because they move through symbol. Sometimes symbol is the only way a truth survives long enough to reach someone who needs it."

Sam listened more intently than she intended to.

"So the words don't matter?"

"The words matter," Maia said. "But not because they trap the meaning. They point toward it. That's different."

They passed through an aisle where several lights had burned out, leaving the shelves in a dim amber shadow. Maia ran her fingers lightly across the spines as she walked, reading titles without slowing.

"Ale told me the story about the mother who cried Pyramid Lake into being," Sam said.

"Stone Mother."

"Yes."

Maia glanced over her shoulder.

"You looked strange when you said that."

"It felt familiar." Sam rubbed her thumb against the side of her index finger. "Like I had heard it before, but not exactly. I can't remember where."

"You probably heard some version in school. A lot of people around here know the name without really knowing the story."

"That's what bothers me."

"What part?"

Sam searched for the answer and found only fragments.

"The children being sent away. The mother waiting. The lake coming from grief." She looked toward the floor. "I don't know. It stayed with me."

Maia stopped beside a narrow shelf of regional history books.

"That happens with old stories."

"What?"

"They recognize something in you before you recognize anything in them."

Sam looked at her.

Maia seemed briefly embarrassed by her own certainty and reached for a book to cover it. "Sorry. That sounded like Ale."

"No," Sam said. "It didn't."

Maia pulled a small hardbound volume from the shelf. Its brown cover had faded near the corners, and the paper smelled faintly sweet with age.

"This one is probably what you want. It's old, and parts of it are dated, so don't treat it like the final word on anything. But it pays attention better than most."

Sam accepted the book carefully.

"Pays attention?"

"That matters more than people think."

The title was simple and worn across the cover. Sam traced it once with her thumb before following Maia to the reading tables near the back of the store.

Three wooden tables stood beneath a round window that looked out toward a narrow alley and a slice of pale sky. Olive-green desk lamps sat at each table, their brass stems slightly tarnished. A promotional display near the wall advertised the store's newest bestseller: *Criminal Lovers: Hot Pursuit.* The cover showed a couple kissing in front of blurred police lights while a body bag rested dramatically in the foreground.

Sam stared at it.

"Subtle."

Maia followed her gaze and sighed.

"That book is outselling every serious title in the store."

"Maybe the body bag adds emotional depth."

"It adds revenue."

Sam laughed, and for the first time since entering the store, some of the weight around her loosened.

Maia gestured toward the table.

"Stay as long as you want. I need to process orders before my employer remembers I was late again."

"Car trouble?"

"Existential car trouble."

Sam smiled and sat down.

Maia returned to the front counter, leaving her alone among the old shelves and low green light.

For a while, Sam read without taking notes.

The book moved through fragments of landscape, migration, ceremony, water, loss, and stories carried by voice before being forced into print by people who often misunderstood what they were trying to preserve. Some passages felt distant and academic. Others felt uncomfortably alive.

Then she reached a section describing a forest beyond ordinary perception.

The words were careful, almost hesitant, as though the writer did not fully trust the account but could not dismiss it either. Tall trees. Unfamiliar animals. A sense of crossing into a place where physical distance no longer behaved correctly.

Sam stopped reading.

Her dream returned at once.

Black trees twisting in wind.

Dust.

Horses emerging from darkness.

The absence moving between them.

Her pulse quickened.

She reached into her purse and pulled out the small journal she had carried for nearly a year. Its cover was soft from use, the elastic band stretched slightly from being opened too often. At first, the journal had been an attempt to understand her grief. Later it became something else.

A record of dreams she did not fully believe were dreams.

She opened to the last written page.

The handwriting there belonged to her, but reading it still made her uneasy. Some entries were practical and fragmented, written just after waking before the details vanished. Others contained sentences she did not remember composing.

She read the final paragraph again.

Black horses. No faces beneath the armor. Something in the middle of them where the world folds inward. A woman with red hair. She says I have to come home.

Sam closed her eyes.

The bookstore faded around her.

She tried to remember the woman's face, but the effort only brought back the feeling of her hand on Sam's shoulder. Warm. Steady. Realer than anything else in the dream.

Her phone rang.

The sound startled her badly enough that her knee struck the table.

She grabbed the phone from beside the book.

"Ale?"

"Where are you?" Ale asked. Her voice came bright and immediate through the speaker. "I'm buying supplies for our wilderness suffering."

"I'm at Maia's bookstore."

"Oh, good. Ask her if my new tarot deck means I'm entering a period of abundance or if my credit card is just delusional."

Sam glanced toward the front of the store where Maia was typing behind the counter.

"I think she's working."

"Maia is always working. It's part of her tragic Victorian librarian energy."

"She can hear you if I put you on speaker."

"Don't you dare. I need her to like me."

Sam smiled despite herself.

Ale continued, "Do you want me to pick you up? I still need a tent big enough for four people and emotionally large enough for my discomfort."

"You're really doing this."

"I have accepted my fate. I am bringing skincare, snacks, and possibly a portable air conditioner."

"For camping?"

"For survival."

Sam looked down at the open book, then at the dream journal beside it.

"Yeah," she said. "Pick me up."

"I'll be there soon. Try not to buy the whole supernatural section before I arrive."

The afternoon light had shifted while she was reading. The round window above the tables now held a softer color, and dust moved gently through the green glow of the desk lamp.

She should have felt calmer after speaking with Ale.

Instead, the dream felt closer.

She closed the book and slipped it into her purse, then gathered the journal without looking carefully enough to notice that it had slid beneath the edge of the table.

At the front counter, Maia was placing shipping labels on padded envelopes.

"I have to go," Sam said.

Maia looked up.

"Did the book help?"

Sam hesitated.

"Yes."

The answer was true, though not in the way Maia meant.

Maia studied her expression without asking another question.

"Keep it for now," she said.

"Are you sure?"

"Bring it back when it stops following you around."

Sam almost laughed, but the words landed strangely.

Outside, a car horn sounded from the street.

"Ale," Sam said.

"That explains the horn."

Sam hugged Maia goodbye, then stepped out into the heat.

Ale's Mercedes idled near the curb. Through the windshield, Sam could see her adjusting lipstick in the mirror with the solemn concentration of someone preparing for public ceremony. In the back seat sat several shopping bags, a cooler, and what appeared to be a boxed portable air conditioner.

Sam opened the passenger door and stared.

"You were serious."

Ale looked offended.

"I am frequently serious. People just miss it because I'm beautiful."

Sam laughed as she got in.

The car pulled away from the bookstore and entered the afternoon traffic.

Behind them, the bell above the bookstore door had barely stopped moving when Maia noticed something near the back tables.

At first she thought Sam had left her wallet behind. Then she saw the journal.

It lay open on the carpet beneath the table, face down, as though it had slipped from her purse unnoticed.

Maia walked toward it slowly.

She knew she should close it without reading. Privacy mattered to her. Words mattered to her. The private ones most of all.

But when she lifted the journal, one sentence had already exposed itself across the page in dark blue ink.

The handwriting belonged to Sam.

The pressure behind it did not.

Maia went still.

She needs me to jump.

The bookstore settled into silence around her. Somewhere near the front, the OPEN sign hummed faintly in the window. Outside, traffic continued along the street as though nothing had changed.

Maia read the sentence once more.

Then she closed the journal carefully, holding it with both hands.

CHAPTER VII
The Other World

Ultimately, anything is possible when belief becomes complete attention. What the mind calls impossible, Puha recognizes only as unfinished.

The moon was immense, suspended above the Other World in the shape of a silver oval whose light drifted through the aqueous sky like a current moving beneath transparent water. Its radiance softened distance and deepened every color below it, illuminating a world untouched by the restraints that governed the material realm.

Across the open land, flowers unlike any found within the World of Form opened and folded in synchronized rhythm. Their petals shifted from copper to fluorescent lavender without wind or shadow touching them, as though color itself possessed breath. Nearby, gigantic bighorn sheep crossed the pale sand in solemn procession while faint currents of electricity traveled continuously through their spiraled horns, illuminating their bodies in soft blue flashes before vanishing again into the night.

At the center of an immense pine forest, the settlement rose.

Golden structures towered above the trees, their surfaces curved and impossibly precise, neither entirely built nor entirely grown. Pines emerged from terraces of polished metal. Roots disappeared into luminous walls that appeared to nourish them rather than resist them. The forest did not end where the city began. Both had been shaped into one continuous form, as though architecture and landscape obeyed the same hidden intelligence.

The structures possessed no visible entrances. Instead, every surface carried shifting symbols and unreadable lines that rearranged themselves endlessly across the gold. Some expanded until they nearly resembled language before folding inward again and dissolving into new patterns. Others reacted subtly to movement below, changing direction as inhabitants passed beneath them, as though the settlement itself were capable of attention.

The roads curved through the settlement with unnatural harmony. No dust gathered upon them. No debris remained where it had fallen.

Even stillness seemed ordered here.

The inhabitants moved through the streets in quiet coordination. They were tall and finely formed, with pronounced cheekbones and elongated chins that gave their faces an old and sculpted stillness. Light flowed through the stones embedded within their garments, causing portions of the fabric to fade transparent before deepening once more into rich color.

No voices could be heard, yet nothing about the settlement felt silent.

Awareness passed continuously between its people without gesture or sound. A glance, a pause, the slightest shift in attention, and entire meanings moved through the open air around them.

North of the settlement, a stream of water levitated high above the earth and descended toward Pyramid Lake in sharp angular turns. Whenever the current bent, it accelerated instead of slowing, gathering impossible momentum at each perfect corner. Within the stream swam cutthroat trout adorned with jade fins and silver eyes, rising and falling through the suspended water in coordinated spirals that reflected the moonlight like fragments of polished stone.

Everything in the Other World carried life beyond itself. Stone listened. Water remembered. Light possessed weight. Even silence seemed alive beneath the surface of things.

This was not merely another world.

It was reality before limitation hardened around it.

High above the settlement, Pamahas stood upon the balcony of one of the great golden structures, looking across the forest toward distant Wono. The immense pyramid hovered above Pyramid Lake, silent against the silver horizon.

Even from this distance its presence dominated the landscape, enduring and immovable.

Beside her stood her brother.

His name was Esa.

Unlike the others below, Esa bore no fully human face. Thick gray fur covered the elongated shape of a wolf's head whose golden eyes carried an age beyond reckoning. Though his body remained upright and powerfully built, nothing within him appeared divided. Wolf and man existed together beneath a single presence so completely reconciled that neither seemed separate from the other.

Long before the Paiute people shaped homes from reed and willow beside Pyramid Lake, before memory divided itself into generations, Esa had guided them toward the World of Form. Some remembered him now only through fragmented stories. Others no longer remembered him at all.

But the land remembered.

For a long while, neither of them spoke. Below them, the settlement continued in perfect rhythm beneath the silver glow of the moon.

Then one trout failed to rise with the others.

The interruption lasted only an instant. A single silver body remained behind within the levitating stream before correcting itself and returning to the choreography. Yet the imbalance carried through the world like a fracture moving silently beneath stone.

Pamahas saw it immediately.

Near the forest edge, a cluster of flowers paused before changing color. Moments later, the symbols upon one of the nearest structures rearranged themselves incorrectly, several lines converging where they should have passed cleanly through one another.

"It is reaching farther," Pamahas said.

Esa's gaze remained fixed upon Wono.

"For many ages," he said, "it drifted without shape. Now it remembers direction."

"The wedding changed it."

"The crossing fed it."

His voice carried neither anger nor surprise. It held only the weight of recognition.

Far below, several inhabitants had stopped walking. Their attention turned toward the distant lake beyond the forest.

Pamahas rested one hand upon the balcony rail.

"We have restrained it for centuries."

"A river held behind stone still seeks the sea," Esa replied. "Delay alters the journey. It does not erase the destination."

For generations beyond counting, Esa and Pamahas had moved carefully at the edges of both worlds, not as rulers imposing will, but as guardians attending to imbalance before it deepened into rupture. They had weakened dangerous crossings before they widened. They had softened certain dreams, redirected certain visions, and closed pathways before human attention fastened too firmly upon them.

They interfered rarely, and never without consequence.

Puha moved through all things. Through creation and decay. Through tenderness and violence. Through the opening of flowers and the hunger of wolves. To interfere carelessly with existence was not wisdom. It was vanity disguised as mercy.

Even darkness belonged to the whole.

But now the darkness was no longer merely moving.

It was multiplying.

The levitating stream flickered faintly. Its sharp geometric angles softened for a brief instant before stabilizing once more.

Pamahas lowered her voice.

"Kewa carried the fracture back with her."

"Yes."

"She was not born from Tahoe like this."

"No," Esa said. "The lake shaped her slowly, the way rot shapes wood beneath bark. By the time the tree falls, the ruin has already lived inside it for years."

Far beyond the forest, the waters surrounding Wono darkened almost imperceptibly.

"There was a time," Pamahas said, "when Lake Tahoe reflected the heavens more clearly than Pyramid Lake."

"The waters there once carried cleaner dreams," Esa replied.

Lake Tahoe rested far beyond Pyramid Lake within the World of Form, separated by mountains, distance, and time. Yet beneath both worlds flowed an old canal, older than human memory, joining the two sacred lakes beneath the earth.

Long ago, both lakes had served together as thresholds between realms. Pyramid Lake became the place of crossing, where attention gathered strongly enough to pierce the boundary between worlds. Tahoe became the place of reflection, transformation, and dream, where consciousness drifted nearest to the unseen.

The Paiute people had once lived near both waters.

Then the shadows gathered.

Not through sudden catastrophe or war, but slowly, through fear, grief, obsession, longing, and the hidden fractures carried silently within living beings. Over generations, the threshold there became unstable. Visions returned altered. Dreams crossed back wrong. Wanderers disappeared into the waters and emerged carrying traces of something that had followed them home.

Eventually, the tribe abandoned the region.

But the corruption remained, and beneath both lakes, the hidden canal continued flowing.

"The shadows learned patience there," Pamahas said.

Esa watched the distant waters surrounding Wono.

"Rot deepens quietly before the tree falls."

Below them, the settlement dimmed slightly. The symbols upon the golden structures slowed. One by one, the jade-finned trout hovering within the levitating stream ceased their spiraling ascent. Then the electricity vanished from the bighorns' horns.

A deep vibration passed beneath the balcony.

Pamahas felt it first through the rail beneath her hand, not as movement, but as pressure gathering somewhere far below the visible world. Across the settlement, the shifting symbols upon the golden structures slowed further, several lines freezing in place before continuing again in broken sequence.

Below them, the levitating stream faltered. One of its sharp angular turns softened unexpectedly, causing the current to spill downward in a glittering arc before forcing itself back into suspension. The trout within it ceased their spiraling movement altogether, remaining motionless inside the water as though listening alongside the inhabitants below.

Far beyond the forest, the surface of Pyramid Lake had begun to darken, though not uniformly.

The change gathered only around Wono.

At first, Pamahas believed the distortion belonged to the moonlight itself. The aqueous sky above the great pyramid appeared strangely blurred, its silver radiance bending inward toward a single point directly above the hovering structure. The stars nearest to it stretched subtly out of shape, their reflections curving along invisible lines.

Then the sky began to turn.

The luminous heavens rotated around Wono in widening circles, drawing streams of pale light inward as though the sky itself had become liquid caught in an enormous unseen drain. The oval moon distorted within the movement, its reflection elongating across the rotation before breaking apart into shimmering fragments.

A vast whirlpool had begun forming above the pyramid.

Pamahas felt the air around the settlement tighten.

The flowers closed.

The electricity vanished entirely from the bighorns' horns.

Far below, the inhabitants stood facing Wono in complete stillness while the enormous vortex deepened overhead, its rotation accelerating with terrifying silence. The aqueous sky folded inward upon itself layer by layer, revealing glimpses of darkness moving beneath the silver currents like shapes struggling to emerge through translucent skin.

"Lake Tahoe," Pamahas whispered.

"The canal no longer weakens what passes through it," Esa said. "It carries it whole."

The settlement dimmed further. The golden structures retained their form, yet the light within them withdrew inward as though something beneath the world had tightened.

Below, the inhabitants remained still.

They listened.

Pamahas felt unease rise within her, though beneath it rested fear. Not for herself. For both worlds.

"She is still not here," Pamahas said.

Esa knew immediately whom she meant.

Sam.

For years Pamahas had entered the human girl's dreams without fully crossing the boundary. She had appeared through symbols, reflections, fragments of impossible landscapes, and flashes of red hair beneath silver light. She had guided without forcing, called without commanding, and opened paths without dragging Sam through them.

But Sam remained within the World of Form, unaware of what she carried.

"She can still transmute it," Pamahas said. "If she awakens fully."

"If her attention survives the crossing."

"She is the only one capable of turning dark energy back toward Puha without tearing both worlds apart."

Esa's gaze remained upon Wono.

"Some souls are born near thresholds. The worlds pull against them from the beginning."

Pamahas turned toward him.

"Then why does Puha leave her sleeping?"

"Because awakening forced too early becomes another form of ruin."

The whirlpool widened further above Wono, descending lower with each rotation until the edge of the vortex nearly touched the uppermost point of the hovering pyramid.

Then Pyramid Lake answered.

The water beneath Wono trembled once before collapsing inward at its center. A deep circular depression formed directly below the pyramid as the lake began rotating around the same invisible axis governing the sky above. Unlike the silver vortex overhead, the movement below appeared heavy and distorted, its waters nearly black beneath the moonlight.

Wono hovered between the converging spirals, suspended in the narrowing space where sky and depth had begun drawing toward one another. Above it, the silver vortex descended through the turning heavens. Below it, the dark whirlpool climbed from Pyramid Lake in wounded rotation, enclosing the great golden pyramid inside a pressure that seemed to bend the distance between worlds.

Pamahas stepped toward the edge of the balcony.

"They are using the canal as passage."

"Yes."

"If they destroy Wono..."

"The boundary between worlds would no longer hold its shape."

Wono had never merely been a place of crossing. It was one of the last points of stillness holding the worlds apart. So long as the pyramid endured, the darkness gathering beyond the threshold remained forced to reach indirectly, through dream, longing, fear, and fracture. But if Wono surrendered completely, the old separation would begin to fail, and what had once needed invitation would no longer require it.

Every fracture would become entrance.

Every fear would become invitation.

Pamahas looked toward her brother.

"Then we must seal the canal."

Esa remained motionless while the spirals tightened around Wono.

The passage beneath the lakes was older than memory. Before the Paiute people walked the shores of Pyramid Lake, before Tahoe darkened beneath corrupted dreams, the waters had moved freely between both thresholds, carrying balance through regions of the world that human beings would never fully understand. To sever that movement was not a simple act of protection. It was a wound that would echo through both worlds long after the danger itself had passed.

Yet the corruption rising from Tahoe had already begun reaching toward Wono with growing strength. If the canal remained open much longer, the darkness would eventually find passage.

"The waters will remember the severing," Esa said at last.

"They already remember the wound."

"The pressure will build."

"It is already building."

Esa closed his eyes briefly, as though listening to something moving far beneath the world itself.

"What is buried beneath delay eventually demands shape."

Far below, a portion of the levitating stream collapsed suddenly, spilling downward before struggling back into its suspended form.

Pamahas lowered her voice.

"Brother."

The word softened the air between them.

Not goddess speaking to god.

Sister speaking to brother.

"We have bent without breaking for longer than humans remember," she said. "We have guided without ruling. But the shadows no longer seek movement. They seek dominion."

The decision entered Esa before he spoke it.

"The canal will be sealed."

Pamahas did not look relieved.

Neither did he.

Esa stepped onto the edge of the balcony, and his transformation began immediately. Bones lengthened with deep resonant cracks. Thick gray fur surged across his body while his spine lowered and widened into the immense musculature of a wolf larger than any earthly creature. The human structure of him collapsed into something older and more complete, though his eyes remained unchanged: golden, still, and older than fear.

Then Esa leapt.

He descended from the balcony into the forest below, landing with enough force to send subtle vibrations through the roads beneath the settlement. The inhabitants parted before him without fear.

Esa ran through the forest beneath towering pines and dimming flowers, across sand where electricity no longer flowed through the bighorns' horns. Each strike of his paws carried him closer to Pyramid Lake with terrifying speed.

When he reached the shore, the lower whirlpool shuddered.

Its outer rotation warped and slackened as though recoiling from his presence. Wono remained suspended between the converging spirals, but the shadows moving through the dark water withdrew slightly, not in defeat, but in recognition of a power they had not yet learned to consume.

Along the shoreline, dozens of translucent oval mirrors appeared floating silently above the sand. They reflected not the lake, but hidden regions of the Other World untouched by corruption: elder forests, luminous caverns, subterranean rivers, and pools beneath starless skies.

From the mirrors emerged the lake creatures.

First came the jade-finned trout. Then aquatic serpents adorned with topaz-colored scales. Other beings followed behind them, stranger and more difficult to name, shaped like fragments of water given consciousness.

They gathered around Esa.

No words passed between them.

He looked upon them, and they understood.

Together they entered the lake.

Far below the surface, where the moon's light dissolved into deep midnight blue, the lakebed shimmered with countless zircon crystals no larger than grains of sand. Their tiny pyramid-shaped surfaces fractured the faint remaining light into subdued glimmers.

At the center of the lake rested the opening.

A vast circular shaft lined entirely in gold descended beneath the earth into darkness. Within it stretched the canal connecting Pyramid Lake to Tahoe, and from deep within that darkness, pressure moved upward.

The creatures converged over the opening without hesitation.

The trout spread themselves across the shaft in perfect symmetry. Serpents coiled along the golden rim. Luminous bodies overlapped until scales softened into molten gold and silver eyes disappeared beneath radiant metallic seams.

One by one, their forms dissolved into the growing seal.

The gold widened, brightened, and hardened completely across the mouth of the shaft.

As the canal closed, a deep vibration moved through Pyramid Lake and continued outward beneath the world itself, passing through water, stone, forest, settlement, and sky with the force of something old recognizing its own interruption. Wono trembled. The levitating stream faltered. The golden structures dimmed sharply before stabilizing once more.

Behind the seal, the pressure from Tahoe struck violently against the barrier.

The gold held.

The darkness surged upward again from beneath the earth, and the seal endured.

Above the lake, the silver whirlpool loosened its hold upon the sky. The lower vortex weakened in uneven rotations, collapsing inward by degrees until the surface of Pyramid Lake began to remember its stillness. Moonlight slowly reclaimed the heavens. The flowers reopened halfway. A faint current returned to the bighorns' horns. The levitating stream resumed its impossible movement toward Pyramid Lake, though weaker now, its once perfect geometry subtly strained.

Esa remained motionless at the shore, his immense wolf form silhouetted against the darkened water.

He had saved the passage from immediate corruption.

But he had also wounded it.

The sacred flow between the lakes no longer moved freely. What had circulated for millennia was now trapped behind gold, pressure gathering where movement had once been effortless. The consequences would not arrive immediately. They would unfold slowly through dream, water, weather, hunger, and memory, reaching the World of Form in ways no one yet understood.

Slowly, Esa turned away from the lake.

The shadows had been delayed, but not defeated. Beyond the sealed canal, Lake Tahoe remained under their influence, and whatever had gathered there would continue searching for another path toward Wono.

High above the settlement, Pamahas watched her brother begin the long walk back from the shore.

For the first time in many ages, neither of them could pretend the war remained distant.

It began long before human memory. Long before Kewa crossed the threshold. Long before the warrior mistook longing for truth. Long before Galilhai entered the boat beneath the stars.

But now it had taken shape.

Somewhere within the World of Form, Wovoka's daughter carried visions she did not yet understand.

Somewhere else, Sam slept beneath dreams she had not yet learned to trust.

And beneath Pyramid Lake, a golden seal held back an old darkness whose hunger had only begun to know itself.

Destiny had not arrived.

It had opened.

CHAPTER VIII

Between California and Nevada

Our spirits don't know about jurisdictions, borders, and other man-defined boundaries. Like all things in this world, these too shall come and go. But our souls are eternal indeed.

Noah closed the browser on his laptop and sat still for a moment, listening to the quiet hum of his room after the screen went dark.

His bedroom was small and painted navy blue, a color his grandmother said made the walls look farther away than they were. A two-panel sliding window faced the street, its light-filtering shades half drawn against the morning brightness. Beside it stood a narrow wooden desk with a black chair tucked beneath it, his notebooks stacked in imperfect towers beside a water bottle, a pair of swim goggles, and the charging cord he always forgot to coil. His twin bed, covered in white linens, had already been made in the hurried way of someone eager to leave.

From the corner, he grabbed his neon-green backpack and slung it over one shoulder.

Downstairs, the house smelled faintly of coffee, warm bread, and the lavender soap Alma kept near the kitchen sink. Noah crossed the living room quickly, hoping to slip out before being noticed, but a soft voice caught him before he reached the front door.

"Hey there, sweetheart. Do you want some breakfast?"

His grandmother, Alma, sat on the coyote-brown leather couch with the morning newspaper unfolded across her lap. She was seventy years old, though the number seemed to sit lightly on her, as though time had passed over her face with care rather than force. Her complexion was fair, her eyes brown and observant, her lips thin and pink. Long, straight white hair framed her face and shoulders. She wore coral pants and a flowery blouse fastened with small white buttons. A delicate silver necklace rested at the hollow of her throat, and pearl earrings caught the sunlight whenever she moved her head.

Noah stopped with one hand already on the doorknob.

"I'm going for a swim, Grandma. I already had a protein bar," he said.

"A protein bar?" Alma lifted her gaze from the newspaper. "Oh dear. That is not breakfast."

"It is if you eat it before noon."

"It is if you want to offend your ancestors."

Noah smiled despite himself.

"I promise I'll have a proper one tomorrow before going camping with Maia and Ale."

"And Sam as well," Alma said, turning a page of the newspaper as if she had merely corrected the weather.

Noah's hand loosened on the doorknob.

"Where did you hear that?"

Alma did not look up immediately. She smoothed the crease of the paper with the back of her fingers, letting him feel the silence before answering.

"It is a small town," she said. "News travels faster than your skipping breakfast."

"Touché."

Her eyes rose then, gentle but difficult to avoid.

"She is going, isn't she?"

Noah shifted the backpack strap higher on his shoulder.

"Yeah. I think so."

"You think so?"

"That's what Ale said."

"And what does Sam say?"

Noah looked toward the window. Outside, the day was already bright enough to bleach the porch boards pale.

"Ale said she was going."

Alma folded the newspaper once, slowly.

"Sometimes people need to be asked things directly, Noah. Especially when everyone around them has gotten used to guessing."

He did not answer. He knew what she meant, and because he knew, he wanted to leave before the knowing became a conversation.

"I'll be back soon," he said.

"Swim where there are other people."

"I always do."

"No, you don't."

He gave her a guilty half smile.

"I will today."

Alma watched him open the door. For a moment, the sunlight divided him from the house, one foot in the dim living room and the other already outside.

"And eat something real after," she called.

"Yes, Grandma."

"And don't pretend you didn't hear me about Samantha."

Noah stepped onto the porch.

"I heard you."

The door closed behind him with a soft wooden sigh.

Outside, Tahoe City was already awake. The morning held the bright, deceptive stillness of late summer, when the air was warm but not yet heavy and the mountains seemed close enough to touch. Tall green pines lined the neighborhood streets, their needles stirring with the lightest suggestion of wind. Birds moved noisily from branch to branch. Cars passed slowly along the road, their tires whispering over sunlit asphalt. Two-story wooden houses, some modest and others built to look modest despite their size, stood among sloping roofs, porch railings, stacked firewood, and flower boxes trembling with color.

Beyond them, Lake Tahoe opened like a blue thought at the edge of the town.

Noah followed the road toward one of the narrow trails he knew by heart. It began behind a row of pines and dropped toward the shore at an angle most visitors overlooked. There were many such paths along the lake, faint and half-hidden, known only to those who had learned them by walking. Some led to beaches or flat rocks where a person could enter the water without being seen from the road. Others ended abruptly above a cliff, offering a beautiful view and no way down, as if the land itself enjoyed reminding strangers that seeing was not the same as reaching.

He liked that about Tahoe. It revealed itself by degrees.

The lake extended across the border between California and Nevada, holding both states in a single body of water as if the names mattered only to maps. To vacationers, it was a place of gleaming ski resorts, summer rentals, crowded cafés, wooden docks, glassy mornings, and photographs taken beneath impossible skies. To Noah, it was less simple. It was where he had learned to swim, where he had cut his foot on underwater granite, where he had kissed someone for the first time and regretted it almost immediately, where storms could arrive over the ridges with no apology. It was beautiful, yes. Everyone said that. But people used the word too easily. They spoke of beauty as if it were harmless.

The trail narrowed quickly. On his left, dry grass and bushes separated the path from the asphalt road above. On his right, rocks marked the edge of a pronounced slope dropping toward the lake. The water flashed between the trees in blue fragments. Heat rose from the dirt in a thin mineral smell. Somewhere below, a dog barked twice and stopped.

Noah walked fast, then slowed without meaning to.

He had been trying not to think about Sam.

That effort had become its own kind of thinking.

He remembered the phone call from Ale after the accident. Her voice had sounded unlike itself, too thin, too breathless, almost formal from shock, as she told him about the freeway, the wreck, the hospital, and Sam's mother. He remembered sitting down on the floor because his legs had become unreliable. He remembered asking questions that Ale could not answer. After that, the town had changed shape around Sam. People lowered their voices when she entered rooms.

Teachers softened deadlines. Friends watched her face for signs of collapse. Adults spoke of resilience as if naming a virtue could compensate for what had been taken.

Noah had done his part too. He had been careful. He had been kind. He had told himself this was love's first discipline.

But lately he had begun to suspect that his kindness had hidden a quieter failure.

He had looked at Sam through the wound before he had looked at her through anything else.

The thought made him uncomfortable. It was not that her grief was imaginary. It had weight. It had changed her posture, her laugh, the rhythm of her attention. There were moments when she seemed to be listening to something beyond the room, and others when she returned so sharply that everyone around her appeared slow and unfinished. But grief was not the whole of her. It could not be. Something else lived beneath it, something older than injury and stranger than endurance. Noah had felt it once or twice when she looked across the lake and went quiet. Not sadness exactly. Not fear. A pressure, perhaps. A depth.

He had not known what to do with that.

Feeling sorry for her had been easier than standing close enough to see what else was there.

A bird called from the trees above him, a brief metallic sound that did not belong to any bird he knew. Noah stopped and looked up.

The branches were still.

He waited. Nothing moved except a small brown pinecone rolling a few inches down the trail before catching against a stone.

He continued.

The air warmed as he descended, but the warmth seemed uneven, gathering in pockets and then vanishing. Halfway down the trail, a cold thread crossed his face so suddenly that he lifted his hand to his cheek. It was gone at once. He looked toward the lake, expecting to see wind advancing over the surface, but the treetops remained calm.

Below, Tahoe shimmered in the morning light.

At first, nothing appeared wrong.

Then he noticed the color.

The lake was not its usual turquoise near the shallows, nor its deep impossible blue farther out. A faint grayness lay across portions of the water, not enough to alarm anyone who had come expecting beauty and intended to find it, but enough for someone raised beside the lake to pause. It did not spread evenly. It gathered in long, thin bands, like smoke pressed flat beneath glass.

Noah moved closer to the cliff edge and narrowed his eyes.

The surface was restless, though there was almost no wind. Small waves crossed each other at odd angles, forming brief patterns that looked intentional before collapsing back into chop.

A group of people sat outside a café near the public parking lot, drinking coffee beneath striped umbrellas. Most of them were turned toward their plates or phones. One man had risen from his chair and was staring toward the water, one hand shading his eyes. A woman beside him laughed, then followed his gaze and stopped laughing. Across the street, two children ran ahead of their parents toward the beach, bright towels bouncing against their shoulders.

Noah descended faster.

The trail turned rocky near the bottom. He caught a branch with his left hand, stepped over a root, and came out between two boulders warmed by the sun. The beach opened before him in a narrow crescent of pale stones and sand. Usually, this part of the shore was loud by midmorning: swimmers calling to each other, coolers being dragged, paddleboards knocking against docks, gulls complaining from the rocks.

Today the sound seemed misplaced.

People were present, but their voices had thinned. Conversations continued in fragments, then faded, then resumed in whispers. A few tourists still held up their phones, smiling uncertainly as they filmed the lake. Others had lowered their devices without putting them away. Near Kings Beach, a white local news van pulled into the public lot, its tires crunching over gravel. A drone moved low above the far end of the shore, steady and insect-like, recording what the people beneath it had not yet agreed they were seeing.

Noah stepped onto the sand.

The first thing he noticed was the smell.

Not rot. Not sewage. Nothing strong enough to send people covering their noses or backing toward their cars. It was subtler than that, a mineral bitterness beneath the ordinary clean scent of water, like wet stone scraped open. It came and went with the small waves. Each time it returned, Noah thought of old coins held too long in a closed fist.

At the waterline, the pebbles were trembling.

He crouched.

The motion was slight, visible only because he had stopped moving. Tiny stones clicked against one another in place. The lake reached for them, withdrew, reached again. The waves were no taller than usual, but they did not break correctly. They seemed to hesitate before touching shore, as if meeting resistance from beneath.

Noah removed his backpack and let it fall beside his feet.

A little girl nearby pointed toward the shallows.

"Mom, look."

Her mother, distracted by a phone call, nodded without looking.

Noah followed the child's finger.

In the clear water near a line of submerged rocks, small silver fish had gathered in a tight circle. They moved together with unnatural precision, turning clockwise, then stopping all at once. For three full seconds they remained suspended, facing outward like needles around an invisible compass. Then the circle broke. The fish scattered into deeper water so quickly that their bodies flashed white and vanished.

Noah stood slowly.

A kayaker farther out lifted his paddle from the water and held it across his lap. He was staring down at the lake beside him. The kayak drifted, but the water immediately around it appeared almost still, a smooth oval amid the chop. Then the stillness loosened and the kayak bobbed again as if nothing had happened.

Noah's pulse climbed.

He told himself there were explanations. There were always explanations. Temperature changes. Algae. Sediment. Wind shear. Boat wakes meeting currents. Fish reacting to shadows.

But the lake did not look ordinary.

It looked watched.

He turned toward the mountains. Their ridges stood clean against the sky, snowless and immense, holding the morning in bright silence. No storm built behind them. No dark weather pressed down from the west. The sun was exposed and hard. Nothing in the visible world justified the gray bands crossing the water or the way the surface seemed to draw breath in sections.

A hush moved along the beach.

Not complete silence. Something more contagious than silence. The subtle pause that comes when many people notice the same wrongness but wait for someone else to name it first.

The drone dipped lower. Its buzz sharpened.

Then, without warning, the sound cut out.

The small machine hung in the air for an impossible fraction of a second, too still to be falling and too lifeless to be flying. Its lights blinked once. Twice. Then it dropped straight into the lake.

Several people shouted.

The splash was small.

Almost immediately, the water closed over it.

A man near the news van cursed and began running toward the shore. Someone laughed nervously. Someone else said it was probably a battery issue. A teenager replayed footage on his phone and muttered, "No way."

Noah barely heard them.

He took one step forward.

The lake touched his shoes. It was colder than it should have been.

A thin ring formed on the surface where the drone had disappeared. Not foam. Not oil. Not anything Noah could name. The ring held its shape against the waves, bright at the edge and dark within, and for a moment the water inside it seemed lower than the water around it, as though the lake had opened an eye and forgotten how to close it.

Noah's hands rose to cover his mouth.

Far beyond the marina, the surface of the lake lifted.

At first, Noah thought it was a swell, though Lake Tahoe did not produce swells like the ocean. But the formation did not collapse. It advanced.

The water ahead of it split into converging lines of silver and gray. Boats rocked violently as the phenomenon passed beneath them. One of the gulls circling above the shore gave a sharp cry and veered inland.

People along the beach began standing. Conversations dissolved into scattered confusion as more faces turned toward the lake. Phones rose into the air. Others simply stared.

The phenomenon remained impossibly far away, yet Noah felt its movement through the stones beneath his feet. The trembling reached the shoreline in faint pulses, subtle enough that most people would mistake them for imagination.

But Noah did not.

Far out across the water, the surface continued rising and folding inward around something unseen.

Not a wave. Not a current.

And it was approaching land with terrifying speed.

Beneath the ordinary blue of Lake Tahoe, something vast moved toward the shore without breaking the surface.

And Noah, holding his breath, refused to believe what he was witnessing.

CHAPTER IX
Conflict Knows No Resolution

War is a product of extreme unconsciousness. The illusion that death and destruction will set us free in whatever form. If we could only see that conflict is the imprisonment of our souls, the perpetuation of our insanity.

Evening descended across the settlement. The woven huts stood scattered along the open land beside Pyramid Lake, their branch frames darkening beneath the last amber light of the sun. A breeze moved through the surrounding fields, bending the tall grasses in soft waves while smoke from the cooking fires drifted into the cooling air.

Near the center of the settlement, the tribe had gathered in a wide circle around the fire.

Clay cups and plates rested upon the ground beside woven baskets filled with roots, herbs, and freshly cleaned fish from the lake. A large copper pot simmered above the flames, releasing the rich scent of fish stew into the evening air. On another night, the gathering might have belonged to laughter, hunger, and the ordinary comfort of bodies drawing close at day's end.

But that evening, no one reached for the food.

Wovoka stood apart from the circle, facing the darkening lake. Since dawn, he had felt something beneath the water that did not belong to its ordinary rhythm. The lake still moved against the shore. The reeds still trembled in the wind. Fish still broke the surface in brief flashes of silver. Yet the hidden current beneath all of it had changed, as though some passage under the world had been interrupted while everyone slept.

He did not know the full shape of what had happened.

That frightened him more than knowledge would have.

For many years, the stories passed down through his father's line had lived inside him like distant thunder. His grandfather had spoken of Wono only after long silences. His father had taught him the old warnings with hands that never trembled, though his voice sometimes did. There were things a shaman inherited that were not meant to be understood all at once. Names. Fragments. Ritual patterns. Warnings carried through generations because forgetting them would have been more dangerous than fear.

The Destiny Dice.

The fall of Tahoe.

The shadows that learned to wear beauty.

The child who would cross.

The distant soul born after forgetting.

He had known these things the way one knows the shape of mountains in darkness. Never fully. Never clearly. But enough to understand they existed.

Then Galilhai had returned from Wono with the lake woman's name upon her tongue.

Since then, the old stories no longer felt distant.

They felt awake.

The older woman sat upon a flat stone beside the fire, a narrow strip of faded red wool resting between her weathered hands. Her silver hair glowed in the shifting firelight while the evening breeze moved across her face. Though her eyes remained closed, her fingers continued folding the cloth with deliberate care, as though listening to something carried deep within its threads.

"The calm before the storm," she murmured.

Wovoka turned from the lake.

No one asked her what she meant. No one needed to.

Galilhai sat near the edge of the firelight, wrapped in a fur blanket though the evening had not yet grown cold. She had spoken little since returning from the Other World. The tribe had welcomed her with relief, but relief had changed once they saw her eyes. Something had crossed back with her, not as possession, not as wound, but as knowledge too large for childhood.

Wovoka looked at her and felt his courage falter.

The scattered whispers faded. Faces turned toward him, amber beneath the firelight, shadowed at the edges. Wovoka stood still until the tribe quieted completely. He had prepared words during the day, then abandoned them. Prepared words belonged to men who understood the shape of what they carried.

He did not.

Still, he had to speak.

"Last night," he said, "during Galilhai's crossing, something old returned to us."

The fire cracked softly.

"She saw what the stories warned us not to forget."

Several members of the tribe looked toward Galilhai. She lowered her gaze, and Wovoka felt the movement like a hand tightening around his chest.

"This was not her doing," he said, with enough force that no one misunderstood him. "She was shown a wound that already existed."

The older woman opened her eyes.

"And now the wound has widened."

Wovoka nodded once.

"For many generations, we have spoken of the Dark Shadows as though they belonged to the edge of memory. Something contained. Something weakened. Something the Other World had already survived." He paused. "I no longer believe that."

Unease moved through the gathering.

One of the younger warriors leaned forward. "You saw them?"

"I saw their pattern," Wovoka replied. "In the fire. In the lake. In the way the water moved before dawn." He glanced toward Pyramid Lake. "And Galilhai saw where that pattern first took form."

"The wedding," Galilhai whispered.

Her voice barely rose above the crackling fire, yet everyone heard it.

Wovoka looked toward her. "Yes."

The tribe grew still.

"The lake woman came from Tahoe," he said. "She entered Wono through longing. Through weakness wrapped around something true. The warrior gave her form, and when she returned to the water, she carried more than herself back with her."

He did not say Kewa's name.

Galilhai had spoken it once already beside the lake, and once had been enough.

"How can one creature do this?" one of the tribe's members asked.

Wovoka looked briefly toward the older woman.

"Because she was never only one creature."

The wind bent the flames sideways for an instant before releasing them again.

"There are stories my grandfather refused to finish aloud after sunset," Wovoka continued. "When I was young, I believed fear had changed them over time. I believed old men sometimes mistook memory for prophecy."

His hands tightened briefly at his sides.

"I do not believe that anymore."

Uneasy glances passed through the circle. Several members of the tribe shifted where they sat beside the fire, while others lowered their eyes toward the sand as though ashamed to admit the same thought had once lived inside them. The younger warriors looked toward the elders for contradiction, but none came. Until that moment, many had carried the old stories the way children carried warnings about spirits hidden beyond the hills: inherited, repeated, yet never fully believed beneath daylight.

"The shadows have grown stronger," Wovoka said. "Strong enough to press against Wono. Strong enough to trouble the guardians of the Other World. Perhaps not enough to overcome them yet, but enough to force their hand."

A young warrior rose halfway from his place beside the fire. "Then we prepare for war."

Wovoka looked at him with visible sadness.

"You speak as though this enemy can be met with arrows."

The young man lowered himself again.

"The shadows are not flesh. They do not enter first through the body. They enter through fracture. Through fear. Through hunger. Through the places where the spirit forgets what it belongs to."

The words settled heavily over the gathering.

A woman seated beside two children drew them closer.

"What do they want?" she asked.

Wovoka looked into the flames.

"The Dice."

A long silence followed.

Then one of the younger men near the edge of the fire frowned.

"The Destiny Dice?" he asked carefully. "When we were children, the elders used to speak of them whenever someone wandered too far beyond the hills alone." A faint, uncertain smile almost reached his lips before disappearing. "They said the Dice watched lost children from beneath the earth and rolled misfortune toward those who ignored the warnings."

Several others exchanged uneasy glances around the fire.

"I thought they were stories meant to keep us near the settlement after dark," another admitted.

The older woman opened her eyes fully.

"That is what becomes of truth when memory weakens," she said. "A warning turns into a story, and a story into something people no longer fear until it begins creating new memories."

The fire shifted violently in the wind.

Wovoka remained silent for a moment before speaking again.

"My father believed they existed. His father before him believed the same. But belief is not the same as understanding."

He looked toward the dark lake.

"For most of my life, I prayed the stories had grown larger than the truth."

No one interrupted him after that.

"The Dice are older than our people," Wovoka continued. "Older than the tribes. Older than the memory of mountains. They are not sacred because they hold power alone. They are sacred because they hold movement before it becomes life."

The tribe listened carefully now.

"There are two Dice. One carries the current of harmony, beauty, peace, and love. The other carries destruction, hatred, conflict, and division. Together they shape the unfolding path of the World of Form."

A man across the circle frowned. "Then it is true. Our lives are already resting in the hands of the Dice."

"No."

The answer came sharper than Wovoka intended. He softened his voice.

"They influence the path. They do not stand above Puha."

The older woman watched him carefully.

"Puha is not a path," Wovoka continued. "It is what allows there to be path, walker, stone, hunger, mercy, and the space between one breath and the next. Even the Dice exist within it."

Far beyond the firelight, the pyramid-shaped stone stood barely visible beneath the rising night, as though the lake itself were listening to the words spoken beside its shore.

"But if the Dark Shadows reached them," he said, "they would not seek balance. They would roll destruction until destruction no longer had anything left to consume."

The young warrior stared into the flames.

"Then we find the Dice first."

Wovoka closed his eyes briefly.

There it was.

The sentence he had feared hearing all day.

"The path to them cannot be taken by strength," he said.

"Then by what?"

Wovoka opened his eyes and looked toward Galilhai.

The tribe followed his gaze.

She became very still.

"No," someone whispered.

Wovoka felt the word strike him more deeply than accusation.

For one frightening instant, he wanted to agree. He wanted to gather Galilhai into his arms and refuse the shape the world was beginning to take around her. He wanted to be only her father and nothing else.

Then the older woman spoke.

"The young pass where the guarded cannot."

Her voice carried the weight of something much older than certainty.

Wovoka swallowed.

"The shadows search constantly for hunger," he said. "For ambition. Fear. Violence. The parts of the spirit that cling tightly to themselves."

His gaze remained upon Galilhai.

"But some souls move lightly enough that darkness struggles to hold them clearly."

The fire softened between them.

"Children sometimes carry this naturally," the older woman said. "Before the world teaches them division."

Galilhai lowered her eyes.

"That is why certain beings may cross farther than warriors," Wovoka continued. "Not because they are stronger. Because they are harder for darkness to grasp."

One of the women shook her head. "She cannot go alone."

"No," Wovoka replied.

Wovoka looked toward the tip of Wono, its upper edges dissolving into the deepening sky while the first faint stars emerged above the horizon.

"There is another part of the old prophecy," he said at last. "One I have never understood fully."

The older woman's expression shifted slightly.

She knew the stories he meant. She also understood that certain truths were not meant to be explained completely, only approached. Some mysteries revealed themselves through living, while others remained unfinished even after a lifetime of seeking them.

"My father called it the distant light," Wovoka continued. "His father called it the soul beyond forgetting. The words changed from one generation to the next, but the meaning remained. In the age when our kind forgets the sacred almost completely, a soul will be born near the end of a long darkness."

Several members of the tribe exchanged uncertain glances.

"A spirit?" someone asked.

"A human being," Wovoka said. "Or something moving through a human life."

That uncertainty unsettled the gathering, but Wovoka did not hide from it.

"They say she will be born in an age of great noise, when people speak across vast distances yet no longer know how to hear themselves. An age when men surround themselves with glowing creations and mistake them for wisdom. When rivers are poisoned for wealth, forests burned for comfort, and people divide one another until they forget they breathe the same air."

The wind pressed against the fire.

"In that age, the spirit will sleep beneath many coverings. But dreams may still reach where waking cannot."

Galilhai looked toward him.

"Pamahas," she whispered.

Wovoka nodded slowly. "Perhaps."

He did not know what Pamahas had seen, or what Esa understood, or whether the distant soul already dreamed somewhere beyond ordinary time. He knew only the prophecy, and that Galilhai's crossing had made it feel less like story and more like a door beginning to open.

"The old stories say this distant soul may carry the same lightness Galilhai carries now," he continued. "A spirit difficult for darkness to fully recognize. Difficult to bind. Difficult to possess."

The older woman watched the fire.

"Such souls are rare," she murmured.

"Does this soul have a name?" one of the elders asked.

Wovoka shook his head.

"Not one that has reached us."

Unease spread through the circle.

Several members lowered their eyes while others stared into the fire as though searching for certainty within its shifting light. Wovoka understood what none of them wished to say aloud. He was asking them to place their faith in a child barely nine winters old and in a distant spirit carried only through fragments of prophecy and dreams no one fully understood.

Even he struggled beneath the weight of it.

A name would have made the prophecy easier to hold. Easier to trust. But the old stories had never offered comfort, only direction.

"Puha rarely announces salvation in ways that satisfy fear," the older woman said. "If it did, no one would need faith."

"If she belongs to the future," another woman said carefully, "does that not mean that our people survive?"

The older woman gave a faint, sorrowful smile.

"You still think the future is a promise."

Wovoka knelt beside the fire and buried his hand into the cool sand. For a moment he remained still, his fingers pressed beneath the surface as though searching for something hidden beneath the earth itself. Then he lifted his hand again, allowing the grains to escape through his fingers in thin shifting streams that vanished back into the ground below.

"In the World of Form, time moves like a trail across the earth. But beyond Wono, time is not a trail. It is water. What has been, what is, and what may come all move together within the same depth."

He rose to his feet and turned back toward the gathering.

"If the Other World falls into corruption, futures that seemed certain may vanish before they ever reach flesh."

The silence that followed was deeper than fear.

It was understanding beginning to form.

One of the elders spoke at last. "Why have Esa and Pamahas not destroyed the Dice?"

The older woman answered before Wovoka could.

"Would you destroy the river because it sometimes floods?"

The elder lowered his gaze.

Wovoka continued walking around the circle.

"For ages, Esa and Pamahas guarded the Dice without forcing their outcome. They understood that power used carelessly becomes another form of corruption. Even protection can wound the world if it tries to rule what Puha allows to move."

He looked around the circle.

"That is why they hid the Dice instead of destroying them. That is why they guide more often than they command."

"And the shadows?" the young warrior asked. "Where did they begin?"

Wovoka drew a slow breath.

"In forgotten places," he said. "Small at first. Weak. No more dangerous than cold pressing against the dunes."

The older woman lowered her eyes.

"But humanity changed them."

No one spoke.

"Each act committed in unconsciousness fed them. Each cruelty. Each hatred. Each war. Every desire to dominate another living thing. The shadows learned from men, and men learned from shadows, though most never knew it."

A child near the fire began crying softly. His mother pulled him against her chest and kissed the top of his head, holding him tightly while struggling to keep her own fear from reaching her face.

"The Dark Shadows became stronger wherever people forgot their connection to Puha. They grew where fear was mistaken for truth. Where beauty became deception. Where longing became possession. Where conflict was worshipped as strength."

Galilhai thought of the warrior inside Wono, holding Kewa's hand as though nothing else existed.

"The lake woman," she whispered.

Wovoka looked toward her.

"She was part of what Tahoe became."

The name of the lake altered the gathering immediately.

Several elders bowed their heads.

"Tahoe was sacred once," Wovoka said. "The old stories say the water reflected more than the sky."

The fire dimmed beside him.

"Then the reflections changed."

His voice lowered further.

"The shadows entered wearing peace."

The tribe listened without moving.

"They lived among the people near Tahoe and learned the shape of their desires. By the time their true nature revealed itself, the lake had already begun darkening."

"What happened there?" someone asked.

Wovoka stared at the fire for a long moment.

"Fire. Death. Dreams that would not release those who entered them. Water reflecting things not standing before it." He paused. "The stories differ in detail, but not in sorrow."

The older woman closed her eyes once more.

"Some spirits remained behind to shield the World of Form from what Tahoe had become," Wovoka continued. "But they could not cleanse it. The corruption had rooted too deeply."

"And the wedding?" Galilhai asked.

Wovoka's expression tightened.

"The wedding was not merely betrayal. It was an attempt. If Kewa had bound herself through Wono to a warrior of the tribe, the shadows might have entered the crossing more fully. Perhaps they hoped to reach what Esa and Pamahas had already hidden."

"The Dice," Galilhai whispered.

"Yes."

The firelight moved across her face.

Wovoka wished he could take the knowledge back from her.

He could not.

"Since dawn," he continued, "the lake has felt different. I cannot tell you exactly what Esa has done, or what Pamahas has seen. But something beneath Pyramid Lake has changed. The hidden flow between waters no longer moves as it once did."

Several members of the tribe turned instinctively toward the dark lake.

"Does that mean Tahoe has reached us?" someone asked.

"It means the guardians have acted," Wovoka replied. "And if they have acted so greatly, then the danger is nearer than I hoped."

His voice remained steady, but those closest to him saw the strain beneath it.

Galilhai saw it most clearly.

Her father was afraid.

Not as ordinary men feared. Not with panic or trembling. His fear moved inside discipline, like fire covered beneath ash. He stood before the tribe because someone had to stand. He spoke because silence would leave them blind.

But she knew, with the strange certainty the Other World had given her, that part of him wanted only to be her father and not the keeper of any prophecy.

The older woman rose from the stone.

Her shadow stretched long behind her.

“Conflict knows no resolution,” she said. “It only teaches hunger to speak another language.”

The words settled over the gathering.

Wovoka looked toward the people before him, people he had known all his life. Men who had fished beside him. Women who had sung beside the fire. Children who still believed tomorrow would resemble today simply because it always had before.

He could not give them certainty.

So he gave them what he still possessed.

Attention.

“We do not meet darkness by becoming it,” he said. “We do not survive by surrendering ourselves to fear. If the shadows feed upon unconsciousness, then every act of awareness becomes resistance. Every refusal to divide ourselves strengthens what the darkness cannot understand.”

The young warrior lowered his head.

“What do we do now?”

Wovoka looked once more toward Galilhai.

“We prepare.”

The word did not satisfy anyone.

“We remember what was nearly forgotten,” he said. “We listen to the lake. We guard the fire. We watch the dreams of our children. And when the path opens, we do not pretend readiness simply because fear asks us to move quickly.”

The older woman nodded faintly.

Above them, the stars spread across the sky in greater number.

No one reached for the stew.

No one asked another question.

Beyond the settlement, Pyramid Lake rested beneath the rising night, its surface dark and endless, carrying beneath it whatever had changed within the hidden places of the world.

Wovoka remained standing until the circle slowly loosened. Families drew close together. The warriors moved among themselves. Elders whispered near the dying fire. Galilhai did not move.

After a long while, Wovoka came and sat beside her.

For several moments neither spoke.

Then Galilhai looked toward the lake.

"Do you know where I have to go?" she asked.

Wovoka followed her gaze into the darkness.

"No."

"But you think I have to go."

His throat tightened.

"I think the world has begun asking something of you that no child should be asked to carry."

Galilhai's eyes remained fixed upon the water.

"And if I say no?"

The father inside him wanted to answer first. The shaman could not allow it.

"Then no must also be heard," he said.

She turned toward him.

He rested his hand against the center of her back, the same way he had when she was smaller and woke frightened by thunder.

"But some paths continue calling even after we refuse them."

The fire settled lower behind them.

Together they watched the lake until the final color disappeared from the sky. Somewhere beyond the reach of sight, the Other World continued moving. Somewhere beneath the earth, the hidden currents had changed. Somewhere within an age not yet born, a distant soul slept beneath dreams that had not yet become memory.

And between all these things, destiny waited, unseen and already moving.

CHAPTER X

Foggy Thoughts

Don't live in the past. Memories, as beautiful as they may be, keep you from rejoicing in the present. Don't live in the future. Dreams, as incredible as they may seem, pale before the joy of your destiny. Life is now and now alone. Start living it.

The sharp vibration of Alma's phone broke the quiet rhythm of the house. She looked down immediately. A warning filled the screen in capital letters.

EMERGENCY ALERT: Avoid contact with Lake Tahoe. Stay at least three hundred feet from the shore. The lake is currently considered unsafe for swimming or other recreational activities. Emergency vehicles are responding. Avoid Highway 28 whenever possible. Hazard lights are mandatory from Incline Village to South Tahoe.

For a moment, Alma simply stared.

Outside the kitchen window, sunlight rested peacefully across the pines bordering the property. The afternoon sky remained clear and intensely blue, untouched by storm clouds or smoke. Nothing within the visible world suggested danger.

Yet something inside her tightened.

"Thomas," she called.

No answer.

She crossed quickly through the living room and entered the smaller room near the back of the house, where her husband spent most afternoons repairing watches.

Thomas sat beneath the bright white circle of a desk lamp, one eye narrowed behind a magnifying loupe while the opened body of a wristwatch rested carefully between his hands. Tiny gears and springs lay arranged across a black cloth pad in perfect rows beside him. Each piece held its place within an order only patience could restore.

"What is it?" he asked, lifting his gaze.

Alma held out the phone.

His expression changed slowly while he read.

"What happened?" he asked.

"I don't know."

She already did.

Not consciously.

But somewhere beneath thought, a quiet certainty had begun gathering the moment she read the warning. It moved through her the way certain dreams lingered after waking, refusing to dissolve completely into ordinary daylight.

"Noah," she whispered.

She tapped quickly through her contacts and pressed the call icon.

The line rang once.

Then silence.

She tried again.

Nothing.

Thomas rose immediately.

"He went to the lake?"

"He said he was going swimming."

Thomas crossed toward the kitchen table and grabbed the Volvo keys from the glass tray near the center.

"I'll go find him."

Alma looked toward the windows.

Though the sky remained clear, the light outside had altered subtly. The brightness no longer seemed to settle naturally upon the trees and rooftops. Instead, it appeared flattened somehow, as though the afternoon itself had become distant.

"Be careful," she said quietly.

Thomas nodded once.

By the time he stepped outside, the smell had already reached the neighborhood.

Not smoke. Something different.

A dry mineral scent moved faintly through the air, carrying traces of wet stone and burned wood beneath it.

Thomas paused beside the car.

Far beyond the houses, above the distant line of Tahoe's waters, something pale had begun unfolding across the basin.

At first, it resembled fog.

Then the shoreline disappeared.

The whiteness rolled across Lake Tahoe in enormous advancing layers, consuming sections of water, docks, beaches, and pine-covered slopes beneath a moving wall of vapor that spread with impossible speed.

It did not drift naturally with the wind. It overtook it.

The fog moved inland the way ocean water moved during storms, folding over itself in immense currents while the basin vanished section by section beneath its advance. Yet it made no sound of water. No crash. No break. No hiss of foam against stone.

Only the silence of something crossing a boundary it had never been meant to cross.

Thomas climbed into the Volvo and started the engine.

As he backed onto the road, the first wave of whiteness reached the neighborhood.

The world ahead of him began dissolving.

Street signs disappeared first.

Then fences.

Then entire stretches of road.

The fog rolled between the houses with terrifying momentum, pouring through trees and climbing over rooftops in slow curling fronts that resembled surf advancing inland. Yet no moisture touched the pavement. The roads remained dry beneath the advancing whiteness.

Nothing about the movement obeyed weather.

The farther Thomas drove toward the lake, the denser the world became.

Not darker. Denser.

The fog carried a strange physical weight within it, as though distance itself had thickened.

Road divisions dissolved beneath the headlights.

At one intersection, Thomas became briefly convinced the road ahead had bent in the wrong direction.

Then the illusion corrected itself.

Even sound behaved incorrectly.

A horn blared somewhere nearby, yet the noise reached him late, muffled and stretched thin across the whiteness. A woman's voice called from the road ahead, then returned again from behind him, as if the fog had caught the sound and sent it back through another path.

The dashboard flickered.

For one brief instant, every illuminated pixel vanished from the display.

The speedometer dropped to black.

The GPS dissolved into static.

Then the interior of the Volvo went completely dark.

A pulse of interference burst violently through the speakers before collapsing back into silence.

Thomas tightened both hands around the wheel.

The road no longer felt connected to the town he knew.

The anti-collision system activated violently.

A warning tone erupted through the car.

The brakes locked.

The Volvo slid hard across the pavement before stopping only inches behind another vehicle materializing suddenly through the rolling white currents.

Thomas caught his breath.

Several cars ahead, red taillights glowed dimly through the fog like submerged embers beneath water.

Traffic had nearly stopped.

All around him, the highway dissolved into confusion.

Drivers abandoned lanes.

Boat trailers sat crooked against shoulders.

Some people had already left their vehicles entirely, moving through the whiteness while shouting names that vanished almost immediately into the vapor, only to return moments later as warped echoes from impossible directions.

Panic spread not through screaming at first, but through hesitation.

People no longer trusted what they were seeing.

The fog distorted proportion.

A man crossing near the shoulder appeared impossibly elongated for half a second before returning suddenly to ordinary shape.

Headlights bent incorrectly within the vapor, curving sideways through the rolling fronts before disappearing entirely.

Nothing held still long enough to remain reliable.

Thomas looked toward the right side of the highway.

Through the moving whiteness, the illuminated Chevron sign emerged faintly from the shifting currents.

The trail entrance.

Noah.

He guided the Volvo carefully toward the station.

The empty lot opened around him like an island suspended inside the advancing fog. Once parked, he reached immediately for his phone.

No signal.

He checked the GPS. Nothing.

For several seconds he remained motionless inside the vehicle.

Outside, the fog rolled continuously across the gas station windows in immense folding layers, thick enough now that even the nearest fuel pumps faded in and out of existence.

Then he noticed something worse.

The fog carried no moisture. His windshield remained completely dry.

Thomas looked toward the invisible shoreline beyond the station.

Something was wrong with the lake.

Not merely disturbed. Unmade.

The rolling whiteness no longer resembled atmosphere.

It resembled the boundary between things dissolving.

He opened the car door.

The smell intensified immediately.

Wet stone. Burned wood. Something metallic beneath both.

And beneath that, another scent altogether.

Cold water rising from impossible depth.

"Please," he whispered quietly into the moving whiteness. "Let him be safe."

Then he stepped into the fog.

Noah ran.

Behind him, Lake Tahoe had disappeared.

The fog consumed the shoreline so completely that water and sky no longer held any visible separation between them. Rolling fronts of whiteness moved across the beach in enormous silent waves, swallowing docks, umbrellas, boats, and people beneath advancing walls of vapor that folded endlessly over themselves.

Noah climbed the rocks near the trail entrance without fully seeing them.

Memory guided him now more than sight.

His hands slipped once against the granite before finding hold along a familiar ledge. He pulled himself upward while the fog surged through the beach below.

For one terrible instant, the whiteness beneath him shifted.

Not movement. Depth.

As though something immense had passed beneath the fog itself.

The pale currents bulged upward briefly around an invisible shape before collapsing inward again.

Noah froze.

The sensation vanished immediately.

A voice shouted somewhere behind him.

The sound reached him twice.

First nearby.

Then again several seconds later from somewhere deeper inside the fog.

Noah turned instinctively.

Nothing.

Only whiteness moving through the trees.

Another cry emerged somewhere below.

Then another echo followed it, stretched thin and distorted, as though the mountain itself had repeated the sound incorrectly.

Noise no longer traveled through distance in straight lines. It folded through the fog and returned altered. A car horn sounded from the highway, broke apart, and came back as three separate tones, each one fainter than the last. Footsteps cracked through brush somewhere to Noah's left, then repeated behind him.

The same footsteps.

His pulse quickened.

The whiteness moved uphill now.

That frightened him more than anything else.

Fog should not climb like water.

Yet the rolling fronts continued pouring upward through the trees and over the stone ridges as though gravity no longer applied to them correctly.

Branches disappeared inside the advancing currents before reemerging several seconds later marked not with moisture, but with pale mineral residue resembling ash.

Noah climbed higher.

He knew these trails.

As a child, he and his friends had spent entire summers exploring the narrow paths overlooking Tahoe. He remembered scraped knees, loose rocks, hidden coves, and the afternoon he slipped from one of the ridges badly enough to leave a scar along his shoulder.

The mountain had always felt enormous to him then.

Now the fog made it feel alive.

Branches emerged suddenly beside his face before disappearing again into white distance. The path beneath him seemed longer than he remembered, bending through stretches of stone that should already have opened toward the road.

Twice he became convinced he had taken the wrong trail.

Then he heard his own breathing echo back at him.

Noah stopped immediately.

The sound returned from somewhere ahead.

Not identical. Slower.

As though another version of him stood somewhere inside the fog breathing slightly out of rhythm.

A deep pressure moved through his chest.

He forced himself upward.

The trail should have reached the roadside already.

Instead, the slope continued stretching ahead through impossible distance.

His foot slipped.

Loose gravel collapsed beneath him.

Noah slammed hard against the rocky slope, his shoulder striking granite before his body rolled sideways through stone and dry pine needles.

Pain burst sharply through his ribs.

For several seconds he remained still, disoriented.

Above him, the rolling whiteness surged silently through the trees.

Then everything stopped.

Not gradually. Instantly.

The echoes vanished.

The mountain fell silent.

Noah lifted himself slowly against the rocks.

The advancing currents of whiteness had frozen.

For one impossible second, the entire basin appeared suspended between realities.

The fog no longer moved.

It hung motionless across the shoreline and forest like an unfinished memory.

Then it began collapsing inward.

The rolling fronts folded violently into themselves, withdrawing across the lake in enormous receding layers that dissolved as they moved. Entire walls of vapor vanished section by section, revealing shoreline, road, forest, and sky beneath them.

The retreat happened too quickly.

It resembled reality correcting itself.

Within seconds, sunlight burst once more across the basin.

Blue sky emerged overhead.

The turquoise surface of Tahoe returned.

Only the final remnants of whiteness remained far above the water, twisting briefly across the lake before dissolving completely.

Noah stared in disbelief.

The silence afterward felt unreal.

As though something immense had briefly occupied the world and then withdrawn beneath it again.

Noah pushed himself upright slowly.

His shoulder burned.

Below him, the town had reappeared.

Cars sat scattered unevenly across the highway.

Several drivers stood outside their vehicles staring silently toward the lake. Police officers moved between lanes attempting to reorganize traffic while paramedics crossed toward an overturned truck farther down the road.

A helicopter circled low above the shoreline.

The fog was gone.

Noah turned slowly toward the water.

Nothing within the visible world explained what he had just witnessed.

Yet the atmosphere still felt wrong.

Not dangerous exactly.

Attentive.

As though the lake had withdrawn something enormous back beneath itself while continuing to watch the shore.

"Noah!"

He spun around.

Thomas emerged from the crowd near the Chevron station.

Relief crossed both their faces immediately.

Noah hurried toward him.

They embraced hard.

"What are you doing here?" Noah asked breathlessly.

"Your grandmother received the emergency alert." Thomas stepped back enough to look at him fully. "We couldn't reach you."

"The service went down." Noah shook his head. "Everything went down."

Thomas studied him carefully.

"You saw it?"

Noah looked toward the lake again.

"I don't know what I saw."

That frightened him more than certainty would have.

A firetruck passed slowly behind them, its lights cutting red reflections across nearby windows.

Along the shoreline, several officers had begun pushing people farther back from the water.

"What happened out there?" Thomas asked quietly.

Noah remained silent for several seconds.

How could he explain it?

The lake had not behaved like water.

The fog had not behaved like weather.

And beneath both, something had moved with enough presence that his body still remembered it.

"It felt like the lake stopped being the lake for a minute," he said at last.

Thomas said nothing.

Together they walked back toward the Volvo.

The drive home unfolded slowly through crawling traffic and flashing emergency lights.

Wireless service returned gradually.

Phones began ringing again throughout the surrounding vehicles while local radio stations attempted to describe the event with language that sounded increasingly uncertain the longer the reports continued.

Possible atmospheric anomaly.

Temporary pressure inversion.

Localized electromagnetic disturbance.

None of the explanations survived their own delivery.

Noah leaned back against the passenger seat and stared through the window.

Pines moved softly beneath ordinary wind.

Tourists had already begun recording videos near the shoreline again.

Yet beneath the restored normalcy, the basin carried a strange incompleteness, as though reality itself had closed too quickly over something that had nearly surfaced.

His phone rang.

Sam.

He answered immediately.

"Oh my God, Noah, are you okay?"

Her voice arrived sharp with concern.

"Yeah," he replied. "I'm with my grandpa."

"We're watching the news," Ale called somewhere in the background. "What the hell happened up there?"

"You're on speaker," Sam added.

Noah rubbed one hand across his face.

"We don't know."

Even now the answer sounded insufficient.

"The fog just disappeared," he continued. "Everything's chaos. Police everywhere. Emergency crews. Nobody knows what caused it."

A silence followed.

Then Sam spoke again.

"We felt it here."

Noah frowned slightly.

"What do you mean?"

Another pause.

"For a second..." Sam hesitated. "I don't know. The house shook a little."

Ale laughed nervously somewhere behind her.

"She almost dropped an entire bowl of popcorn and now she's turning it into prophecy."

But Noah noticed Sam did not laugh.

"You sure you're okay?" she asked.

Noah looked once more toward the lake beyond the passing trees.

The water flashed blue between the pines.

Yet for a brief instant, he thought he saw something darker beneath the reflected sky.

"I don't think Tahoe is," he said quietly.

Neither Sam nor Ale answered immediately.

Then Sam exhaled softly.

"Please, be safe."

The call ended.

For several minutes neither Noah nor Thomas spoke.

Traffic continued inching through the basin while emergency vehicles moved steadily toward the shoreline.

Eventually Noah opened the glove compartment searching absentmindedly for a charging cable.

A photograph slid loose and fell against his leg.

He picked it up carefully.

His mother.

The image had faded slightly near the corners from age. She stood beside the family boat smiling toward the camera while afternoon sunlight moved through her dark hair. Noah stared at the photograph longer than he intended.

"What's this doing here?" he asked.

Thomas glanced briefly toward the picture.

"Oh. I forgot to tell you. I've been digitizing the old family albums for your grandmother's birthday."

Noah nodded quietly.

He continued staring at the photograph.

Certain memories resisted time.

Others dissolved each year no matter how tightly he tried to preserve them.

He could still remember the warmth of his mother's perfume when she kissed him goodnight before leaving for the lake that evening long ago. Wood sage and sea salt. He remembered her earrings catching the light. He remembered his father rubbing his hand gently across the top of his head.

But the face itself remained unfinished.

Whenever Noah tried to hold the memory clearly, something within it blurred.

As a child, he used to panic at that.

Later he learned that grief altered memory the way water altered stone. Not through violence. Through repetition.

For years, he had been tempted to live inside those memories completely.

Pain offered strange forms of comfort. There was familiarity in sorrow, especially when sorrow carried the last clear shape of someone loved. The past could begin to feel safer than whatever remained unfinished ahead.

But Noah had slowly understood something else.

Memory was not meant to become a dwelling but a bridge.

He looked once more toward the lake beyond the trees.

Whatever had moved beneath Tahoe that afternoon felt older than tragedy.

Older than memory itself.

Yet strangely, thinking about his parents no longer tightened something inside him the way it once had.

The feeling passing through him now resembled gratitude more than loss.

He slipped the photograph gently back into the glove compartment.

"You mind if I put on some music?" he asked.

Thomas smiled faintly.

"That's the purpose of a copilot."

Noah scrolled through his phone before selecting a song.

A low drumbeat filled the car.

Then Phil Collins' voice emerged softly through the speakers.

Thomas laughed under his breath.

"Still listening to old man music?"

Noah leaned back against the seat.

Outside the window, Tahoe flashed blue beneath the late afternoon sun while the mountains watched silently over the basin. The slow, intensifying drums from the stereo filled Noah's ears.

"I can feel it coming in the air tonight. Oh, Lord."

The trees closed once more over the water.

Somewhere far beneath Tahoe, something moved.

CHAPTER XI

True Wisdom is Silent

It is difficult for human beings to hear truth because the mind is always speaking first. Yet the universe has never raised its voice. Wisdom arrives quietly, and only those capable of stillness ever notice it.

Wovoka suspended the tribe's ordinary activities the following day. No hunting parties departed into the desert. No nets were lowered into Pyramid Lake. Even the children moved more quietly between the woven huts, sensing the heaviness that had settled across the settlement since Galilhai's return from Wono. Beneath the visible rhythms of the tribe, something unseen had shifted. The lake still breathed against the shore. Wind still moved through the reeds. Yet everyone felt the same unspoken truth pressing quietly beneath the day.

Something had begun.

As evening approached, the older woman entered Wovoka's hut carrying a small wooden box beneath her arm. A triangular symbol had been carved into its surface long ago, its edges worn smooth by time and touch.

Inside the hut, Wovoka sat beside a mortar of crushed herbs with his eyes closed.

The older woman lowered herself across from him without speaking immediately. The silence between them carried familiarity deeper than comfort. Outside, the wind brushed softly against the hanging drapes of woven hide.

"At dawn your thoughts were already standing inside tomorrow," she said at last.

Wovoka opened his eyes slowly.

"She is still a child."

The older woman rested the wooden box beside the mortar.

"So were you when fear first found you."

"That was different."

"No." Her voice remained calm. "It only feels different because now you love what may be taken."

The words settled heavily inside the hut.

Wovoka lowered his gaze toward the herbs between his hands. For most of his life, fear had appeared to him as something distant, almost transparent. He had learned to watch it rise without surrendering himself to it. But this fear moved differently. It entered him through memory. Through love. Through the sight of Galilhai sleeping beneath fur blankets when storms crossed the desert. Through the sound of her laughter before the world became larger than childhood.

"I do not know how to stand before them carrying this uncertainty," he admitted quietly.

The older woman began grinding leaves slowly within the mortar.

"You do not stand before them as certainty," she replied. "You stand before them as attention."

The herbs released a bitter fragrance into the air.

"People mistake fear for weakness because they do not understand stillness. A frightened mind runs toward tomorrow searching for ground that does not yet exist. Wisdom remains where breath already is."

Wovoka listened.

Outside the hut, the final light of evening had begun softening across the settlement.

"She will accomplish what is required of her," the older woman continued. "The danger is not the path ahead. The danger is your desire to walk it for her."

For a moment, neither of them spoke again.

Then Wovoka looked toward the wooden box resting beside her.

"What did you bring?"

The older woman slid the lid aside.

Inside rested a dark green paste flecked with crushed white flowers and powdered roots.

"The lake remembers certain plants," she said. "And some plants remember the lake."

Wovoka understood.

Tonight Galilhai would cross again.

The tribe began its descent toward Pyramid Lake shortly before sunset.

No music accompanied them this time.

During Galilhai's first crossing, celebration had surrounded the procession like firelight around warmth. But now silence moved among the people instead. Even the younger warriors walked without speaking, their expressions hardened not by confidence, but by the strain of helplessness. Many still struggled to accept that the fate of the tribe might soon rest upon a child.

The shoreline awaited them beneath a sky of fading gold.

Wono rose from the lake in the distance, dark and motionless against the horizon.

Near the water, the tribe formed a wide circle around the fire while Wovoka stepped forward beside the older woman. Between them rested a woven blanket upon the sand.

One by one, the people approached it.

A hunter placed down his favorite spear.

A woman removed a necklace of polished shell beads from around her throat.

Another laid down a dyed shawl passed to her by her mother.

Objects accumulated slowly upon the blanket: tools, ornaments, carved bone figures, weapons, woven fabrics worn smooth by years of wind and dust.

No one explained the ritual aloud.

Nothing needed explanation.

The gesture carried acknowledgment. If conflict approached, then no possession could remain more important than attention itself. To cling too tightly to objects while the spirit fractured inward was to weaken before the battle had even begun.

Galilhai watched quietly from beside the fire.

The wind moved strands of dark hair across her face while the final sunlight touched the surface of Pyramid Lake behind her. Though fear still existed somewhere within her, it no longer ruled her in the same way. Since returning from the Other World, she had begun noticing how thoughts arrived and departed like weather crossing open land. They seemed less permanent now. Less solid.

She placed one hand gently against the center of her chest and closed her eyes.

The sounds surrounding her gradually loosened.

The crackling fire drifted farther away. Voices dissolved into distant currents. Even the coldness of the evening air softened against her skin until only the rhythm of her breathing remained.

Then even that began to disappear.

Not absence. Stillness.

Something warm unfolded slowly behind her ribs, spreading outward through her body with quiet precision. The sensation moved downward through her arms, her stomach, her legs, until the roughness of the sand beneath her feet seemed impossibly vivid. She could feel each grain separately against her skin.

Light gathered faintly behind her closed eyes.

Not images. Movement.

Color shifting without shape.

Wovoka approached carrying the mortar.

The tribe watched silently while he knelt beside his daughter and dipped his fingers into the dark green paste. Carefully, he traced narrow lines along her arms and forehead. The mixture smelled of bitter roots, lake water, and crushed flowers left too long beneath moonlight.

Galilhai did not move.

Wovoka settled beside her afterward, mirroring her posture.

Around them, the fire continued breathing softly against the darkening shore.

Wovoka lowered himself inward.

The transition came quickly.

The lake receded.

The fire receded.

His body thinned into attention until sensation no longer belonged entirely to flesh. Beneath the silence, he felt movement gathering somewhere far beyond ordinary distance.

Pressure.

Darkness turning beneath water.

Gold.

A narrowing path.

Then another presence.

Immense.

Ancient.

Watching.

Not language.

Recognition.

Wovoka felt Pyramid Lake trembling beneath unseen weight. He felt Wono standing against something vast pressing from beyond the boundary between worlds. He saw flashes of Tahoe beneath blackened water and a sealed passage deep beneath stone where pressure continued building in silence.

And somewhere beyond all of it, faint but unmistakable, another soul flickered briefly against the darkness.

Distant.

Unawakened.

Waiting.

The vision vanished before he could reach further.

Wovoka opened his eyes sharply and inhaled.

Night had fully arrived.

After a long while, Wovoka rose and walked with Galilhai toward the small reed boat resting at the edge of the shore while the tribe remained behind them beside the fire, silent beneath the shifting glow of the flames.

Neither father nor daughter spoke immediately.

The water moved gently around the hull as Wovoka steadied it against the sand.

At last, Galilhai looked up at him.

"You would come with me if you could."

The words were not a question.

Wovoka smiled faintly, though grief moved visibly beneath it.

"Yes."

"But you cannot."

He shook his head slowly.

"The shadows would feel me beside you."

Galilhai lowered her gaze toward the lake.

For a moment, Wovoka almost spoke against the journey entirely. The impulse rose through him with terrifying force. He imagined carrying her away from the shore, abandoning prophecy, abandoning destiny, abandoning every burden except fatherhood.

But the world had already begun moving.

And love could not stop it simply because it feared loss.

Galilhai stepped into the boat.

Wovoka pulled the fur blanket gently around her shoulders the same way he had during her first crossing. This time, however, his hands lingered longer.

"I am afraid," he admitted quietly.

Galilhai looked surprised.

"You?"

He nodded once.

“Courage does not remove fear. It only teaches you not to obey it.”

The water shifted softly against the wood.

Galilhai reached forward and embraced him.

“I will return,” she whispered.

Wovoka closed his eyes briefly.

When they separated, he pushed the boat slowly into the lake.

Neither of them spoke again.

The vessel drifted farther into Pyramid Lake beneath the immense night sky, its small frame moving so quietly across the surface that it seemed less carried by water than absorbed into it. Around the hull, delicate ripples spread outward in widening circles of silver, catching fragments of starlight before dissolving again into the darkened lake. Along the shore, the tribe remained motionless beside the fire, watching until distance slowly consumed both boat and child beneath the vastness surrounding Wono.

Yet the ripples continued.

They traveled beyond the ordinary reach of movement, crossing the surface of the lake with impossible persistence, as though the water itself had ceased recognizing the separation between moments. The night deepened around them. Stars trembled faintly within the current. Reflection and memory folded together beneath the silent breathing of the lake.

Far away, beneath another sky unknown to Wovoka and his people, Pyramid Lake rested once more beneath the stars.

A young woman floated silently upon the water, suspended between wakefulness and dream while the cold lake pressed softly against her skin. The shoreline lay distant behind her, reduced to scattered silhouettes and faint points of artificial light shimmering far beyond the desert darkness. Above her, unfamiliar constellations stretched across the modern sky, though the lake beneath her remained ancient enough to remember what human beings had forgotten.

For a long while, nothing moved.

Then another sound reached her across the water.

Faint at first, so distant she almost mistook it for wind moving through the mountains, a low howl drifted across the lake beneath the stars, carrying with it a loneliness so ancient that it did not seem to belong to the same world surrounding her. The sound raised the hair along her arms. Beneath it came other fragments barely audible against the water: the cry of unseen birds, the soft strike of wood against waves, voices too distant to become language.

Then the water behind her rose suddenly and struck the center of her back with startling force.

She gasped sharply and turned within the lake.

At first, she believed the moonlight itself had distorted. The surface of the water no longer reflected the same night surrounding her. Another sky had appeared within it, older somehow, deeper, crowded with unfamiliar stars whose pale light shimmered across the darkened lake in elongated currents.

Then she saw the boat.

It emerged soundlessly across the surface, gliding through the water where moments earlier nothing had existed. The vessel appeared impossibly small beneath the enormity of the ancient sky surrounding it, its wooden edges illuminated faintly by silver reflections drifting across the lake. Wrapped in fur beneath the night air sat a young Paiute girl whose stillness carried something both fragile and immeasurably distant.

The girl slowly lifted her head.

Their eyes met across the water. In that suspended instant, the lake no longer felt divided by centuries, nor by memory, nor by death, nor by birth. Past and future touched one another so completely that neither seemed capable of existing separately from the other. The young woman felt something move through her chest that surpassed fear or confusion, a sensation closer to recognition than surprise, as though some forgotten part of her had suddenly remembered itself without warning.

Inside the boat, the girl stared back with equal astonishment, her dark eyes reflecting the same impossible awareness.

Neither of them spoke.

The water trembled softly between them.

Then the vision began to dissolve.

The ancient stars faded first, their reflections breaking apart across the lake like disturbed silver. The outline of the boat thinned into darkness, and the ripples surrounding it disappeared one by one beneath the returning surface of the water until only the ordinary night remained once more around the young woman floating alone within Pyramid Lake.

Yet even after the lake had stilled completely, the feeling remained.

Somewhere beyond the visible world, beyond the boundaries separating memory from destiny, two lives had recognized each other across the hidden depth of time itself.

CHAPTER XII

A Leap of Faith

Faith has little to do with religion. Instead, Faith is something deeply personal between the Creator and the creation. It's discovering that maker and thing are ultimately one.

Morning sunlight filtered softly through the blinds of Noah's bedroom, drawing pale golden lines across the navy-blue walls while the quiet hum of the ceiling fan turned lazily above him. For a few seconds after waking, he remained still beneath the sheets, suspended in that peaceful confusion where dreams and reality had not yet fully separated. Then remembrance arrived all at once.

It was his birthday.

A smile crossed his face immediately.

Noah reached for the digital watch resting beside his bed and checked the hour. In less than two hours, Sam, Ale, and Maia would arrive to pick him up for their camping trip to Pyramid Lake. The thought alone filled him with a boyish excitement he no longer tried to hide from himself. Ever since Sam had returned to Tahoe, ordinary moments had begun carrying a strange brightness around them, as though life itself had quietly recovered something it had once misplaced.

A knock sounded gently against the door.

"Come in," Noah answered.

Alma entered carrying a small rectangular box wrapped carefully in dark blue paper. A yellow ribbon crossed over the top.

"Happy birthday, Noah," she said warmly.

"Thank you, Grandma."

He stood up and hugged her while she handed him the gift.

"You really didn't have to get me anything."

"It's nothing extravagant," Alma replied. "Just something useful."

Noah sat on the edge of the bed and slowly untied the ribbon before opening the box. Inside rested a polished Swiss-made multi-tool knife with his initials engraved discreetly on the handle.

His eyes widened.

"This is actually amazing."

"I thought it might come in handy today."

"It definitely will."

Before Alma could answer, Thomas's booming voice erupted from downstairs.

"Jaha jakaru!"

Alma laughed immediately.

"He's hungry already."

The phrase, spoken loudly in Guaraní, echoed through the house with familiar warmth. Noah had heard his grandfather speak the language his entire life, though Thomas reserved it mostly for emotional moments, stories, prayers, and meals. Over the years, the sounds themselves had become part of the emotional architecture of home.

Downstairs, breakfast waited across the kitchen table beneath the morning light. The room smelled of coffee, eggs, toasted bread, and bacon. Cream-colored walls reflected the brightness pouring through the windows, while the dark wooden cabinets and white curtains gave the kitchen a warmth that felt untouched by modern restlessness.

At the center of the table rested a white ñanduti tablecloth Alma had purchased years earlier while visiting Thomas's family in Paraguay. She often said the fabric reminded her that beauty survived longest in places where people still made things slowly, by hand, with patience and love woven directly into them.

Noah sat between his grandparents while they sang happy birthday softly and slightly off-key. He laughed through most of it.

For a brief moment, the world felt extraordinarily simple.

The doorbell rang shortly after breakfast ended.

Noah kissed Alma on the cheek before heading toward the entrance.

"Call us when you get there," she reminded him.

"I will."

The moment he opened the door, sunlight flooded the hallway behind Sam.

She stood on the porch wearing a sleeveless green dress and black sandals, her loose hair moving gently with the breeze. The brightness of the morning deepened the warm amber color of her eyes, and for a second Noah simply stared at her without speaking.

"There's the birthday boy," Sam said, smiling before kissing him lightly on the cheek.

"Thanks," Noah replied, suddenly aware of how fast his heartbeat had become.

Her closeness unsettled him in ways he secretly enjoyed. He leaned toward her instinctively, hoping to kiss her properly this time, but Ale's impatient voice exploded from the SUV parked outside.

"Can you two stop acting like a low-budget romance movie and get in the car already?"

Noah laughed under his breath while resting his forehead briefly against Sam's.

"Somebody woke up violent."

Sam smiled and placed her hand softly against his chest before stepping away.

The drive northeast unfolded beneath clear skies and rising heat. Ale sang loudly through most of the trip while Maia remained immersed in a romance novel in the backseat. Noah and Sam spent the first hour talking quietly about music, college, and the strange cultural differences between the East and West coasts, but as the Sierra Nevada slowly gave way to the solemn openness of the desert, Sam found herself speaking less and listening more.

The landscape seemed to expand in ways she could feel physically.

Tahoe possessed beauty, but Pyramid Lake belonged to something older. The farther they traveled, the more the world around them appeared stripped of distraction. Mountains rose from the earth with immense silence around them, untouched by the constant movement of cities, advertisements, schedules, and screens. The desert did not compete for attention. It simply existed, vast and patient beneath the sky.

Sam rested her forehead lightly against the passenger window while watching the empty terrain drift past.

For years, she had carried the quiet feeling that something essential was missing from her life. Not materially. Emotionally. Spiritually. She had seen people move through their days with a tired urgency that made even happiness seem brief, as though life had become something to manage rather than inhabit.

Her mother had never lived that way.

Some of Sam's earliest memories involved watching her stop entire afternoons simply to help someone else. A neighbor. A cashier. A stranger sitting alone. Her mother listened to people with a kind of attention that made them feel visible again, as though being fully present before another human being constituted its own form of grace.

After her death, Sam realized what she missed most was not only her mother's love, but the largeness of spirit with which she had moved through the world.

And lately, especially after returning to Tahoe, Sam had begun feeling that something beyond ordinary life was calling to her with increasing intensity, though she could not explain why.

By late morning, Pyramid Lake finally appeared beyond the desert.

The sight of it silenced the vehicle almost immediately.

The lake stretched beneath the sun like an inland sea surrounded by mountains and pale stone, its waters impossibly blue against the dry Nevada landscape. Ale eventually drove offroad for several miles before parking near the shoreline.

The heat outside was intense.

As the group stepped from the SUV, a large golden eagle descended suddenly from above and landed on a weathered signpost nearby. The enormous bird folded its dark wings slowly while observing them with unsettling calm.

"Look at that thing," Noah whispered. "It's incredible."

Maia reached carefully for her phone.

"I've never seen one this close before."

Neither Ale nor Noah noticed that the eagle's gaze remained fixed entirely on Sam.

Something inside her tightened.

The desert wind moved softly through her hair while the bird continued watching her with ancient stillness in its eyes. For reasons she could not explain, standing there beside Pyramid Lake did not feel like arriving somewhere unfamiliar. It felt like returning to a place she had somehow forgotten.

“Do you have the camping permits?” Ale asked Noah while unloading camping equipment.

“Yeah. They’re in the glove compartment.”

Pyramid Lake had belonged to the Nu-Mu for longer than memory could measure. Even now, the lake seemed to carry something of their presence within its depths, as though memory itself still moved beneath the surface.

The group spent the next hour setting up camp beneath the burning sun. Ale complained dramatically through most of it while Noah teased her relentlessly from a distance.

“You attached one mosquito net,” Maia reminded her after nearly tripping over one of the tent loops.

“And drove all the way here,” Ale defended herself. “Do you know how emotionally exhausting that was?”

“Yes,” Noah answered. “German engineering truly is humanity’s greatest burden.”

Their laughter drifted briefly across the shoreline before dissolving into the wind.

The rest of the day unfolded peacefully. They swam in the lake, cooked fish over a small fire, and watched the desert gradually soften beneath the descending sun. As evening approached, the mountains surrounding Pyramid Lake darkened into deep blue silhouettes while the water absorbed the changing colors of the sky with dreamlike clarity.

Sam spent long stretches simply observing the lake.

The place affected her in ways she could not explain rationally. The silence surrounding Pyramid Lake did not feel empty. It possessed density, presence, almost consciousness. Standing near the water made her strangely aware of herself, not only physically, but inwardly, as though something beneath the surface of ordinary life had begun watching her in return.

Night arrived slowly.

By midnight, the Milky Way stretched across the heavens with astonishing clarity. The campfire had collapsed into dim embers, and the shoreline rested beneath a silence so complete that even the smallest sounds seemed magnified within it.

Inside the tent, Sam remained awake.

At first she blamed the unfamiliar sleeping conditions, but deep down she already understood that something else was keeping her from rest. For weeks, her dreams had grown increasingly vivid. Pamahas's presence no longer felt symbolic or distant. Sometimes Sam woke with the sensation that another world existed dangerously close to her own, separated only by some fragile boundary she could neither see nor understand.

Tonight, the feeling was stronger than ever.

Carefully, she unzipped the tent and stepped outside without waking the others.

The desert air had turned cold. A soft wind moved across the shoreline while the lake remained perfectly still beneath the moonlight. Sam removed her jacket and left it draped across one of the folding chairs before walking slowly into the water wearing only denim shorts and a black lace-up bikini top.

The warmth of the lake startled her immediately.

It felt warmer than the air itself.

She continued farther inward until the water reached her waist. Above her, countless stars reflected across the unmoving surface with such clarity that the boundary between heaven and earth seemed momentarily uncertain.

Sam closed her eyes.

The silence surrounding her was unlike anything she had ever experienced. It did not feel vacant. It felt expectant.

A painful longing rose quietly inside her chest.

All her life, she had searched for something she could never fully name. Not success. Not romance. Not escape. Something larger. Something capable of restoring meaning to a world that increasingly felt fractured and spiritually diminished. Ever since her mother's death, Sam had feared that humanity had forgotten how to truly see one another, forgotten how to stand still long enough for life to reveal its deeper shape.

Then she noticed the red light.

Far across the lake, a crimson flare drifted against the darkness. Sam opened her eyes fully.

At first, she thought it might belong to another campsite, but the light moved slowly across the water. A small boat emerged around it before disappearing once more into the night.

Her pulse quickened.

The flare appeared again.

This time she saw the figure inside the vessel.

A young girl sat alone beneath the stars, guiding the reed boat across the water with a single oar while a torch burned beside her.

The sight hollowed something inside Sam with sudden, unbearable force.

She had never seen the child before, and yet recognition flooded through her so intensely that it bordered on grief. The small figure rowing silently across the lake seemed impossibly familiar, as though some forgotten part of Sam's life had waited years for this exact moment to arrive.

The water around her trembled softly.

Dreams returned to her in fragments. Red light drifting across black water. A distant child. A voice calling from somewhere beyond waking life. Until now, Sam had dismissed those visions as products of exhaustion and loss. But standing there beneath the immense silence of Pyramid Lake, she understood with terrifying clarity that the dreams had never belonged entirely to sleep.

A sudden splash erupted behind her.

Sam turned sharply toward the shore. The tent, the SUV, and the folding chairs remained exactly where they should have been, yet all of it seemed strangely distant now, as though ordinary reality itself had begun receding from her reach.

When she looked back toward the lake, the boat was closer. The water surrounding it shimmered like molten gold, illuminated by something moving beneath the surface.

The girl continued rowing toward her through the golden water while the torchlight trembled softly against the darkness. As the boat passed behind the pyramid-shaped rock, it vanished from sight.

Without fully understanding why, Sam rushed back toward shore, grabbed a towel from one of the chairs, and began climbing toward a nearby cliff overlooking the lake. Some instinct deeper than reason compelled her upward, toward height, toward perspective, toward whatever impossible thing was unfolding beneath the night sky.

Behind her, Noah emerged from the tent moments later and immediately noticed her absence.

"Sam?"

A violent gust exploded across the beach, hurling sand into the air.

He shielded his eyes and spotted her running toward the cliff.

"Sam, wait!"

The wind intensified with impossible speed. Gusts collided violently across the shoreline while sand spiraled upward through the darkness in towering sheets. Noah struggled forward against the storm, panic rising steadily inside him.

"Sam! You could fall!"

But the wind swallowed his voice.

By the time Sam reached the top of the cliff, the lake below had transformed completely.

Pyramid Lake glowed with a faint golden radiance beneath the night sky while the storm raged everywhere except upon its surface. The water remained smooth and untouched by the violence surrounding it, as though the lake existed within a reality separate from the world above it.

Noah finally reached her moments later.

Then he saw the boat.

The small vessel drifted directly below them now, carrying the young girl across the luminous water while the torch burned steadily beside her.

The child lifted her gaze toward Sam.

The girl cried out from the boat in a language Sam could not understand. Still, the meaning arrived inside her almost instantly, as though the lake itself had translated it.

Jump.

Though separated by distance and roaring wind, her voice reached them with impossible clarity.

Sam stared downward in silence.

The little girl lowered the torch slowly into the liquid gold of the lake. The flame disappeared beneath the surface without resistance, as though the water itself had accepted it willingly. For a brief moment, the glowing surface thinned like drifting clouds, and far beneath it Sam thought she saw the golden apex of Wono suspended in another world below the lake, impossibly distant and yet terrifyingly clear.

Then, without hesitation, the child leaped from the boat and vanished beneath the golden surface without producing so much as a splash.

Noah stepped beside Sam at the edge of the cliff.

Their hands found one another instinctively.

For a brief moment, he became painfully aware that whatever waited below them might take them somewhere from which ordinary life could never fully return. Yet standing beside Sam beneath the storm, he also understood with equal certainty that letting her face the unknown alone was impossible for him.

"Are you sure you want to do this?" he asked softly.

Sam looked toward the glowing lake once more.

Toward the impossible stillness that now resembled a pristine mirror of liquid gold.

Toward the feeling that her entire life had been moving silently toward this moment beneath the surface of things.

She thought of her mother, of the way she had given herself to others without demanding certainty in return, trusting that meaning revealed itself only to those willing to surrender themselves honestly to life.

Perhaps faith had always been that.

Not answers.

A willingness to cross the threshold before understanding what waited beyond it.

"Yes," Sam whispered.

She tightened her hand around Noah's.

Then together, they jumped.

Their bodies disappeared beneath the golden surface while the desert storm continued screaming across the cliffs above them. Yet moments later, even the wind began to fade, and the ancient waters of Pyramid Lake, having received what had been offered to them, returned quietly to their immense and solemn silence.

CHAPTER XIII
The Power of Truth

Don't pollute what is with labels, opinions, and judgment. Instead, see the truth in it by observing it impartially and acknowledging it in its entirety. Then, in a state of honor, appreciation, and acceptance, you will discover its genuine essence. Now that's truth indeed.

The lake released them gently. Sam emerged first, drawing a desperate breath as golden water streamed down her face and shoulders. Noah surfaced beside her moments later, coughing violently while his hands searched instinctively through the glowing surface for stability. For several seconds, neither could fully understand what they were seeing. The storm was gone. The violent wind that had consumed Pyramid Lake moments earlier had vanished completely, replaced by a silence so profound that even the movement of the water around them seemed restrained by it.

The air itself felt different here, lighter and strangely conscious, as though the world surrounding them possessed awareness of their arrival.

Sam wiped the water from her eyes and slowly turned toward the shore.

Galilhai stood waiting for them several feet away, barefoot against pale sand that shimmered faintly beneath the silver light surrounding the lake. Her dark hair moved softly across her shoulders while the fabric of her dress drifted gently around her legs despite the absence of wind. There was no fear in her expression now. Only recognition, as though she had always known this moment would arrive.

Then she lifted her arm toward the horizon.

Noah followed her gaze first, and the breath disappeared from his lungs.

Far across the water, Wono rose into the heavens.

The pyramid no longer resembled stone. Its immense surfaces radiated a living golden light that shifted constantly across the colossal structure like sunlight moving beneath translucent water. From this distance, its scale felt almost incomprehensible. The geometric perfection of its ascending faces imposed a strange authority upon the landscape around it.

Several streams of water floated freely through the air surrounding the pyramid.

They moved in enormous spirals around Wono with slow and dreamlike elegance while thousands of silver fish traveled peacefully within them. Some currents descended toward the lake while others disappeared into the upper reaches of the sky itself, resembling luminous veins carrying life through the body of a sleeping god.

Galilhai said something softly in her own language while gesturing toward the enormous golden pyramid rising across the lake. Though Sam and Noah could not have repeated the words aloud afterward, their meaning entered them with perfect clarity.

Wono.

The Other World.

Sam remained motionless.

Something deep within her had recognized this place immediately, though not through memory in the ordinary sense. The feeling moved beneath thought itself, ancient and intimate at once, as though some forgotten part of her had suddenly awakened after years of silence.

Beside her, Noah struggled to absorb the impossible reality surrounding them. Colors appeared deeper here. Light possessed texture. Even the surface of the lake seemed alive in ways he could neither explain nor fully endure.

Then Galilhai smiled faintly.

"There she is."

Across the shoreline, several mounted figures emerged slowly from the distant trees.

At their center rode Pamahas.

Her white horse moved across the sand with unnatural grace, its silver mane flowing continuously behind it like liquid moonlight. Several riders surrounded her in complete silence. At first Noah believed they were men dressed in ceremonial armor, but as they approached, the details of their forms became clearer.

Their upper bodies resembled enormous birds of prey covered in bronze and white feathers, while the lower halves of their bodies remained unmistakably human. Semi-transparent currents of golden energy moved slowly around them, enveloping their figures in a faint radiance that pulsed softly against the darkness of the forest behind them.

Noah felt Sam's hand tighten around his arm.

"What is this place?" he whispered.

"I think I've seen it before," Sam answered quietly, unable to pull her eyes away from Wono. "Not exactly like this. But somewhere inside my dreams."

Noah turned toward her.

Before he could speak, Galilhai looked back at them with gentle amusement.

"You do not always need words here," she said. "Thought moves differently."

Noah stared at her in confusion.

"You can hear us?"

"At first, it frightened me too," Galilhai admitted softly.

The riders finally reached the shoreline.

Pamahas dismounted slowly from her horse, and Noah immediately understood that no dream he had ever experienced could have prepared him for her presence. She stood nearly a head taller than either of them, yet nothing about her height felt disproportionate. Instead, it carried the same natural authority as mountains and oceans. Her long red hair moved continuously around her body as though responding to invisible currents flowing through the world itself.

When her eyes met Sam's, an overwhelming calm moved through her body instantly.

"You crossed successfully," Pamahas said.

Her voice carried unusual depth beneath it, soft and melodic yet ancient in ways Sam could feel more than understand.

"We jumped into the lake," Noah replied carefully. "How are we here?"

Pamahas looked toward the floating streams surrounding Wono before answering.

"In your world, people often mistake the visible for the complete," she said softly. "They touch only the surface of life and believe they have touched its entirety."

Her gaze returned to them.

"Life does not end where sight does."

The words settled heavily inside Noah despite their simplicity. Questions continued gathering within him, yet their urgency had begun dissolving since his arrival. The Other World itself seemed to weaken the frantic need to explain everything immediately. Thought behaved differently here. It moved more slowly, more deeply, as though awareness itself had detached from the constant noise that dominated the World of Form.

One of the mounted guardians approached silently beside them and lowered itself slightly.

Up close, Noah could see golden patterns moving beneath the creature's feathers like living light beneath translucent skin.

Galilhai climbed easily onto one of the horses beside Pamahas while Sam and Noah mounted behind another guardian whose broad body radiated immense warmth beneath its soft feathers.

Without command, the riders began moving.

The shoreline disappeared gradually behind them while the forest ahead opened beneath towering silver trees whose enormous branches shimmered softly against the strange sky above. Streams of luminous water flowed silently between the roots, illuminating the earth below with faint currents of moving gold.

Then Noah finally lifted his eyes upward.

Far above them stretched another world.

An immense layer of transparent water moved across the heavens like a suspended ocean resting above reality itself. Through it, Noah could see mountains, moonlight, and the distant outline of Pyramid Lake. The World of Form drifted there silently beyond the liquid barrier, distorted occasionally by slow currents overhead.

"We are beneath it," Noah whispered.

Pamahas rode ahead without turning.

"You are within it," she replied quietly.

Sam continued staring upward in silence.

For the first time, she understood why the dreams had always felt incomplete. The worlds had never truly been separate. One simply existed beyond the perception of the other, concealed beneath distraction, fear, and the limitations of ordinary sight.

Far above them, the reflection of Stone Mother drifted slowly across the liquid sky.

"That lake above us," Noah said softly. "That's Pyramid Lake."

"The form of it," Pamahas answered.

She gestured toward the glowing waters behind them.

"And this is the essence."

The riders continued deeper into the forest while strange creatures watched silently from the distance between the trees.

Some resembled pale deer formed from drifting mist, while others carried translucent wings within which entire constellations appeared to move slowly like living galaxies suspended beneath glass.

Yet despite the impossible beauty surrounding them, Sam gradually became aware of something else.

A presence that did not feel as though it were approaching, but waiting.

The horses slowed.

Ahead, beneath an enormous tree whose roots rose from the earth like ancient stone walls, a massive black wolf rested in silence.

At first Noah thought the creature was part of the landscape itself. Its fur absorbed light rather than reflecting it, blending almost seamlessly with the shadows surrounding the roots of the tree. The sheer size of the animal dwarfed the forest around it.

Then the wolf opened its eyes.

Gold moved within them, not color but light itself.

The entire forest seemed to grow quieter in response.

A single leaf drifted downward through the silver air before settling gently upon the creature's snout.

The wolf rose slowly.

Every movement carried impossible restraint, as though the world itself adjusted carefully around him.

Then the shape began to change.

Dark fur receded like flowing water while bone and light shifted soundlessly beneath the surface of the body. The enormous creature rose gradually onto two legs, its form reshaping itself with slow and impossible grace until a towering humanoid figure stood beneath the ancient tree, broad-shouldered and powerful, with the head of a great black wolf still gazing upon them through luminous golden eyes.

His skin resembled sunlit earth after rain, while faint golden currents moved beneath it like distant fire beneath stone.

Yet it was not his appearance that overwhelmed them.

It was his presence.

Standing near him felt almost unbearable, not because of fear, but because nothing false seemed capable of surviving in his presence. Sam felt every hidden grief, memory, fear, and longing inside her becoming visible without judgment, seen completely and accepted completely at once.

“I am Esa,” he said.

His voice moved through the forest like deep water.

Galilhai lowered her head immediately while even the mounted guardians remained perfectly still.

Noah tried to speak but found himself incapable of forming words.

Esa looked toward them with profound calm.

"You crossed far to arrive here," he said. "But no distance truly separates our worlds."

As he spoke, Sam became aware of something extraordinary surrounding him. The trees, the water, the wind moving softly through the branches overhead all seemed connected to his presence somehow, not controlled by him, but aware of him in the same instinctive way living things recognize sunlight, gravity, or breath.

Then Esa looked toward Galilhai.

"You carry the memory of your people with honor."

Emotion filled the young girl's eyes instantly.

Finally, Esa turned toward Sam and Noah.

"What you call life," he said quietly, "is only one movement within a much greater current."

The words entered Noah before thought could reach them.

Questions still existed inside him, but they no longer felt sharp or desperate. In Esa's presence, certainty itself seemed less important than awareness.

Sam stared at him silently.

For the first time since her mother's death, the emptiness within her no longer felt abandoned.

It felt unfinished.

Esa stepped closer.

The warmth surrounding him resembled sunlight passing through water.

"Darkness approaches both worlds," he said. "Yet darkness has never been the true danger."

The forest listened.

"The danger has always been forgetting what you are."

Silence followed.

Somewhere far above them, beyond the liquid sky of the World of Form, distant thunder rolled softly across another reality.

Pamahas approached beside her brother then, and together they emanated a strange completeness impossible to describe in ordinary language, like two halves of something once whole.

In that moment, Sam finally understood the feeling she had carried her entire life. The longing. The absence. The quiet certainty that something sacred had been forgotten.

It existed here.

And standing beneath the silver trees of the Other World, surrounded by waters older than memory, Sam understood at last that Pyramid Lake had never called her away from the world she knew.

It had called her toward something the world could no longer see.

CHAPTER ∞

Puha is Love

"I am,
I am complete.

For me to exist,
fragmented I come to be.

In pieces revealed,
as one I find me.

I am,
I am complete."

— Puha reflected itself.

CHAPTER XIV
Lost and Found

We came to this world to find ourselves, to be ourselves. So, we should not be distracted by superfluous objectives and elaborate acting. They are unnecessary layers that obstruct the beauty of our souls, the holiness of our spirits.

"Did you hear that?" Maia's voice emerged sharply through the darkness of the tent. Her trembling hands searched beside the sleeping bag until they found the black flashlight resting near her backpack. After several frantic attempts, the beam finally burst alive.

Ale shielded her eyes immediately.

"Oh my God."

"I heard screams outside," Maia whispered. "Sam and Noah are gone."

For a moment, Ale simply stared at her.

"What do you mean gone?"

"There's a storm outside. I can barely see anything."

The flexible poles supporting the tent bent violently beneath the pressure of the wind while thousands of grains of sand scraped continuously against the fabric. The sound surrounded them like restless static.

Maia pulled the oversized yellow hoodie tighter around herself, the blue letters across the front, NEVADA: THE BATTLE BORN STATE, creasing as her hands trembled near the pocket. Beside her, Ale had thrown on the dark green waterproof jacket she kept near the entrance of the tent, though one sleeve still sat twisted at her wrist from the hurry of putting it on.

Ale looked around quickly.

Sam's blanket lay empty.

Noah's backpack remained beside the entrance.

Then Maia pointed downward.

"Their phones."

Near the corner of the tent, two dark screens rested silently beside Ale's car keys.

A cold pressure gathered inside her chest.

Without speaking further, the two girls pushed their way outside.

The storm had already begun weakening. Wind still crossed the shoreline in sudden bursts, but the violence from moments earlier had faded into an unnatural stillness that unsettled Maia more deeply than the storm itself. The lake stretched beneath the moonlight in almost perfect silence.

Ale approached the SUV first and unlocked it automatically as she neared the driver's door.

"Hold on," she said. "I'm turning on the headlights."

The engine awakened softly.

Bright white beams cut across the darkness and reached toward the shoreline before dissolving against the black water.

"Sam!" Maia shouted suddenly. "Noah!"

Only silence returned.

Ale stepped back out of the vehicle slowly.

"They're not here."

The headlights disappeared as she shut the SUV off again.

Darkness reclaimed the beach almost immediately.

Then Maia froze.

"There."

Far out upon the lake, something drifted silently across the water.

The two girls climbed instinctively toward higher ground overlooking the shore. As they reached the cliffside, the shape below became clearer.

A small reed boat floated alone beneath the moonlight.

Empty.

Ale narrowed her eyes.

Then her entire body stiffened.

Beneath the dark surface of the lake, something enormous revealed itself. At first it appeared only as distorted gold trembling beneath the water, but as the waves briefly settled, the shape clarified with terrifying precision.

The apex of a colossal pyramid.

Its golden surfaces radiated faintly through the depths like submerged sunlight from another reality. Even fractured by the movement of the lake, the structure's scale felt impossible, ancient, sacred beyond understanding.

Then the water shifted again, and the vision dissolved back into darkness.

Ale stepped backward slowly, unable to pull her eyes away from the dark water below.

"That was real," she whispered.

Maia said nothing.

Far beneath them, the empty boat continued drifting silently across the lake while the surface of the water returned gradually to darkness. Whatever doorway had revealed itself beneath Pyramid Lake was gone now.

Maia knew it then.

Sam and Noah were no longer here.

Not hidden somewhere along the shoreline.

Gone.

Beside her, Ale remained silent, but Maia could already sense the same realization beginning to emerge inside her as well.

The wind moved softly across the cliffs.

"We need to go to Sparks," Maia said suddenly.

Ale turned toward her.

"Why?"

Maia hesitated briefly, still staring toward the lake below.

"Because Sam came to me about something a few days ago."

She tightened her arms around herself against the cold desert wind.

"I think it explains what we just saw."

Neither of them spoke again while descending toward the shoreline. By the time they reached the SUV, the desert had become unnaturally still.

The drive toward Sparks unfolded beneath empty roads and a sky crowded with stars. Ale kept both hands tightly around the steering wheel while Maia remained turned toward the passenger window, her thoughts moving somewhere far beyond the road ahead. Rational explanations continued collapsing inside her one by one. She knew what she had seen beneath the lake. More unsettling still, some part of her had recognized it immediately.

Wono.

The name alone unsettled her.

The red SUV finally stopped outside the bookstore shortly before dawn.

At night, the building appeared older somehow. The large windows reflected only darkness while the faded wooden sign above the entrance creaked softly beneath the wind.

Maia unlocked the front door.

The familiar scent of old paper, dust, and cedar greeted them immediately. Ale remained close behind her while Maia crossed toward the front desk and switched on a small brass lamp beside the computer. A circle of warm amber light spread softly across the counter.

"What exactly are we looking for?" Ale asked quietly.

Maia removed her glasses briefly and pressed her fingers against her eyes as though trying to steady her thoughts.

"A book," she said at last.

Ale stared at her across the amber light of the desk.

"After everything we just saw... you brought me here for a book?"

Maia looked back toward the darkened shelves surrounding them.

"I think it's the reason Sam came here."

She sat at the computer and typed rapidly through the inventory system while Ale wandered restlessly between the nearby shelves. Then Maia suddenly stopped.

Her breathing changed.

Without saying a word, she rose from the chair and disappeared between the aisles near the back of the store. Moments later, she returned carrying a massive blue volume nearly the size of an atlas.

Dust drifted softly from its cover as she placed it upon the desk.

Ale helped clear space for it instinctively.

When Maia opened the book, both girls froze.

Spread across the center pages stood a detailed illustration of Pyramid Lake beneath a dark ceremonial sky. Galilhai rested barefoot inside a narrow reed boat drifting silently across the water while distant fires illuminated shadowed figures gathered along the shoreline in ritual dance. Beneath the lake itself, partially obscured by darkness and depth, the golden apex of Wono emerged from the abyss. The enormous blocks, the luminous surfaces, even the shape of the pyramid's ascending faces matched perfectly with what Ale and Maia had witnessed beneath Pyramid Lake only hours earlier.

Above the image, black letters stretched across the page.

THE SACRED WONO

Ale felt the blood drain slowly from her face.

"That's it," she whispered.

Maia nodded.

A long silence passed between them before she finally spoke again.

"Sam came here a few days ago," Maia said quietly.

Ale looked up from the illustration.

"I know. I picked her up afterward."

Maia hesitated briefly before continuing.

"She wasn't here browsing."

Her fingers rested softly against the open page.

"She came asking about Stone Mother. About dreams. About Pyramid Lake."

Ale's expression changed immediately.

"Why didn't you tell me?"

Maia lowered her eyes.

"Because I thought it was only curiosity."

Then she opened one of the desk drawers beside her and carefully removed a black journal.

"She forgot this here," Maia said softly.

Ale looked down immediately.

"That's Sam's."

Maia nodded.

The journal appeared worn from use, its edges softened beneath fingerprints and folded pages. A blue ribbon rested between the center sheets as though Sam had been interrupted in the middle of writing.

Maia handed it to Ale carefully. The journal opened naturally near the center, revealing several handwritten entries.

Then Ale began reading aloud.

First dream

October 29th, 2020

I'm walking beside Pyramid Lake at night. A tall woman with red hair is standing on the water. I can't see her face clearly, but I know she wants me to follow her.

Second dream

December 30th, 2020

I'm holding hands with a little girl in the woods. I think she might be Native American. Somehow, I feel like I've known her for a very long time.

Third dream

June 14th, 2021

The black riders came back. Their armor has dark openings at the center that feel wrong somehow, like looking into empty space. I hide behind a tree until the red-haired woman touches my shoulder and wakes me up.

Fourth dream

June 15th, 2021

The little girl is standing barefoot inside a boat beneath a cliff. The lake is glowing gold below us. She wants me to jump.

Ale lowered the journal slowly.

"The first dream," she whispered, "that was the night her mother died."

Fear moved visibly through her now.

"What if she actually jumped?"

Maia crossed quickly around the desk and guided Ale into one of the chairs nearby before filling a small paper cup with water from the dispenser beside the wall.

"She didn't kill herself," Maia said softly, handing her the cup. "At least... I don't think she did."

Ale looked up at her.

"Then where is she?"

Maia glanced toward the open book resting across the desk.

The golden pyramid seemed to glow faintly beneath the amber light of the bookstore.

"I think she crossed."

The silence that followed felt heavier than anything either of them had yet experienced that night.

Maia continued turning the pages slowly, though part of her no longer wanted to know what else the book contained. The stillness inside the bookstore felt charged with the unbearable sensation that something impossible was steadily becoming real. Then another illustration appeared across the yellowed paper.

Galilhai.

The young girl stood barefoot inside a narrow wooden boat drifting across Pyramid Lake beneath a dark ceremonial sky. Fires burned along the distant shoreline where shadowed figures gathered in ritual dance beside the water, their movements illuminated by flickering orange light. Galilhai held a single wooden oar against her chest while beneath the lake itself, partially obscured by darkness and depth, the golden apex of Wono emerged from the abyss.

Faint violet currents resembling strands of living spirit descended through the water beneath the boat, stretching downward toward the hidden pyramid below.

Ale stared silently at the image.

"That's her," Maia whispered. "The girl from Sam's dreams."

Together they continued searching through the book while the darkness outside slowly softened toward dawn. Most of the pages contained fragmented stories, ceremonial drawings, or descriptions of rituals connected to water, dreams, and sacred crossings between worlds. Yet several pages near the back had been violently removed.

Maia ran her fingers carefully along the torn binding until something caught her attention.

A number written in blue ink across the inner cloth of the spine.

Her expression changed immediately.

"That's strange."

"What?"

"That's one of the store inventory codes."

Maia returned quickly to the computer and entered the sequence.

Only one result appeared.

No title, author, or publication information.

Only a location.

The basement safe.

Ale looked toward her uncertainly.

"Why would missing pages from that book be hidden in a safe?"

"I don't know."

Maia already did not like where her thoughts were leading.

The basement smelled faintly of humidity and old cardboard. Stacks of unopened boxes lined the walls while a black iron safe rested beneath the staircase beside a dim floor lamp.

Ale watched nervously as Maia entered the combination.

"You've opened this before?"

"Mr. Schneider forgets the code constantly," Maia replied, distracted by the numbers beneath her fingers. "He made me memorize it in case he ever needed help."

A metallic click echoed softly through the basement.

The safe opened.

Inside, several rare books rested carefully arranged upon velvet-lined shelves. Yet what immediately caught Maia's attention was a thin brown folder positioned directly on top of them.

The same inventory number had been written across the label.

She opened it carefully.

Loose pages rested inside, their ancient paper, typography, and texture perfectly matching the damaged book upstairs.

Maia felt her pulse quicken.

Back upstairs, the missing pages fit perfectly into the damaged section of the book.

The text itself was fragmented and partially faded, more prophecy than history. Certain passages spoke of a sacred object shaped in the image of Wono, created long ago as a bridge between worlds and entrusted to the care of the living. Other sections described an approaching imbalance connected somehow to Lake Tahoe, though much of the writing had deteriorated beyond comprehension.

One phrase appeared repeatedly throughout the pages.

The flow of life must continue.

Maia read the line several times silently.

Elsewhere, a final passage referred cryptically to someone through whom the sacred object would eventually emerge into the World of Form. No name appeared. Only a symbol resembling an unfinished circle surrounding a pyramid of gold.

Ale looked up from the pages slowly.

"What does any of this mean?"

Maia closed the book carefully.

Outside, the desert night remained untouched by morning. Darkness pressed softly against the bookstore windows while the wind moved through the empty streets of Sparks with a low and distant whistle.

"I don't know yet," she admitted quietly.

But deep inside, she already understood one thing with certainty.

Whatever had taken Sam and Noah beyond Pyramid Lake was not finished with them.

And somewhere beyond the visible world, something had already begun moving toward them all.

CHAPTER XV

Vital Priorities

There is only one thing that matters: whatever you are doing at this moment. Put your heart and soul into it, and it will be marvelous. The how will always be more important than the what, even when that thing is to not do a thing.

Pamahas guided them through the settlement without haste. The town rested high above the lake, protected by miles of dense forest whose silver trunks rose like pillars from the luminous earth. The buildings along the street appeared grown rather than constructed, their golden facades fused seamlessly with stone, roots, and living wood. Symbols moved slowly across the walls in currents of light, disappearing and reforming as though the structures themselves were thinking in silence.

Galilhai walked beside Sam with quiet fascination, stopping every few steps to study the shifting inscriptions before hurrying forward again, afraid they might change before she could fully observe them. Wonder followed her naturally here. She did not search for explanations or resist what the Other World offered her. It settled around her with the familiarity of remembered water, as though some forgotten part of her spirit had already walked these streets long before her body reached them.

Noah noticed everything differently.

He measured distance instinctively. Streets, corners, pathways between buildings, the direction of the lake, the position of Wono in the distance. Since arriving in the Other World, part of him had continued trying to understand the place through orientation and structure, as though the unknown could become safer once mapped in his mind. Yet nothing here remained fixed long enough to be possessed intellectually. Every time he thought he understood the shape of something, the world revealed another layer beneath it.

Sam sensed the tension inside him and quietly took his hand.

He held onto hers immediately.

Above them, the sky began to transform. At the eastern perimeter of the heavens, beyond immense walls of pale stone and suspended sand, the sun emerged slowly into view. At the same time, from the opposite horizon, the moon rose with equal magnitude. Neither body diminished the other. Both moved toward the center of the liquid sky with solemn inevitability, and as they approached one another, the settlement gradually grew still.

Figures standing near fountains of suspended water lowered their heads. Children paused beside glowing doorways. Even the bird-headed guardians near the forest edge remained motionless beneath the approaching convergence above them.

Noah lifted his gaze.

"What is happening?"

Pamahas looked upward.

"Noon."

The word carried unusual weight inside the silence.

When the sun and moon met above the town, the entire Other World seemed briefly suspended between breaths. Then light moved through everything, not violently, not like fire or lightning, but with a tenderness so complete that it seemed to pass through the settlement rather than over it. It entered the streets, the forest, the lake below, the golden buildings, and the bodies standing beneath the joined celestial bodies.

The world did not darken beneath the eclipse. It inverted.

Gold deepened into graphite. Silver leaves transformed into fields of rose and yellow. The distant forest bloomed in impossible colors while the lake below darkened into crimson glass. The altered radiance touched everything with strange intimacy, revealing not an opposite world, but the hidden face of the same one.

Noah looked down at his hands.

His skin had changed.

The pale tone he had known his entire life had become a deep cinnamon warmth spreading naturally across his arms and fingers. In the polished surface of a nearby wall, he caught the reflection of his own eyes and saw their gray-blue color had deepened into rich brown. He stared silently at himself, not afraid exactly, but unsettled by the impossible familiarity of his altered body.

Sam studied him carefully.

The transformation did not make him unfamiliar. If anything, it stripped something away. The careful ease he carried around others, the humor he used to soften difficult moments, the quiet instinct to make himself dependable before admitting fear, all of it seemed suddenly more transparent beneath the altered light of noon.

"You're still you," Sam said softly.

Noah looked toward her.

"That's what scares me."

The honesty in his voice unsettled her more deeply than fear would have.

For most of his life, Noah had believed goodness was something earned through effort. By being patient enough. Useful enough. Reliable enough. He had learned to become the person others could lean on, and because people had leaned on him, he had rarely asked whether steadiness was the same as peace. Standing beneath the joined sun and moon, he felt exposed before himself in a way he had never experienced before. Noon had not transformed him into someone else. It had revealed the part of him that had spent years trying quietly to deserve his place in the lives of those he loved.

Sam stepped closer and touched his forearm gently.

"It's beautiful," she whispered.

Noah lowered his eyes toward her hand against his skin.

"You didn't change."

Sam looked at herself instinctively. Her arms, her hands, the amber warmth in her eyes, all remained untouched by the inversion surrounding them. Beside her, Galilhai also stood unchanged beneath the eclipse, small and solemn within the transformed world.

The child noticed it too.

She gently pulled at the fabric of Sam's dress.

"Why are we the same?"

Sam looked down at her, unable to answer.

Pamahas knelt beside Galilhai. The eclipse had transformed her as well. Her flowing red hair now carried pale blue tones like moonlight moving beneath water, while her skin had become almost porcelain beneath the merged radiance overhead. Yet despite the strangeness of her altered appearance, sadness remained visible within her eyes, ancient and immeasurable.

She took Galilhai's hands carefully into her own.

"Some things do not wait for noon to reveal themselves," Pamahas said quietly.

Galilhai lowered her gaze, thoughtful beneath words she could not yet fully understand.

Then Pamahas looked toward Sam.

"You have spent much of your life listening to what others ignore."

The statement entered Sam with painful precision. For years, she had mistaken her longing for absence alone: the death of her mother, the loneliness that followed afterward, the quiet sensation that the world had forgotten something sacred and continued living anyway. Yet the Other World had begun revealing another possibility to her, one both terrifying and beautiful. Perhaps her longing had never been emptiness. Perhaps it had always been recognition.

Noah watched her silently.

For the first time, he understood something essential about the difference between them. Noah carried responsibility naturally. He protected, repaired, steadied. But Sam moved toward suffering differently. She listened to it. Entered it. She wanted not merely to survive the fractures of the world, but somehow to heal them. That frightened him, because people willing to walk toward broken things often disappeared into them.

The joined eclipse burned overhead.

Far below the settlement, Pyramid Lake became visible between two buildings. Wono hovered above the water in crimson brilliance beneath the inversion of noon, no longer gold but burning like the exposed heart of another reality. Forests of rose and yellow separated the town from the lake while currents of luminous water drifted through the air surrounding the great pyramid in vast spirals.

Then birdsong rose through the trees.

At first the sound seemed distant and delicate, but as the melody deepened, the forest itself responded. Leaves shifted slowly across thousands of branches until a massive glowing triangle emerged within the canopy, its three points aligned perfectly between the town, the lake, and Wono itself. The entire Other World seemed joined by invisible geometry. Water influenced light. Light influenced sound. Sound moved through life. Somewhere beneath all of it, Puha gathered and scattered itself endlessly, not as an idea, but as the living relationship between every visible thing.

Noah stared at the glowing triangle in silence.

The world was not explaining itself.

It was revealing itself.

Pamahas rose slowly to her feet.

"The time has come," she said.

The stillness surrounding them changed. Until then, the Other World had unfolded like revelation. Now it became direction.

Pamahas extended one hand, and a woven basket appeared within it, formed from pale yucca fibers threaded with delicate lines of gold. She approached Noah and carefully removed a small object wrapped in white cloth. When the cloth unfolded, he forgot to breathe.

A miniature Wono rested within Pamahas's hands.

The artifact was no larger than his palm, yet it carried the same impossible presence as the great pyramid suspended above the lake below. Its surfaces glowed with living gold while intricate engravings moved faintly across its ascending faces like currents beneath metal. At the apex, a concentrated light pulsed softly, almost like a heartbeat.

Pamahas placed it carefully into Noah's hands.

The weight startled him. Not physically alone. The object carried a density that seemed to extend beyond matter itself, as though responsibility had taken form within his grasp.

"The flow between Tahoe and Pyramid Lake has been wounded," Pamahas said softly.

Noah immediately thought of the fog rolling across Lake Tahoe the previous day.

"The disturbance," he whispered.

Pamahas nodded once.

"For a long time, the lakes spoke to one another beneath both worlds. But the passage had to be sealed before darkness entered through it."

She looked toward the crimson pyramid suspended above the distant waters.

"Now the imbalance has begun spreading."

Noah closed his fingers carefully around the miniature Wono.

"What do you need me to do?"

Pamahas studied him quietly before answering.

"Return to the World of Form. Take this to Lake Tahoe and surrender it into the deepest water you can reach."

Noah absorbed the instruction in silence.

Beside him, Sam turned sharply toward Pamahas.

"He has to leave?"

The fear in her voice emerged before she could conceal it.

Pamahas looked toward her with visible sorrow.

"Yes."

The eclipse above them suddenly felt colder.

Sam looked at Noah, and for the first time since arriving in the Other World, she felt truly afraid. Not of Wono. Not of the Dark Shadows. Not even of the unknown waiting ahead. She was afraid of separation, afraid that this impossible world revealing truth so mercilessly might take from her the one person who still made her feel anchored to the life she understood.

Noah stepped toward her.

"I'll do it," he said quietly. "But I'm coming back."

Pamahas remained silent.

Noah understood the silence immediately. Promises behaved differently here. Words carried consequence. The Other World listened.

Still, he did not withdraw the promise.

"I'm coming back," he repeated.

Sam's eyes filled slowly with tears.

"You always say things like that when you're scared."

A faint smile touched Noah's face before disappearing again.

"I know."

The honesty broke something inside her more completely than reassurance would have.

She stepped into him and wrapped her arms around his body with sudden force. Noah held her tightly against him while the altered light of noon drifted silently across the settlement around them.

"I thought I wanted something greater than my life," Sam whispered against his chest. "Now all I can think about is losing part of it."

Noah closed his eyes.

"You're not losing me."

"You don't know that."

"No," he admitted softly. "But I know what I'm supposed to do right now."

That was Noah. Not fearless, not extraordinary because prophecy had named him, not eager for wonder or power, but capable of turning toward the fragile thing placed before him and carrying it as far as he could. Sam understood that then, and the knowledge only made loving him more painful.

She looked up at him through tears.

The miniature Wono glowed faintly between their bodies.

"I love you," she whispered.

Noah inhaled slowly, as though the words had entered somewhere deeper than his lungs.

"I love you too," he said. "I think I did long before I understood what it meant."

She kissed him beneath the joined sun and moon, not desperately, but with the sorrowful tenderness of someone realizing that love could not prevent separation. It could only make separation meaningful.

When they finally pulled apart, Galilhai had stepped quietly beside them.

The child looked up at Noah.

"You will return?"

Noah knelt before her.

"I'll try."

Galilhai studied him carefully. In her eyes lived another shore, another crossing, another impossible departure no child should ever have witnessed.

Then she removed a small braided reed thread from within her dress and gently tied it around Noah's wrist.

"So the lake remembers you," she said.

Emotion rose unexpectedly inside him.

"Thank you," he whispered.

Pamahas lifted one hand.

At the corner of the street, an oval mirror appeared in silence. It possessed no frame. Its surface floated several inches above the ground while faint silver currents moved slowly beneath the glass. Only Noah appeared reflected within it. Sam, Galilhai, and Pamahas stood absent from the mirror entirely, as though the passage had already chosen whom it would allow through.

Noah rose slowly.

The miniature Wono remained warm within his hand.

Pamahas approached him one final time.

"When fear grows too large," she said quietly, "return your attention to what is directly before you. Life rarely asks for more than one honest step at a time."

Noah nodded.

Then he looked toward Sam.

She stood beneath the eclipse unchanged, tears moving silently down her face while the transformed colors of noon surrounded her like another reality trying unsuccessfully to conceal the truth of who she was. Noah wanted to say something profound enough to ease the fear between them, but nothing came. So he simply held her gaze for several seconds longer before turning toward the mirror.

The surface trembled gently as his fingers touched it. Cold passed through his hand first, then light, then the impossible sensation of falling through his own reflection. The mirror absorbed him slowly until no trace of his body remained within the Other World.

Sam stood motionless after he vanished.

For several moments, no one spoke.

Then above the settlement, the sun and moon slowly began separating once more.

Noah reappeared in open sky.

Wind tore violently across his body as he plunged downward through clouds toward the waters below. The miniature Wono burned warmly within his grasp while the reed thread around his wrist fluttered wildly against the rushing air. For one suspended instant, Noah existed between worlds.

Then Pyramid Lake struck him.

The impact exploded through water and darkness as his body disappeared beneath the surface. Bubbles surged violently around him while the force of the descent pulled him deeper into the lake. Still, his hand never released the miniature pyramid.

For several terrifying seconds, he could not tell which direction led upward.

Then the reed thread brushed against his skin.

Noah kicked desperately toward the faint silver light above him. His arm broke through the surface first, the miniature Wono raised intact against the night sky. Moments later, he emerged gasping violently for air.

The shoreline rested not far away.

Stone Mother stood motionless in the distance, eternally watching the horizon for the children she had lost long ago.

Suddenly, bright headlights swept across the water.

Noah turned.

A red SUV stood near the shore. Ale and Maia had stepped out onto the beach, frozen beneath the beam of light. Maia held a large book tightly against her chest while both girls stared toward the lake in complete disbelief.

Noah looked down at the miniature Wono glowing faintly in his hand, then back toward the shore.

He had returned to the World of Form carrying proof that reality was far larger than humanity had ever dared to imagine.

CHAPTER XVI

Ambiguous Communications

There is one language that doesn't need translation, nor does it need interpretation. It's called love, and it's everywhere. Speak it fluently, and it will transform your life and those around you.

Ale and Maia hurried down from the SUV, struggling to keep their footing as the loose sand shifted beneath them. The headlights remained aimed toward the lake behind them, illuminating the shoreline in pale white bands that dissolved gradually into darkness. Neither girl spoke while running back toward the abandoned campsite.

The wind that had consumed the shore earlier had vanished completely, yet the silence left behind unsettled Maia more deeply than the storm itself. The impossible no longer felt distant. It had followed them back from the lake.

By the time they reached the tent, Ale immediately disappeared inside while Maia dropped beside the fire pit they had used earlier that evening.

Several half-burned logs still rested where they had left them after dinner. Maia gathered them carefully into the center of the shallow pit while repeatedly glancing toward the lake behind her.

A moment later Ale emerged triumphantly from the tent.

"Found them."

She lifted a small matchbox in one hand while carrying a plastic bottle of lighter fluid in the other.

Maia nodded quickly.

"Good. Hurry."

Ale knelt beside her and poured the liquid across the dry wood. The sharp chemical smell spread immediately through the cold desert air. When the first lit match touched the logs, fire rose eagerly into the darkness.

Firelight spread across the campsite, staining the sand and tent walls in restless orange.

The tent behind them flickered softly beneath the movement of the flames while shadows stretched and collapsed continuously across the beach.

Maia opened the large blue volume beside the fire.

The pages trembled slightly beneath her hands.

Maia had managed to understand only fragments of the missing passages. Fire was not regarded as warmth alone within the text, nor merely as light against darkness. The flames were described almost as living thresholds, capable of drawing the attention of things existing beyond the visible world.

Certain rituals warned that if a connection were established successfully, the fire itself could begin to respond. Shadows might shift independently from the bodies casting them. Wind could arrive without warning. Even the movement of ash carried meaning.

The deeper the communication reached into the Other World, the more the world around them seemed to forget its natural order.

Maia still did not fully believe what she was reading.

But after seeing the apex of Wono beneath the lake, disbelief no longer protected her from possibility.

"We need to hold hands," Maia said quietly while kneeling beside the open book. "And keep our arms straight."

Ale lowered herself beside her.

"I cannot believe this is happening."

Neither could Maia.

The two girls intertwined their hands and extended their arms outward while the fire crackled between them. Behind their bodies, the fabric of the tent transformed into a shifting screen of light and shadow. Every movement of the flames distorted their silhouettes across the canvas in slow and restless motion.

Hundreds of sand-colored pages filled the immense volume, carrying prayers, ceremonial instructions, fragmented prophecies, and symbols Maia had spent years studying academically but never expecting to use. While the chapter titles had been translated into English, most of the text remained written in Nu-Mu.

Maia reached nervously into the book and removed a folded pronunciation chart she had placed there earlier.

"Okay," she whispered. "I think I can read this."

The title at the top of the page read:

THE FIRE COMMUNION

The first words leaving Maia's mouth sounded unlike anything Ale had ever heard before. The syllables flowed rhythmically, soft and fluid yet strangely heavy beneath the silence surrounding the fire. Though Ale could not understand their meaning intellectually, the sounds stirred something instinctive inside her, as though the language belonged less to speech than to memory.

Certain syllables lingered strangely within the silence after Maia pronounced them, vibrating faintly around the fire a fraction longer than ordinary sound should have allowed. Even the desert itself seemed to listen.

The fire shifted.

Maia continued reading.

The deeper she moved into the passage, the stranger the words became. Certain sounds seemed almost impossible to pronounce correctly, yet somehow her voice adapted to them naturally, guided less by knowledge than intuition. Gradually, her breathing slowed. The nervous hesitation that had accompanied her at the beginning of the ritual began dissolving into something calmer, more focused, as though the language itself were carrying her forward.

"You need to repeat after me," Maia said softly.

Ale swallowed hard.

"Okay. One word at a time."

Maia nodded.

Together, they began repeating the phrases one by one.

At first the words felt awkward against Ale's mouth, foreign in ways that made her painfully aware of every movement of her tongue and breath. Yet after several repetitions, something unsettling began happening. The sounds no longer felt invented. They felt remembered.

Maia continued carefully through the passage, terrified of mispronouncing even a single word. The arrangement of sounds carried an unfamiliar certainty beneath them, as though the ritual depended less on meaning than on being remembered.

The fire responded gradually.

The flames no longer rose randomly from the wood, but leaned and twisted with strange intention, bending subtly whenever Maia pronounced certain syllables correctly. Tiny sparks drifted upward without disappearing, hovering momentarily above the pit like suspended embers refusing to die. Even the temperature surrounding them shifted unpredictably. One moment Ale felt heat pressing against her face. The next, cold moved through her so sharply that goosebumps rose across her arms beneath the jacket.

The lake behind them had disappeared entirely from her awareness.

There was only the fire.

The language.

The shadows.

As the final phrases left their mouths, the flames suddenly surged upward. Fire spiraled violently sideways despite the absence of wind.

Ale felt cold move slowly across the back of her neck.

Something was changing.

Slowly, she turned her head toward the tent behind them.

A new shadow had appeared across the fabric.

Not theirs. A pyramid.

The enormous triangular shape stretched silently above their distorted silhouettes while the shadows cast by their intertwined hands curved strangely near its center, resembling part of a symbol neither girl fully recognized.

Ale's breathing became shallow.

"Maia..."

Maia stared at the shifting image without answering.

The flames rose higher.

The shadow of the pyramid sharpened while its apex began turning slowly upon itself, distorting the fabric of the tent like something trying to emerge through it.

Then suddenly a freezing hand touched Ale's shoulder.

She screamed.

The ritual shattered instantly.

The fire collapsed violently inward while both girls stumbled away from the pit.

"What are you doing?" Noah asked.

Ale spun around.

Noah stood behind them soaked completely through, water dripping continuously from his clothes onto the sand.

"Jesus Christ, Noah!" Ale shouted, clutching her chest. "Do you always crawl out of lakes like dead people?"

Noah blinked in confusion.

"I'm sorry."

Maia stared at him in complete silence while her eyes slowly lowered toward the object glowing faintly within his hand: the miniature Wono.

"You actually crossed," she whispered.

Noah looked between them.

"How do you know about that?"

Ale laughed nervously.

"Honestly, after tonight, that's probably the least insane question anybody could ask."

Noah finally sat beside the fire, shivering beneath the cold desert air. Ale disappeared briefly into the tent before returning with a blanket she wrapped tightly around his shoulders.

"Thanks."

"No problem."

Then Maia spoke.

"We saw it too."

Noah looked toward her immediately.

"The pyramid."

"We climbed the cliff looking for you and Sam," Maia continued quietly. "For a moment, we saw the apex beneath the water."

Noah lowered his eyes toward the miniature Wono in his hands.

"So it really crossed into this world."

Maia nodded silently.

Then, beside the fire and the dark waters of Pyramid Lake, Noah began telling them everything that had happened after the leap into the lake: Galilhai, the Other World, Wono, Pamahas and Esa, the eclipse beneath the liquid sky, and the Destiny Dice waiting somewhere beyond the reach of the World of Form.

As Noah spoke, the fire crackled steadily between them while the night around Pyramid Lake seemed to grow heavier with every revelation.

Ale listened in complete silence.

For once, even she had no sarcastic response waiting behind her fear.

When Noah finally spoke Sam's name again, something inside her tightened visibly.

"She stayed there?"

Noah nodded.

"She went with Galilhai."

"To do what?"

"She has to recover something called the Destiny Dice."

Ale shook her head slowly.

"This sounds insane."

"It is insane," Noah answered. "But it's real."

Maia looked toward him carefully.

"And Esa and Pamahas sent you back?"

Noah's eyes lifted immediately.

"You know their names?"

Maia adjusted her glasses nervously.

"I've spent years studying Nu-Mu cosmology. Most historians dismiss the stories as symbolic mythology, but some texts describe them differently."

Noah looked back toward the lake.

"They didn't feel symbolic."

The miniature Wono pulsed faintly within his hand.

Ale began pacing anxiously through the sand.

"This cannot actually be happening."

Her voice trembled now.

"Sam is trapped in another world fighting… whatever those things are."

"Dark Shadows," Noah said quietly.

Ale stopped walking.

Even the name disturbed the air around them.

Noah leaned forward toward the fire.

"They're coming for both worlds."

The silence following his words felt unbearable.

Finally, Maia looked toward the miniature pyramid.

"And that's supposed to stop them?"

"Not permanently," Noah answered. "Pamahas said it's supposed to restore the flow between Lake Tahoe and Pyramid Lake."

The fog and the strange disturbances surrounding the lakes no longer felt like isolated events, but fragments of the same unseen wound spreading quietly through both worlds.

Ale wrapped her arms tightly around herself.

"What if Sam never comes back?"

Noah looked into the fire.

For the first time since returning from the Other World, fear reached him fully, not fear of the Dark Shadows or even death itself, but the unbearable possibility of time continuing without Sam beside him.

"She will," he said quietly.

Yet even he could hear uncertainty moving beneath the words.

Then the wind returned violently, bending the flames sideways while sand spiraled across the campsite. The force extinguished the fire instantly, scattering glowing logs and ash through the darkness.

Ale shut her eyes as Maia pulled the book instinctively against her chest, and when the sudden violence finally passed, the three friends found themselves staring silently at the remains of the fire pit where the embers still glowed faintly beneath the drifting sand.

Noah rose slowly to his feet.

The ashes had arranged themselves into the shape of a rider mounted upon a black horse. The figure's face remained hidden beneath long drifting shadows while two glowing red points burned where its eyes should have been.

Ale stepped backward immediately.

Maia felt her stomach tighten.

The fire had not shown them a vision. It had delivered a warning, and in the dying red of the embers, the three of them understood that the war Pamahas had spoken of was no longer waiting beyond the veil. It had found the shore.

CHAPTER XVII

Pernicious Intentions

Know a man's mind, and you'll know his intelligence. Know a man's heart, and you'll know his intentions. Shine the light of your soul on a man, and he will become known to himself.

Galilhai ran ahead briefly before stopping beside one of the elevated terraces overlooking the settlement. Beyond the curved golden rooftops and towering pines, waterfalls descended upward from the distant lake into floating streams that crossed through the forests in luminous curves. Schools of silver fish swam calmly within the suspended currents while strange birds with translucent wings circled around them without sound.

Sam approached the edge slowly.

Even after everything she had witnessed since crossing Pyramid Lake, the Other World still resisted ordinary understanding. Nothing here appeared separated from anything else. The forests, the water, the sky, and the monumental presence of Wono rising beyond the distant cliffs all seemed connected through invisible movement, as though the entire world breathed with one shared pulse.

Galilhai looked back toward her and smiled.

"It listens," the child whispered.

Sam frowned slightly.

"What does?"

Galilhai lifted her gaze toward Pyramid Lake.

"Everything."

From the moment she had met Galilhai, something inside Sam had shifted in ways she still struggled to name. The feeling extended beyond affection, sympathy, or responsibility. It resembled instinct, a certainty that the child's safety mattered more than her own fear. Galilhai had crossed time, water, and worlds with a courage too quiet for her age, and the thought of anything harming her awakened in Sam a tenderness that frightened her by its force.

Around them, the settlement continued its quiet movement beneath the liquid sky. Reflections from the suspended streams overhead drifted across the golden surfaces surrounding the street while distant voices echoed somewhere beyond the trees, softened almost beyond recognition by the immense openness of the Other World. Sam could not escape the growing sensation that the reality around her was observing them gently, patiently, as though waiting for her awareness to catch up with something it had always known.

Then one of the nearby walls began to ripple.

The metallic surface softened like disturbed water as a narrow opening emerged across it, widening gradually until the silhouette of a small tree became visible beyond the passage. Pamahas stepped through moments later, and even the distant sounds of the settlement seemed to quiet around her presence.

Sam could never fully grow accustomed to her.

Beauty alone did not explain the effect Pamahas had on the world around her, not the flowing red hair, the quiet elegance within each movement, or the impossible harmony of her features. Something deeper moved through her, something closer to the solemn presence of the lake at night or the first note of music capable of awakening grief one had not known was waiting inside the body.

"Come with me," Pamahas said softly. "There is something you must see."

Another opening revealed itself along the opposite wall, wider than the first and illuminated by the distant sound of falling water beyond it. Sam reached for Galilhai's hand, and together they crossed through the shimmering threshold.

A colossal waterfall descended beside them in a silent curtain, falling along the outer edge of a vast observatory suspended hundreds of feet above the lake below. The chamber possessed no visible pillars, beams, or foundation. Three sides opened completely to the Other World, while the ceiling hovered high above them in impossible stillness, separated from the floor by nothing but air and light.

Sam stepped forward carefully, her hand tightening around Galilhai's.

Far beneath them, forests stretched across the mountains surrounding the lake. Rivers of silver light crossed through the wilderness. Clouds drifted beneath the cliffs instead of above them. Only when Sam reached the edge did she understand where they stood.

They were beneath the apex of Wono, though the immense structure hovering above them no longer felt like the summit of a pyramid. It resembled a crown suspended over the world below.

Above them, the crown of Wono hovered in impossible stillness, separated from the greater body of the pyramid by a vast open space through which luminous water descended endlessly into the world below. The torrents emerged not from rivers or clouds, but from somewhere hidden within the suspended crown itself, glowing softly as they crossed the void before gathering beneath the monument and continuing outward into Pyramid Lake.

Sam could not understand where the water began, nor how the crown remained suspended above the abyss without collapsing into the lake beneath it. Yet nothing about the spectacle felt unnatural. The movement carried the solemn precision of something older than gravity, older perhaps than the moment the worlds first separated from one another. Watching the endless current descend through the heart of Wono, Sam felt that creation itself was unfolding continuously before her eyes, not as a distant event from the beginning of time, but as a living process still taking place.

The suspended crown was shaped like a smaller inverted pyramid made from the same radiant substance as the monument below, though its colors moved in opposition to the greater structure. Where Wono glowed gold, the crown deepened into crimson. Where shadow touched the lower pyramid, the crown gathered light until it burned softly from within.

Sam stared upward without speaking.

The scale overwhelmed ordinary thought. Wono no longer resembled architecture. It did not feel built, even by divine hands, but revealed, as though it had existed before any living thing learned to distinguish between stone, water, body, and spirit.

The water continued descending through the open space between crown and pyramid, and as Sam watched it, the movement became difficult to understand as water alone. It resembled circulation, breath, memory entering form, life feeding life across the invisible seam between worlds.

"This is where the flow begins," Pamahas said.

Her voice nearly vanished beneath the waterfall, yet Sam heard her clearly.

"Puha moves through all realities, but here it takes direction."

Sam felt Galilhai lean closer against her side.

"What happens if it stops?" Sam asked.

Pamahas did not answer immediately. Her gaze remained fixed upon the falling water, and for the first time Sam noticed something in her expression that resembled sorrow, not sudden sorrow, but something much older, something endured for so long it had become part of her beauty.

"At first," Pamahas said, "the world continues. People wake, eat, speak, love, harm, forgive. The visible things remain visible."

She turned slightly toward Sam.

"Then the hidden things begin to wither."

The words moved through Sam slowly. She looked out across the lake, the forests, and the distant slopes illuminated by strange light, feeling the meaning before she fully understood it. In the World of Form, people had learned to trust what they could touch and measure. They believed life failed only when bodies failed, when structures fell, when water dried, when breath stopped. But standing beneath Wono, Sam sensed that loss could begin much earlier, in the invisible places where reverence, attention, memory, and love were quietly severed from the world.

For the first time in her life, Puha did not feel like a belief someone might choose or reject. It moved before her in water and light, in the connected breath of lake, mountain, creature, sky, and stone. It was not outside life, asking to be worshipped from a distance. It was the relationship that allowed anything to exist with anything else.

Pamahas lifted one hand toward the eastern horizon.

"In the World of Form, they call them the Lehman Caves now," Pamahas said. "Long before that, the Nu-Mu knew them as the Hollow Beyond Wono."

Sam followed the direction of her gaze. Far beyond the forests, past jagged slopes and fields of pale mist, distant mountains rose in solemn layers toward the edge of the sky. The distance between Wono and the caves felt immense, not only geographically, but spiritually, as though the journey itself would require them to move from the heart of creation toward a place where creation had begun to darken.

"The Dark Shadows guard the region," Pamahas continued. "Esa and I can bring you near, but not all the way. If we enter their watch too closely, they will feel us before you arrive."

Galilhai looked toward the distant mountains with unusual stillness.

"So we walk alone?"

"Not alone," Pamahas said, resting her gaze on the child. "But without us."

Sam understood the difference, and it made the fear inside her quieter rather than smaller.

"What are they?" she asked. "The Dark Shadows."

Pamahas lowered her hand. For a moment, the waterfall seemed louder.

"They are intention emptied of love."

The answer unsettled Sam more than a description of monsters would have.

Pamahas looked toward the distant caves again.

"They do not create. They consume. They enter fear, hunger, vanity, cruelty, grief left untended, power desired without wisdom. In your world, they do not always appear as shadows. Often they arrive as thoughts people believe belong only to themselves."

Sam felt Galilhai's small fingers tighten around hers.

The idea frightened her because it did not place darkness somewhere safely distant. It did not belong only to caves, monsters, or the Other World. It could move through ordinary choices, through language, through the small corruptions people justified until their hearts could no longer recognize what they had surrendered.

"That is why they want the dice," Sam said.

Pamahas nodded once.

"The Destiny Dice do not command life as a tyrant commands servants. They incline possibility. They open certain roads and close others. Much still depends upon the living, upon attention, courage, weakness, mercy, pride, love. But if the Dark Shadows reach them, destruction will no longer need to force its way into the World of Form. It will enter through destiny itself."

Sam looked again toward the distant mountains, and the beauty surrounding her suddenly felt almost unbearable. The forests, the waterfall, the strange birds circling beneath the observatory, Galilhai breathing softly beside her, all of it seemed fragile not because life was weak, but because life was sacred enough to be wounded.

"What keeps them away now?" she asked.

"A chamber beneath the caves," Pamahas replied. "Crystal grown from the first light Wono ever cast into stone. Esa and I sealed the dice there long ago, when the shadows first learned to hunger for direction."

She paused, and the silence carried more truth than reassurance.

"The crystal has begun to crack."

Sam closed her eyes briefly. She imagined a chamber under the earth, light sealed in stone, darkness waiting around it with the patience of something that did not need sleep. The image entered her with such clarity that she nearly felt the cold of the cave against her skin.

"If they take them," Sam asked, "does everything end?"

"Not forever," Pamahas said.

The answer did not comfort her.

"Puha restores what collapses into itself. Nothing truly leaves the whole. But restoration is not mercy to those who vanish before it comes."

Sam opened her eyes.

Below them, the water continued falling.

The sound no longer seemed peaceful alone. It sounded necessary.

Entire generations could disappear. Children, families, memories, songs, homes, faces lifted toward morning light, hands held beside hospital beds, laughter across kitchens, strangers helping strangers without knowing why. The vastness of what could be lost moved through Sam until she could no longer think of the World of Form as abstract, flawed, distracted, or spiritually asleep. It was wounded, yes. Often cruel. Often careless. But it was also full of beings who loved without understanding the sacredness of what they were doing.

Galilhai looked up at her.

"We won't let them take it," the child said softly.

Sam forced herself to breathe.

"No," she answered, though her voice trembled. "We won't."

The waterfall behind them shifted.

Water separated silently, opening like a veil.

Esa entered the observatory.

He remained in his neutral form, broad and powerful, neither fully man nor fully wolf. His body carried the height and shape of a man, but the head of the great black wolf remained, its golden eyes reflecting the light of Wono with depth that seemed to hold more than sight. Dark fur moved along portions of his arms and shoulders, while faint currents of gold traveled beneath his skin like fire glimpsed under stone.

Despite his imposing form, peace entered with him, not a peace imposed from above, nor one that denied danger, but something quieter and older, the kind that exists beneath fear once fear has finally exhausted itself.

Esa came to stand beside them at the edge of the observatory. He did not greet them with words, and no one seemed to expect him to. In his presence, silence gathered meaning quickly. Sam felt that he did not merely know answers. He knew the deeper place from which questions arose, and because of that, many of the questions inside her began changing before she could ask them.

Together, they watched the Other World beneath the descending light.

The forests darkened into deeper shades of emerald while the cliffs surrounding the lake burned crimson beneath the shifting sky. The suspended crown of Wono reflected rivers of gold across the water below until Pyramid Lake seemed illuminated from within. In the distance, herds of pale animals moved through the trees like drifting mist, and above them, streams of levitating water carried fish through the open air in slow and glimmering arcs.

Sam wrapped an arm around Galilhai's shoulders without realizing it, and the child leaned into her.

A tear moved down Sam's cheek. It did not come from sorrow exactly, nor from fear, though both lived inside her now. It came from recognition, from the sudden awareness that life was not valuable because it lasted, nor because it promised safety, nor because it spared anyone grief. Life was valuable because, for a time, it allowed one thing to touch another. A mother to comfort a daughter. A child to trust a stranger. A lake to hold the memory of a people. A world to continue despite everything inside it that tried to forget its own holiness.

Standing beneath Wono, with the waterfall descending beside her and the shadow of the Lehman Caves waiting somewhere beyond the mountains, Sam finally understood what her mother had spent her life trying to teach without ever reducing it into doctrine. Love did not stand apart from existence. It was the current by which existence remembered itself.

What an incredible gift life is, Sam thought.

Beside her, Esa's voice emerged softly for the first time since entering the observatory.

"Indeed," he said, gazing toward the endless waters below. "It is."

CHAPTER XVIII

Expeditious Departure

Don't rush things. Instead, cultivate patience, and all those things will come of their own accord. Even then, nothing outside you can give you any more than what you already are. In this state, how can you feel rushed?

Morning arrived slowly over Pyramid Lake, not with warmth or renewal, but with the hollow stillness that follows catastrophe before grief fully reveals itself. Pale desert light spread across the shoreline in thin bands of silver and muted gold while the remnants of the camp rested beneath the windblown silence like evidence abandoned after an accident.

Noah stood beside the extinguished fire pit securing the final tent straps around their carrying bag while Maia folded blankets near the SUV. Alejandra moved repeatedly between the campsite and the vehicle collecting anything they might accidentally leave behind, her eyes scanning the ground with the tense concentration of someone already imagining investigators searching the area days later.

None of them had slept properly, and Sam's sleeping bag still rested near the edge of the campsite, partially unzipped and untouched.

Every time Noah closed his eyes, he saw the Other World again: forests illuminated beneath liquid skies, streams suspended in the air like threads of light, and the immense golden form of Wono floating above waters untouched by human history. Yet those visions no longer carried the overwhelming wonder they possessed hours earlier. Now they were inseparable from Sam's absence.

The sight of the sleeping bag seemed to affect all of them differently. Maia avoided looking toward it entirely. Ale kept glancing at it involuntarily before forcing her attention elsewhere. Noah, meanwhile, could not stop associating it with the final moment he saw Sam standing near Wono before the threshold between worlds consumed her.

Ale finally exhaled sharply and broke the silence.

"We need to talk about what we're going to say."

Noah looked up. "To who?"

"To everybody," she replied, visibly irritated that the answer was not obvious. "To Sam's dad. To our parents. To literally anyone who asks where she is."

Maia stopped folding the blankets while the wind moved softly across the lake.

Ale crossed her arms tightly against the morning cold before continuing. "Because right now we don't even have a story. We have nothing. If she doesn't come back soon, people are going to start asking questions, and once they start asking questions, this whole thing becomes a nightmare."

"She is coming back," Noah said.

Ale stared at him. "You keep saying that like you know it for a fact."

"I do know it."

"How?"

Noah hesitated.

The truthful answer sounded irrational even inside his own mind. He could not explain why he felt so certain. The conviction existed somewhere beneath logic and evidence, deeper than thought itself. Ever since Sam crossed into the Other World, he had continued sensing her presence faintly, as though some invisible thread remained stretched between realities.

"I just know," he murmured.

Ale looked away in frustration. "That's not something we can tell detectives, Noah."

The word detectives immediately altered the atmosphere surrounding them.

Maia slowly rose from beside the blankets. "Do you really think it could get that serious?"

Ale laughed quietly, though there was no humor in it. "Maia, if a nineteen-year-old girl disappears during a camping trip and three people come back without her, it becomes serious immediately."

Nobody answered.

The sound of waves brushing softly against the shoreline filled the silence between them while Ale continued speaking, more quietly now, as though the reality of the situation was settling deeper into her chest while she verbalized it.

"At first her dad is probably just going to think she lost signal or forgot to charge her phone. Maybe he waits a few hours. Maybe until tonight. But eventually he starts calling everybody. Then he realizes nobody has heard from her. Then he asks where we last saw her." She paused briefly. "And what exactly do we tell him after that?"

Maia lowered her gaze.

They could not explain Wono. They could not explain the Other World. They could not explain Pamahas or the threshold beneath Pyramid Lake or the fact that Sam had willingly disappeared into another reality because a wolf-headed god believed she could save existence itself.

Every version of the truth sounded indistinguishable from madness.

The exhaustion hanging over the group deepened with every passing minute. Beyond the mountains, the machinery of the ordinary world had already begun moving toward them with questions they could never answer honestly.

Maia finally walked toward Sam's sleeping bag and crouched beside it slowly. The fabric still carried traces of the night cold.

"She trusted us," Maia said softly.

The statement settled heavily between them.

Ale closed her eyes briefly while Noah looked toward Pyramid Lake stretching beneath the brightening dawn with ancient indifference, its surface reflecting pale currents of sunlight that seemed too calm for a place connected to so much hidden knowledge. Somewhere beyond the visible shoreline stood Wono, silent and immovable beneath the desert sky.

Noah instinctively touched the object resting inside his jacket pocket.

Even through the fabric, he could feel its warmth.

The miniature Wono had remained with him since his return from the Other World, and although its size had not changed, the object no longer felt small. Its presence carried an almost oppressive density now, as though something vastly larger existed folded impossibly within it.

Ale noticed the movement immediately.

"You've been checking that thing every five minutes."

Noah lowered his hand. "It feels different."

"How?"

"I don't know." He searched unsuccessfully for the right words. "Heavier."

Ale studied him carefully. "You mean physically?"

"No," he admitted. "Not physically."

Maia looked toward him with growing fascination despite everything else weighing on them. "Do you think it's reacting to Tahoe?"

The possibility unsettled Noah because he had already wondered the same thing.

He glanced once more toward Pyramid Lake before climbing into the SUV.

"We should go."

The drive south unfolded through long stretches of desert highway beneath an increasingly brilliant morning sky. Pyramid Lake gradually disappeared behind them while the terrain expanded outward into vast plains of pale earth and distant mountain ridges softened by heat and light. Inside the SUV, exhaustion lingered heavily over the group despite the coffee cups balanced between backpacks and camping supplies.

Ale stared ahead at the highway for several seconds, her fingers tightening around the steering wheel while the desert rolled endlessly outside the windows.

"Okay," she said finally. "Let's think about this realistically. The campground probably has cameras near the entrance. At the very least they'll have our license plate entering and leaving."

Maia shifted uncomfortably in the passenger seat. "Do campgrounds out there even use cameras?"

"Some do. Especially after vandalism." Ale exhaled slowly. "And even if they don't, there are gas stations between Pyramid Lake and Tahoe. Traffic cameras too."

Noah remained quiet, watching the empty highway disappear beneath the vehicle.

"If Sam's father reports her missing," Ale continued, "the first thing investigators are going to establish is who saw her last. That's us."

Maia lowered her gaze toward her phone resting silently in her lap. "Sam's dad also trusts us."

"That's what makes this so bad," Ale murmured.

For several moments, only the sound of tires moving across asphalt filled the silence between them.

"What if we wait?" Maia asked quietly. "Maybe Sam comes back before any of this even matters."

Noah immediately looked toward her. "She will."

Ale glanced briefly at him through the rearview mirror.

"Noah," she said carefully, "you went somewhere impossible last night. You talked to people who shouldn't exist. You crossed into another reality and came back carrying..." Her eyes drifted briefly toward his jacket pocket. "Whatever that thing is. I'm trying very hard to stay calm right now, but you have to understand that certainty isn't the same thing as proof."

Noah looked out toward the distant mountains.

"I know."

Maia swallowed faintly. "Do we tell her dad we've heard from her?"

Ale's expression tightened immediately. "No. Absolutely not."

"Why?"

"Because then we'd have to fake messages. And once police get involved, they can subpoena phone records."

Maia blinked. "You really have thought about all of this."

Ale gave a tired laugh lacking any humor. "That's because somebody has to."

Noah leaned his head lightly against the cold window glass while Pyramid Lake continued disappearing farther behind them.

"Maybe we don't say anything yet," he murmured. "Maybe we just wait."

"And if she doesn't come back in two days?" Ale asked.

Noah did not answer.

Somewhere beyond human perception, Sam now walked through another world beneath unfamiliar skies while, here, ordinary systems of law and procedure waited to interpret her absence through paperwork and suspicion.

The contrast made the ordinary world feel fragile.

After another stretch of silence, Maia spoke quietly.

"What if she can't come back?"

Ale's grip tightened slightly around the steering wheel.

Noah opened his eyes immediately. "She will."

"But what if she can't?" Maia insisted softly. "What if the Other World changes people? Or time works differently there? Or—"

"She's coming back," Noah repeated.

His certainty unsettled both girls again.

Ale glanced at him through the rearview mirror. "You sound like somebody already convinced you."

Noah looked down at his hands.

The truth was that Pamahas had not promised anything directly. Yet every memory of her carried a strange gravity that continued reshaping his understanding of reality itself. He remembered the way she moved through the Other World with absolute familiarity, as though the world itself adjusted naturally around her presence. He remembered the golden settlements hidden among the forests, the streams flowing weightlessly through the sky, and Esa standing near the edge of the elevated terraces with eyes that carried something older than humanity.

Most disturbing of all was how normal everything had eventually begun to feel while he was there, as though some forgotten part of himself recognized that world more deeply than this one.

The thought sent unease quietly through his chest.

The highway gradually began ascending into the Sierra Nevada while the desert receded behind them and the terrain transformed into rocky slopes and immense pine forests stretching across the mountainsides beneath the strengthening sunlight. The air itself seemed different now, colder and cleaner, carrying traces of sap and stone through the partially opened windows.

Maia rested her chin against the passenger door while watching the landscape change.

"It's strange," she murmured.

"What is?" Ale asked.

"I spent years reading stories about hidden worlds and sacred places and ancient beings connected to nature." A faint smile appeared briefly before disappearing again. "I always thought the appeal came from escaping reality." She looked toward Noah. "But now reality itself feels stranger than all those stories."

Noah understood exactly what she meant.

Since leaving Pyramid Lake, the ordinary world had begun feeling unnaturally thin, as though something enormous existed just beyond visibility waiting to reveal itself completely.

Even the mountains now seemed different.

Not merely beautiful. Watching.

The first glimpse of Lake Tahoe appeared between the trees nearly three hours later.

The vast alpine waters stretched across the Sierra Nevada like polished blue crystal beneath the late-morning sun, surrounded by towering forests and snow-covered summits glowing softly in the distance. Yet despite the overwhelming beauty of the landscape, Noah immediately felt the same sensation that had disturbed him upon approaching Pyramid Lake the previous night.

Presence. The lake did not feel empty.

Ale slowed the SUV slightly as the road curved along the mountainside overlooking the water.

"No matter how many times I come here," Maia whispered, "it never looks real."

The clarity of Tahoe was almost unnatural. Sunlight penetrated so deeply through the water near the shoreline that submerged rocks and fallen trees remained visible far below the surface, giving the impression that the lake possessed no depth at all despite being one of the deepest bodies of freshwater in North America.

Noah touched the miniature Wono again.

Warmer. Definitely warmer.

Ale noticed immediately. "It's happening again?"

He nodded faintly.

Neither girl asked for clarification. At this point, all three of them had begun accepting impossible things with disturbing ease.

"We're close to Emerald Bay," Ale said after a while. "The boat rental should be nearby."

Maia turned slightly toward Noah. "Did Pamahas tell you exactly where we're supposed to drop the object?"

"She said to take it to the center of the lake." Noah paused briefly, hearing her voice clearly inside his memory. "'Look for the Lahontan cutthroat trout made of emeralds. It will let you know you've reached the right place.'"

Ale shook her head slowly. "I still can't believe sentences like that sound normal now."

"They don't," Maia replied quietly. "That's the problem."

The parking lot overlooking Emerald Bay was nearly empty when they arrived. Only a handful of scattered vehicles rested beneath the towering pines while sunlight filtered through the branches in shifting patterns across the pavement. Beyond the stone guardrails, Lake Tahoe extended outward with such overwhelming clarity that the shoreline below almost appeared unreal.

Ale parked near the edge of the overlook and shut off the engine.

For several seconds, nobody moved.

The silence inside the SUV felt strangely complete after hours of driving.

Maia was the first to step outside.

Cold mountain air greeted her immediately, carrying the scent of pine sap, wet stone, and freshwater drifting upward from the bay below. She walked instinctively toward the overlook, and the full immensity of Emerald Bay revealed itself beneath the late-morning sun.

The recessed waters curved inward between the mountains in the shape of a vast turquoise crescent while dense forests descended toward the shoreline in immense green layers. Near the center of the bay, Fannette Island rose silently from the water like an isolated memory preserved outside time itself.

"My God," Maia whispered.

Noah remained beside the SUV, his hand unconsciously resting against the object inside his jacket pocket.

The miniature Wono felt almost burning now.

Ale adjusted her sunglasses and looked toward the descending trail leading through the forest below.

"Vikingsholm is down there."

The path curved steeply through dense pine trees toward the shoreline beneath them. From above, portions of the old Scandinavian estate were barely visible through the foliage.

As the three of them began descending the trail, gravel crunched softly beneath their shoes while filtered sunlight moved between the trees in long shifting bands. The farther they descended, the quieter the world became. Even the distant sounds of vehicles along the highway gradually disappeared until only the breeze and occasional birdsong remained.

Then Maia noticed the eagle.

The massive bird descended silently above the trees before gliding across Emerald Bay with broad brown wings illuminated by sunlight. A cold sensation moved through her chest immediately. Maia felt suddenly certain she had seen the eagle before, though the thought itself sounded irrational the moment it formed. There was something deeply unsettling about the stillness in its movements, the strange awareness lingering behind its eyes.

But she said nothing.

Because she no longer trusted coincidence.

As they stepped beyond the final curve of the trail, Vikingsholm Castle revealed itself fully beneath the filtered mountain light. Massive granite walls rested beside the shoreline with solemn permanence while the sod-covered rooftops blended into the surrounding forest so naturally that the estate appeared grown from the mountain itself rather than constructed by human hands.

Behind the castle, Lake Tahoe shimmered like liquid crystal beneath the sky.

The atmosphere surrounding the estate felt wrong in a way none of them could properly explain. The silence was too complete. Even the breeze moving through the trees seemed strangely muted near the shoreline.

The miniature Wono had become almost painfully hot against his chest.

Ale noticed immediately. "Again?"

Noah nodded faintly.

Maia was the first to notice movement behind one of the narrow windows overlooking the lake.

Someone was watching them.

A few seconds later, the heavy wooden doors of the castle opened slowly.

The elderly man who emerged carried himself with visible physical difficulty, supporting part of his weight against a dark wooden cane polished smooth with age. Long silver hair rested against his shoulders while deep lines crossed his honey-toned face beneath the mountain sunlight. Though age had weakened his body considerably, his eyes retained the sharpness of someone whose body had aged faster than his memory.

The man descended the stone pathway carefully before stopping several feet away from the group. His gaze moved briefly across Maia and Ale before settling entirely on Noah.

Then his eyes lowered toward Noah's jacket pocket.

Toward Wono.

The color drained subtly from the old man's face.

"No..." he whispered.

Noah stepped forward.

"Who are you?"

The old man tightened his grip around the cane before finally lifting his eyes again.

"Honi," he said quietly. "My name is Honi."

A cold wind moved softly across the shoreline behind them.

Honi continued staring toward the sacred object hidden beneath Noah's jacket with unmistakable fear.

"There is far less time remaining than I hoped," he murmured. "And if Wono has returned to Tahoe now..." His eyes drifted briefly toward the vast waters of the lake behind the castle. "Then the darkness beneath this place has already begun to awaken."

CHAPTER XIX
Into the Darkness

When we face our fears, we learn how small they are. They rise from the mind like smoke, take shape in the mirror of our dread, and vanish when the soul refuses to turn away.

The magical woods ended a few miles east of Wono, where the valley narrowed and the first shoulders of the mountains rose from the earth. There, where gold-leafed branches gave way to blackened trunks, the Dark Woods began.

A fallen tree lay across the mold-soft ground, immense and ancient, its exposed roots twisted like the fingers of something long dead. Esa stood upon it in his wolf form, larger than any beast born in the World of Form, his silver-gray fur stirring with the warmth of his breath. Steam drifted from his snout into the cold morning air. His brown eyes, bright with command, moved over the hundreds gathered before him.

Pamahas waited beside him on her white horse. The animal's three eyes shone with a troubled intelligence, each one reflecting the dim gold light that filtered through the trees. Behind her stood the mounted guards of the settlement, armored and still, their bodies surrounded by a luminous field that cast a low radiance over bark, leaf, and stone. Beyond them, the creatures of the Other World kept watch in grave silence: bears formed from copper, coyotes forged from titanium, and mountain lions whose lapis-lazuli bodies carried the deep blue memory of water carried by Wono.

Samantha and Galilhai stood near the front of the assembly, their feet sinking slightly into the damp earth. Sam wore white fabric like Pamahas', fine as mist and bright as moonlit water. Around her right arm rested a gold shoulder bracelet shaped into a triangle. Galilhai wore a short vanilla-colored dress and a turquoise tassel hairband, from which hung a small pendant echoing the same sacred geometry.

The two girls looked almost ceremonial, as if the Other World had dressed them not for travel, but for offering.

Esa lowered his head, and the murmuring of the gathered beings ceased.

"This is Galilhai," he said. His voice moved through the forest with the weight of stone and thunder. "Her heart is pure. Nothing made wholly of darkness can see her. Kindness has placed a veil over her, and through that kindness, a portion of Pamahas' own essence lives in her."

Pamahas turned her gaze toward the child.

"She will be accompanied by Samantha," she said. "A soul of light, though grief has tried to convince her otherwise. The shadows will not easily perceive her. Beneath the sorrow of her life, she carries a gift that can mend what has been wounded. Her hands can call healing forward."

A small puddle lay at Sam's feet. In it, her reflection appeared with startling clarity, untouched by the murk of the ground around it. She saw her own face, pale with fear, framed by the strange white fabric of the Other World. But beneath that fear, something unfamiliar looked back at her. Something patient. Something that had survived.

She thought of the many years in which pain had named her before she could name herself. She had believed herself unlucky, abandoned, and broken by a life that had taken more than it had given. Now, listening to Pamahas speak, Sam felt that belief loosen. Not disappear. Not yet. But loosen.

Perhaps her suffering had not been emptiness.

Perhaps something sacred had been hidden beneath it, waiting for the hour when darkness would force it into the open.

Esa lifted his head again.

"Pamahas and I will guide Galilhai and Samantha through the first part of the Dark Woods," he continued. "We will make sure they cross the border alive."

"But we cannot go with them to the end," Pamahas said. "Our presence burns too brightly. If we continue beyond the appointed place, the Dark Shadows will feel us and gather. Once Samantha and Galilhai reach the far side of the woods, Esa and I must return to defend the settlement."

Esa's gaze passed over the guards and the waiting animals.

"The cavalry will hold the perimeter. The mountain lions will patrol the valley and carry warning at the first sign of movement. The coyotes will divide into packs and take the high ground around our home. The bears will raise barricades from fallen trees and stone. The Dark Shadows may come whether the Destiny Dice are recovered or not. We will be ready."

No one spoke.

Even the leaves seemed to withhold their trembling.

The Dark Woods stretched between the enchanted valley and the eastern desert. No human soul had ever crossed them and returned. Esa and Pamahas had entered them once, long ago, when the Destiny Dice were taken from the sight of living beings and hidden inside the Hollow Beyond Wono. They had survived because they knew the secret paths, and because the woods had not yet grown as hungry as they were now.

The place was not a forest in the manner of the World of Form. It was a labyrinth with roots. A snare of black timber, false distances, vanishing trails, and paths that folded back upon themselves without mercy. Those who entered could wander for days without moving a single mile. They could hear water where there was no water, see light where no sky remained, follow voices that remembered the sound of loved ones, and die with their hands full of leaves.

Yet the Destiny Dice lay beyond them.

And without the Dice, the fate unfolding toward Pyramid Lake would have no counterweight.

Samantha climbed onto Esa's back, burying her hands in his thick fur. Galilhai mounted behind Pamahas and wrapped her small arms around the woman's waist. The white horse shifted beneath them, stamping once into the wet soil.

The assembly remained still as the four departed.

No farewell was spoken aloud. Farewell had no place in a mission from which the world itself might not return.

They crossed the last stretch of the magical forest in silence. Around them, luminous flowers closed as they passed, their petals folding inward like hands in prayer. The gold-threaded grasses bent away from the east. Birds with translucent wings fled into the higher branches. The nearer they came to the border, the more the living world seemed to withdraw its blessing.

Then the land changed.

The trunks ahead stood black and ashen. Their bark twisted from root to crown as if some invisible force had wrung them dry. Branches crowded the sky, knitting themselves into a ceiling that swallowed the light. Nothing grew straight. Vines curled against their own direction. Stones leaned as if listening. Even the shadows seemed warped, refusing the natural obedience of shape.

Sam tightened her grip on Esa's fur.

A line of trees marked the threshold. Between them drifted a thick black fog, slow and deliberate, moving not with the wind but with the will of something hidden. From somewhere far within came the faint sound of weeping. Then a scream, thin and distant. Then silence.

"There is no reason to fear," Esa said without turning. "Fear is an illusion."

"Stay alert," Pamahas added softly. "But stay calm."

Esa fixed his gaze upon the trees before them. For a moment nothing moved. Then several trunks began to unwind. Their bodies uncoiled from one another with a low wooden groan, opening a narrow passage into the dark.

The horse refused.

It reared its head and stamped backward, all three eyes wide. Its breath came fast, clouding the air. Galilhai leaned forward and placed one small hand against its neck.

"It is all right," she whispered.

A quietness passed from the child into the animal. The horse lowered its head. Its breath steadied.

Sam closed her eyes for a heartbeat.

When she opened them, they had entered the Dark Woods.

The last light behind them thinned at once, shrinking into pale threads caught between the trees. The fog slid over the ground and curled around Esa's claws, around the horse's hooves, around the hem of Sam's white garment. The soil beneath them was wet and soft, smelling of mold, old rain, and buried things.

Something moved to Sam's right.

She turned sharply.

Another movement answered from the left. Then above. Then ahead.

Tiny yellow eyes opened in the canopy, in the bushes, between roots, inside hollows where no creature should have fit. They blinked out of rhythm, appearing and disappearing in the blackness like sparks trapped behind a veil.

What is happening? Sam thought.

"They are ada'a," Pamahas answered from ahead, her voice entering Sam's mind as clearly as speech. "Crow-like things. They feed on whatever death leaves behind, and on whatever weakness exposes."

Sam swallowed.

"Are we about to become their meal?" she asked.

"No," Pamahas said. "They cannot see you or Galilhai. They see only Esa and me, and they are afraid of what our essence can summon."

"Puha," Galilhai whispered.

Pamahas looked back at her. "Yes. They fear Puha."

A sudden flapping shook the canopy. The yellow eyes scattered and vanished deeper into the trees.

The stillness that followed was worse.

They continued through the warped forest, slow and careful. The ground sloped and dipped without warning. Stones jutted from the soil like broken teeth. Fallen trunks blocked the path, though Sam could not tell if they had fallen long ago or placed themselves there moments before. The darkness flattened every shape until depth became uncertain. A root looked like a snake. A shadow looked like an opening. A narrow space between two trees seemed to widen when ignored and close when watched.

Even Pamahas' horse moved with difficulty. Its hooves searched for truth in the ground and did not always find it.

After a long while, Galilhai raised her head.

"Do you hear water?" she asked.

Sam listened. Beneath the low groaning of the trees came another sound, faint but steady. Running water.

Pamahas stopped her horse.

"We are near the heart of the woods," she said.

Esa's ears lifted.

"A stream cuts through this place," he said. "It divides the eastern dark from the western dark. The crossing is dangerous. Creatures live in that water and feed from it. They will sense us."

"Then they will attack," Pamahas said.

Sam looked toward the sound, though she could see nothing beyond the crowded trunks.

"What do we do?"

"Pamahas and I will cross first," Esa said. "You and Galilhai will keep your distance and find another place to pass. Remain close enough to see us, but not so close that our battle reaches you."

Pamahas turned in the saddle and touched Galilhai's cheek.

"Do not lose sight of us if you can help it," she said. "This place wants separation. It wants every living thing alone with its fear."

The child nodded, though her eyes had darkened with worry.

The creek appeared ahead of them as a silver-black wound in the earth. It rushed over jagged stones, violent and cold, its current foaming white where it struck the rocks. The sound of it filled the air until thought itself became difficult.

Esa and Pamahas moved toward the nearest crossing.

Sam and Galilhai followed the bank downstream, searching for a place where the water narrowed. The noise hammered against Sam's ears. She pressed one hand against the side of her head and tried to think. The woods answered with distractions: a voice behind her, a shape between the trees, a flash of light that disappeared when she looked at it directly.

Do not let the noise distract you, Pamahas thought from a distance. Look for the silence underneath the noise.

Sam breathed.

Beneath the roar of the creek, beneath the trembling of leaves, beneath the panic rising in her chest, she found a small stillness. It did not remove the fear. It gave her somewhere to stand inside it.

"There," she said.

A large rock broke the current halfway across, its dark surface slick with water. Beyond it, several smaller stones formed an uneven path toward the opposite bank.

Sam took Galilhai's hand.

"We cross here."

She stepped into the creek.

Cold seized her foot at once. Pain shot up her leg as if the water were made of knives. She gasped and nearly lost her balance. The current shoved against her knees, heavy and relentless.

"Climb on my back!" she called.

Galilhai obeyed without hesitation, wrapping her arms around Sam's neck. Sam bent forward under the child's weight and took another step. Then another. Water struck her thighs, splashed her chest, soaked the white fabric until it clung to her skin.

"I cannot see them," Galilhai said, her voice small against the roar. "Where are they?"

"We will meet them on the other side," Sam said, though she could no longer see Esa or Pamahas either. "Hold on."

Upstream, Esa entered the creek with his head low and his claws digging against stone. Pamahas rode beside him, her horse struggling against the force of the water.

The first stingray rose without a ripple.

At first, Sam mistook it for part of the creek itself. Its scarlet body reflected no light. Water slid across its back without disturbing the surface, as though the creature existed half inside the stream and half somewhere beneath reality. Strange markings pulsed faintly beneath its skin, resembling veins filled with molten metal.

Then its eyes opened.

Not two. Dozens.

Small black eyes blinked across the underside of its body, each one moving independently, searching the darkness like drowned souls trapped inside living flesh.

It unfolded from the creek like a scarlet banner torn from the depths, vast and glistening, its fins spreading wider than the body of the horse. A metal stinger curved behind it, bright as a blade.

Pamahas leaped from the saddle before it could strike.

She landed on the creature's back and drove her fist into its flesh. The blow thundered over the water. She struck again. The stingray twisted, thrashing beneath her, its body slamming against the current. Esa lunged toward it, jaws open, but the creature folded itself downward and vanished beneath the surface, dragging Pamahas under.

Esa roared.

The water erupted around him.

More stingrays rose from the stream, a dozen scarlet bodies circling the wolf. Their metal tails flashed through the dimness. Esa turned with brutal speed and seized the nearest one in his jaws. Venom spilled black from the wound and hissed where it touched the water.

Beneath the surface, Pamahas fought in silence.

The stingray dragged her through the cold dark, its body crushing her against stone and current. Her hair streamed around her face. Bubbles fled from her mouth. She wrapped one arm around the creature's fin and struck with the other, again and again, until her fist broke through its hide. The thing convulsed. Its stinger whipped blindly. Then its body slackened.

Pamahas kicked free and burst through the surface, drawing a violent breath.

She saw Esa surrounded.

She swam toward him, seized one stingray by its tail, and pulled it backward before it could pierce his flank. Esa tore through another. Pamahas struck the next so hard its body folded in the water. The creek turned red, then black, then white again as the current carried the dead away.

For a moment, it seemed the crossing had been won.

The creek quieted.

Not completely, but enough for the silence beneath the noise to reveal itself again.

The dead stingrays drifted away in the current. Black venom unraveled through the water like ink dissolving through silk. Even the trees appeared motionless, listening.

Pamahas stood chest-deep in the stream, breathing hard. Her white hair clung to her skin. For an instant, she looked toward the opposite bank, toward the place where Samantha and Galilhai struggled through the darkness.

A strange sadness crossed her face.

As though some hidden part of her had already seen what was about to happen.

Then the largest stingray rose behind Esa.

Its body emerged slowly, almost without sound.

Unlike the others, this creature carried no markings. Its flesh was pale beneath the water, nearly translucent, and within it moved long shadow-like shapes that twisted where veins should have been.

Its stinger lifted.

For a brief instant, the entire forest seemed to hold its breath.

Then the weapon shot forward.

Esa sensed the movement and sprang aside. The blade missed his throat by the width of a breath. He twisted in the air and came down upon the creature, sinking his fangs deep into its back. Bone, metal, and flesh cracked beneath the force of his bite.

The stingray died in the same instant its stinger found another body.

Pamahas looked downward first.

Almost with confusion.

The metal barb protruded from her abdomen, trembling slightly with the force of the strike. Around it, golden light flickered beneath her skin, struggling to remain whole.

Only then did the pain reach her face.

Pamahas stopped moving.

Esa released the creature and turned.

She stood waist-deep in the current, one hand pressed to her abdomen. The metal barb had passed through her. Dark blood moved between her fingers and was taken at once by the water.

For the first time since entering the woods, Esa looked afraid.

He reached her as her knees weakened. The current struck her body and tried to pull her down, but Esa placed himself beside her and lifted her against him. She clutched his fur, her fingers trembling.

He carried her to the shore.

The white horse stood nearby, shaking, its three eyes fixed upon its rider. Galilhai's touch was no longer there to calm it.

Esa lowered Pamahas onto the black soil. Her glow, once steady as sunrise over sacred water, flickered beneath her skin. Each breath cost her more than the last.

"No," Esa said.

It was not a command. It was not thunder. It was the voice of a brother who had reached the edge of his power and found it useless.

Pamahas lifted one hand and touched the fur along his face.

"This is not the end," she whispered. "I will be with you in the light of Puha."

Esa lowered his head until his brow touched hers.

Her eyes remained on him for one final moment. Then they closed.

The light in her body went out slowly, as if a flame had consumed the last of its wax.

The forest felt it.

The darkness deepened. The creek grew louder. The trees leaned closer, their branches tightening overhead.

Esa raised his head and howled.

The sound rose above the water, above the branches, above the hidden things waiting in the trees. It was grief and fury together, old enough to belong to the beginning of the world.

Across the stream, Sam reached the opposite bank and collapsed to one knee, Galilhai still clinging to her back. Both of them were soaked, shaking, and nearly blind in the darkness.

Then they heard the howl.

Galilhai slid down from Sam's back. Her face had gone pale.

"Pamahas?" she called.

No answer came.

Sam stood, water dripping from her clothes, her breath ragged.

Something is wrong, she thought. Very wrong.

The branches above them began to move.

Slowly, the trees closed the space between the creek and the woods. Roots lifted from the soil and settled again, nearer than before. Vines descended like black cords. The path behind them narrowed. The path ahead seemed to vanish.

Then the yellow eyes returned.

Hundreds of them opened in the dark, blinking from the canopy, the bushes, the hollows, and the crooked spaces between the trunks. They no longer watched from a distance.

They gathered.

Sam understood then.

Something had died in the Dark Woods.

And the woods were preparing to eat.

CHAPTER XX

Unsolicited Company

Do not seek answers outside when they have already begun to speak within you. Bring your attention inward, and what waits beneath thought will make itself known.

For several seconds, no one moved. The old man's words remained among them like something dropped into still water, widening beyond what any of them could understand. Noah felt the weight of the miniature Wono inside his pocket, though he had not touched it. The object seemed suddenly heavier, as if it had heard itself named by a stranger and answered by becoming more real.

The path to Vikingsholm Castle lay behind the old man, half hidden among pines and afternoon shadow. Beyond the trees, Lake Tahoe remained wide and blue and deceptively calm. Nothing on its surface suggested terror. Nothing in the clean mountain air confessed that the world had begun to open in places it should have remained sealed.

Noah's hand moved toward his pocket.

The old man noticed.

His face was narrow and weathered, marked by years spent beneath sun, wind, and solitude. A pale scar curved across his right cheek in the shape of a small moon, pulling the skin around one eye slightly lower than the other. When he turned his head, Noah saw a crimson tattoo at the side of his neck: Wono, rendered in three small triangular strokes, as if the pyramid-shaped rock had been reduced to a secret only the skin could carry.

Alejandra stepped closer to Noah without looking at him. Maia stayed half a pace behind, studying the man with the quiet suspicion of someone already assembling evidence.

Noah stared at him in disbelief.

"Honi," he said slowly, "how do you know about Wono?"

The old man looked at him.

Mouth shut.

"How do you know what he has?" Alejandra asked. Her voice was controlled, but not calm. "How do you know where we are going?"

Honi's gaze shifted toward the lake.

"Some things announce themselves before they arrive."

"That is not an answer," Maia said.

"No," Honi replied. "It is the beginning of one."

Noah looked from Honi to the castle beyond him. Vikingsholm stood among the pines with an old-world stillness, its stone and timber body resting near the edge of Emerald Bay as though it had been placed there by a memory from another continent. Its rooflines and carved wooden details seemed beautiful from a distance. But now, after Honi's arrival, the beauty felt watchful.

"You said you were waiting for us," Noah said.

"I said I knew you were coming."

"That is not better."

A faint smile passed over Honi's mouth, then disappeared.

"The wind changed before dawn. The pines turned their needles east. The lake kept a second rhythm beneath its waves. And near the shore, the ravens would not land."

Maia's eyes narrowed.

"You read bird behavior and concluded that three strangers were walking toward Vikingsholm Castle with a supernatural object in someone's pocket?"

Honi looked at her then, and for the first time, the old man seemed less like a caretaker and more like someone accustomed to being doubted by people who had mistaken certainty for intelligence.

"I read what still knows how to speak."

Alejandra exhaled softly.

Noah did not know whether to trust him. The scar, the tattoo, the knowledge of Wono, the way he spoke as if the landscape itself reported to him, all of it felt impossible. But impossible had ceased to be useful as a category. Too much had already happened. Too much had crossed the boundary between story and flesh.

"Are you Nu-Mu?" Noah asked.

Something in Honi's expression tightened.

"I was born among the Nu-Mu," he said. "But I no longer have a place among them."

"Why?" Maia asked.

Honi's gaze moved back toward the castle.

"Because people forgive many things before they forgive a man who hears what they cannot."

"That still does not answer the question," Maia said.

"No. It answers the part of it you need for now."

For a moment, the four of them stood in the uneasy quiet between refusal and necessity. Then Honi turned toward the castle.

"You want a boat," he said. "You want to reach the heart of the lake. And you believe water and distance are the only things standing between you and what you came to do."

Noah felt the chill of those words settle between his shoulders.

"It isn't?"

Honi did not look back.

"Come with me."

Alejandra caught Noah's sleeve before he could move.

"We should not follow him blindly," she whispered.

"I know."

"Do you?" Maia asked under her breath.

Noah looked at both of them. He had no good argument. Every choice before them had become a different kind of danger. Staying outside solved nothing. Running would only delay what already seemed to know their direction. And Honi, whatever else he was, knew about Wono.

Noah nodded once.

They followed.

The path to Vikingsholm descended through pines whose long shadows crossed the ground in narrow strips. The castle grew larger as they approached, revealing details that had been softened by distance: dragon-headed carvings along the wooden rails, hand-shaped beams darkened by age, window frames worked with delicate precision, and stone walls that seemed to hold the day's warmth even as the air began to cool. Nature did not merely surround the estate. It leaned into it. Pine branches shaded the roof. Moss gathered in the seams of stone. The house appeared less built than permitted to remain.

Under different circumstances, Alejandra might have stopped to admire it. Maia might have asked questions about the architecture. Noah might have taken out his phone and photographed the way sunlight touched the upper windows.

But none of them spoke.

The quiet around the castle felt curated, almost unnatural, as if every ordinary sound had been asked to wait outside.

Honi led them through a side entrance rather than the main doors. Inside, the air smelled of old timber, dust, lake dampness, and faint smoke, though no fire burned nearby. The rooms carried the warmth of human design: carved wood, patterned textiles, iron fixtures, furniture arranged with care. Yet beneath the domestic beauty, something else pressed upward. A hidden age. A preserved unease.

"We need to get on the water quickly," Noah said as they followed Honi down a narrow corridor.

"You need to understand the water first."

"We do not have time for riddles," Alejandra said.

Honi stopped at the end of the hall, before a heavy wooden door partly concealed by a hanging tapestry. He pulled the fabric aside. The door behind it was darker than the surrounding walls, fitted with a bronze lock discolored by age.

"Esa and Pamahas did not tell you everything," he said.

Noah's body went still.

"How do you know those names?"

Honi removed a bronze key from a cord around his neck. Its handle was shaped like a circle broken by a triangle.

"I know many names that no longer wish to be spoken near this lake."

Maia stepped forward.

"You are avoiding every direct question."

"And yet," Honi said, inserting the key into the lock, "you are still here."

The lock turned with a dull internal click.

The door opened onto darkness.

A narrow staircase descended beneath the house, its stone steps damp at the edges. Cold air breathed upward from below, carrying the smell of moss, rust, and something mineral, like wet bone. Honi took an oil lamp from a hook near the doorway and lit it with a match. Flame trembled inside the glass.

"I do not like this," Alejandra said.

"Good," Honi replied. "That means something in you is still listening."

Lamp in hand, he descended.

Noah followed first, then Maia, then Alejandra, who kept one hand on the wall. The stone was slick beneath her fingers. With each step, the sound of the upper house retreated. The creak of wood, the hush of wind against windows, the distant blue openness of Tahoe, all of it faded until only the lamp and their breathing remained.

At the bottom, the chamber widened.

It was larger than Noah expected, though the low ceiling made it feel buried rather than spacious. Webs hung from beams in gray veils. Moisture had entered through hairline cracks in the stone walls, feeding patches of moss that spread like dark bruises. Old furniture stood beneath cloth covers. Wooden crates rested in corners. A rusted lantern lay on its side near a wall, its glass broken inward.

In the center of the room stood a long glass display case.

Dust covered it so completely that it looked less like furniture than a coffin.

"What is this place?" Noah asked.

"A room that does not officially exist," Honi said.

He crossed to the display case and wiped a red cloth across the glass. Dust lifted in a thick cloud. Alejandra coughed and stepped back.

"This chamber was added after the estate was built. Not in the public plans. Not in the records shown to visitors. The first owner wanted a place where a discovery could be kept without becoming a story told by every mouth around the lake."

"What discovery?" Maia asked.

Honi did not answer immediately.

He continued wiping the glass, slowly revealing what lay beneath.

At first, Noah saw only a curved shape, pale and enormous.

Then the full object emerged.

A tooth rested inside the case.

It was nearly forty inches long, thick at the root, tapering toward a point still sharp enough to seem recently pulled from a living mouth. Its surface was not smooth. Fine ridges ran along it like growth rings in ancient wood. Near the base, dark stains had settled into the calcified grooves, too old to be blood and too deliberate to be dirt.

Beneath the tooth lay a charcoal illustration, its paper yellowed by age. The drawing depicted a lake creature with a long serpent-like tail, wide fins, a heavy reptilian head, and a mouth crowded with teeth like broken knives. The artist had drawn the eye too carefully. It held a malice that seemed excessive for imagination.

At the bottom of the page, in faded block letters, someone had written:

THE MONSTER OF LAKE TAHOE

Alejandra stared at the case.

"That is not real."

"No," Honi said. "That is what people say when reality has become inconvenient."

Maia leaned closer, careful not to touch the glass.

"Where did this come from?"

Honi rested both hands on the edge of the case.

"In the early nineteen-thirties, during a summer so hot that people said the lake itself had begun to sweat, a fisherman took the owner of this estate onto the water. Her name was Annika Pedersen. Wealthy. Admired. Generous in public. Careful in private. She loved this bay more than she loved most people, though some believed she loved the fisherman as well."

Alejandra looked at him.

"Were they lovers?"

"That depends on whether you trust gossip more than silence."

Maia gave him a sharp look, but said nothing.

Honi continued.

"They went farther from shore than they should have. The lake was calm when they left. Too calm. The fisherman had brought a harpoon because he believed something large had been taking fish from the deeper water. Not a bear. Not a bird. Not anything with a name people could agree on."

The lamp flame flickered.

Noah looked down at the tooth again.

"They saw it?"

"They survived it," Honi said.

A silence followed.

"When the creature rose, it struck the boat from below. The fisherman drove the harpoon into its mouth. The rope caught around one of the teeth. The animal dove. He held on, or the rope tangled around his arm, depending on which version you believe. Either way, the tooth tore loose before the creature vanished into the depths."

"And they brought it here," Maia said.

"Annika did. The fisherman died before winter."

Alejandra crossed her arms, suddenly cold.

"How?"

"He stopped sleeping. Said he could hear something scraping beneath the floor at night, though his cabin stood nowhere near the water. Then he walked into the lake before sunrise and did not come back."

Noah felt the miniature Wono warm faintly inside his pocket.

He looked at Honi.

"What does this have to do with us?"

Honi's expression changed, not dramatically, but enough. The guarded storyteller receded. The man who had been waiting for them returned.

"The creature is not merely an animal. It is old lake hunger given a body. For many years, it remained where the deep water kept its secrets. Then it found the hidden passage between Tahoe and Pyramid Lake."

"The underground canal," Noah said.

Honi nodded.

"Long before men tried to name these waters as separate things, they knew each other beneath the earth. A sacred flow moved between them. What happened in one could trouble the other. What was sealed in one could search for the other."

Maia looked from the tooth to Honi.

"Esa closed the canal."

Honi's eyes shifted toward her.

"So you know that much."

"We know enough," she said.

"No," Honi replied quietly. "You know what you were told."

The words struck harder than they should have.

Noah remembered Esa's presence, Pamahas' certainty, the impossible logic of the Other World. Until now, he had accepted their guidance as the nearest thing to truth available. But Honi's voice carried something dangerous: not contradiction exactly, but incompletion.

"What are you saying?" Noah asked.

"When Esa sealed the passage, he protected Pyramid Lake from what was moving through it. But the seal did not erase what had already crossed partway. It trapped anger between waters. It interrupted a current older than memory. And anything powerful enough to live in that darkness would not mistake interruption for mercy."

Alejandra's face tightened.

"The monster is in Lake Tahoe."

"It has returned to Tahoe," Honi said. "And it knows the small Wono is here."

Noah's hand closed over his pocket.

The chamber seemed to shrink around him.

"How?"

"The same way I knew," Honi said. "Everything sacred gives off a disturbance when carried into a wounded place. You brought a fragment of Wono to the edge of a lake that has been listening for it."

Maia turned away from the display case and looked toward the staircase, as if calculating how quickly they could escape.

"And you waited until we were underground to tell us this?"

"I waited until you saw proof," Honi said.

"This is not proof. It is a tooth in a case and a story from a man we do not know."

Honi stepped back from the glass.

"Then look closer."

For a moment, Maia did not move.

Then, despite herself, she leaned toward the case again.

The tooth shifted.

Not much. Barely the width of a fingernail.

But the movement was real.

Alejandra gasped.

A thin line opened near the base of the tooth where the old dark stain had settled into the grooves. Something wet gleamed there, black and viscous, gathering slowly as though the tooth still remembered the mouth from which it had been torn.

Noah stepped back.

The miniature Wono grew warmer in his pocket.

The lamp flame bent toward the display case.

Honi covered the tooth again with the red cloth, and the room seemed to breathe out.

"It has never been dead," he said.

No one spoke for several seconds.

Above them, from somewhere in the house, came a faint groan of settling wood. Alejandra flinched.

"What are we supposed to do?" she asked.

The question sounded smaller than she intended.

Honi looked at Noah, then at the place where his hand still guarded his pocket.

"You still need to reach the island."

"The creature will stop us," Noah said.

"It will try."

"And if it gets Wono?" Maia asked.

Honi's face hardened.

"Then the lake will no longer need a monster. It will become one."

The words settled over them with the cold finality of stone.

Noah thought of the water outside, bright beneath the sky. Tourists had once walked these paths with cameras and picnic bags. Children had stood on the shore and admired the impossible blue. Boats had crossed Emerald Bay as if the lake were scenery, as if beauty could not also be a mask.

He pulled the miniature Wono from his pocket.

Its golden surface gave off a faint light, dim but steady. In the underground chamber, surrounded by dust, moss, hidden history, and the tooth of something that should not exist, the small pyramid seemed less like an object than a burden choosing its bearer.

Honi bowed his head slightly, not to Noah, but to Wono.

"So," Alejandra said, her voice unsteady, "how do we get past it?"

Honi lifted the lamp.

"We do not get past it."

Maia stared at him.

"You cannot be serious."

The old man turned toward the stairs, and the shadows moved across the moon-shaped scar on his cheek.

"If the monster is already waiting, then avoidance is only another name for delay."

Noah closed his fingers around Wono.

Outside, beyond stone and timber and pine, Lake Tahoe remained calm.

Honi began climbing the stairs.

"We will have to face it."

Far beneath the blue surface of the lake, where sunlight thinned into green darkness and the cold held its breath, the creature moved across the lakebed.

Its body was long and scaled, dark as wet pine shadow, with wide fins that stirred the silt without sound. One gap broke the cruel architecture of its mouth, where the stolen tooth had never grown back. Through that opening, a thick purple tongue shifted, covered in thorns that opened and closed like tiny mouths.

Above it, the lake remained beautiful.

Open. Welcoming.

The creature raised its reptilian head.

Somewhere beyond the shore, the miniature Wono burned like a small sun inside the old wound of the world.

The monster tasted its light.

CHAPTER XXI

The Wave of a Star-Spangled Banner

We don't have to be afraid of the unknown. Eventually, it will be known, and we'll act accordingly.

Night had settled peacefully across the mountains surrounding Pyramid Lake. The moon hung low above the desert, bathing the ridges and canyons in silver light while the lake itself rested in silence, reflecting fragments of stars across its dark surface. The wind had grown unusually gentle. Even the sagebrush seemed reluctant to move beneath its touch. It was the kind of stillness that often preceded change, though few recognized it until afterward.

Shilah sat alone upon a rocky ridge overlooking a narrow canyon several miles from the tribal settlement. At twenty years of age, he had already earned a reputation among the Nu-Mu as one of the most gifted hunters and warriors of his generation. Yet there was nothing boastful about him. The desert had taught him patience long ago. Every successful hunt began with observation. Every mistake began with certainty.

A brown owl rested beside him upon the stone.

The bird had appeared years earlier and simply never left. Some among the tribe believed it to be a messenger. Others considered it a guardian spirit. Shilah had never concerned himself with naming the relationship. The owl accompanied him because it chose to do so, and that was enough.

Together they listened to the desert.

Far below, the canyon stretched eastward through the mountains before disappearing into the immense darkness of the Great Basin. Countless generations had crossed those lands. Travelers, hunters, dreamers, wanderers. The desert remembered them all and spoke of them to no one.

The owl suddenly shifted its weight.

Its feathers tightened.

Shilah noticed the change immediately.

A moment later, he heard it as well.

Voices.

At first they were little more than distant sounds carried by the wind. Yet something about them felt strange. The rhythm was unfamiliar. The words rose and fell in ways he had never encountered before. No neighboring tribe spoke like that.

The owl turned its head toward the canyon.

Shilah rose slowly.

Curiosity carried him forward.

He descended along the ridge with practiced caution, navigating between weathered rocks and narrow ledges until he reached a large stone overlooking one of the canyon passages below. There he crouched and listened.

The voices were clearer now.

Two men.

Speaking a language completely unknown to him.

For a moment he wondered whether he was hearing spirits.

Then came laughter. Human laughter.

Shilah carefully climbed onto the rock and raised his head above its edge.

What he saw below rooted him in place.

A fire burned in the center of a small camp.

Several horses stood nearby, tethered to wooden stakes. Strange supplies surrounded the campfire. Metal objects reflected the flames in brief flashes of silver and gold. Blankets, bags, tools, and other unfamiliar items covered the ground.

Yet none of those things captured Shilah's attention.

His gaze fixed upon a tall pole standing beside the camp.

Attached to it was a piece of fabric unlike anything he had ever seen.

The cloth moved continuously beneath the wind, unfolding and gathering itself with a strange dignity. Wide bands of red and white stretched across its surface, while a dark blue field occupied one corner. Within that darkness rested numerous white shapes resembling stars scattered across the night sky.

The fabric rose and fell.

Rose and fell again.

Its movements felt purposeful.

Almost ceremonial.

Shilah could not explain why, but the object unsettled him.

Every tribe possessed symbols. Certain markings carried meaning beyond their physical form. A sacred object was never merely an object. It represented attention. Belief. Intention accumulated across many generations.

Though he had never seen this banner before, he sensed immediately that it carried immense significance to those who followed it.

The realization disturbed him.

His attention shifted toward the men seated beside the fire.

Their clothing matched.

Blue garments covered their bodies. Thick belts circled their waists. Long metal objects rested within arm's reach. The weapons looked unlike bows, spears, or anything familiar to him. Even from a distance, they seemed dangerous.

One of the men stood and stretched.

The firelight illuminated his face.

Pale skin.

Reddish beard.

Eyes unlike any Shilah had ever seen.

The stranger said something to his companion. The second man laughed and pointed toward the darkness beyond the canyon.

Toward the west. Toward Pyramid Lake.

An inexplicable chill passed through Shilah.

Perhaps the men intended no harm.

Perhaps they were merely travelers.

Yet the sensation growing within him felt similar to standing beneath darkening clouds before a storm. The danger was not visible. It had not arrived. Still, some deeper part of him recognized its approach.

The owl released a low call.

Shilah took the warning seriously.

Without making a sound, he descended from the rock and retreated into the darkness.

The voices gradually disappeared behind him.

The banner did not.

Even after the camp vanished from sight, he continued seeing it in his mind. Red. White. Blue. Moving beneath the wind like a declaration he could not yet understand.

The journey back to the settlement felt shorter than usual.

Moonlight guided his path across the desert while the owl followed silently overhead. By the time the first huts emerged from the darkness, Shilah had reached only one conclusion.

The world was changing.

Whether the tribe was ready or not.

Most of the settlement slept.

Small fires glowed between the huts, their embers casting soft orange light upon the ground. Near the center of the village sat Wovoka.

The shaman appeared alone.

His eyes remained closed.

One finger moved slowly through the sand before him, tracing lines and curves whose meaning was not immediately obvious. The patterns intersected repeatedly, creating pathways that emerged, diverged, and returned again.

Shilah approached quietly.

Before he could speak, Wovoka smiled.

"You found them."

The young warrior stopped.

"You knew?"

"The wind knew."

Wovoka opened his eyes.

"The lake knew. The mountains knew. I simply listened."

Shilah glanced toward the eastern horizon.

"They are unlike anyone I have ever seen."

"Yes."

"They carried strange weapons."

"Yes."

"And a banner."

Something changed in Wovoka's expression.

Not surprise.

Recognition.

"You saw it."

Shilah nodded.

"I do not know what it means, yet I could feel its importance."

The shaman studied him for a moment.

"Then you understood more than you realize."

The wind moved softly through the settlement.

The fires crackled.

Somewhere beyond the huts, a child shifted in sleep.

Shilah looked down at the patterns Wovoka had drawn in the sand.

"What are these?"

"Possibilities."

The answer raised more questions than it answered.

"Can you see the future?"

"No."

Wovoka smiled faintly.

"Anyone who claims certainty about the future understands neither time nor Puha."

"Then what are you looking at?"

"Directions."

Shilah remained silent.

Wovoka's finger traced one of the paths.

"When a snowflake falls upon the mountain, winter has not yet arrived. Yet the wise hunter begins preparing immediately."

His finger moved to another line.

"When the first leaf releases itself from a tree, autumn has not yet claimed the forest. Yet the wise traveler begins gathering firewood."

He looked toward the eastern darkness.

"When the first foreign banner enters the land, history has not yet changed. Yet the wise people begin paying attention."

The words settled heavily between them.

Shilah felt his stomach tighten.

"There are more coming."

It was not a question.

Wovoka nodded.

"Yes."

"How many?"

"I do not know."

"Can we stop them?"

The shaman's gaze drifted toward Pyramid Lake.

The water reflected moonlight beneath the stars.

"Can you stop the sunrise?"

"No."

"Can you stop a river from seeking the sea?"

"No."

"Then do not waste your strength trying to stop what has already begun."

A sudden gust of wind swept across the settlement.

Sand spiraled through the air.

The patterns drawn before Wovoka vanished instantly.

Every path disappeared.

Every possibility erased.

When the wind passed, only smooth earth remained.

Shilah stared at the empty ground.

The lesson required no explanation.

Eventually Wovoka rose to his feet.

"The world changes form endlessly," he said. "Most people notice only after the transformation is complete. They mistake the fruit for the seed and the wave for the wind that created it."

His gaze remained fixed upon the darkness beyond the mountains.

"Something has begun moving toward us, Shilah. Not only in this world, but beyond it."

The owl landed upon the warrior's shoulder.

Neither man spoke again.

Above them, the stars continued their ancient journey across the heavens.

Far to the east, beneath a banner neither of them could ignore, another campfire burned against the darkness.

The Dark Woods had turned into a madman's nightmare.

The strange harmony that had once defined the forest was unraveling before Sam's eyes. Shadows moved where shadows should not move. Distant sounds emerged from no discernible source and then vanished before their origin could be located. The luminous vegetation that covered portions of the forest floor pulsed unevenly, casting uncertain colors across the twisted trunks while countless yellow eyes appeared and disappeared among the darkness like fragments of some enormous living consciousness observing their every movement. Fear pressed against her from every direction, making it difficult to think clearly, yet she understood that remaining motionless would accomplish nothing. Whatever was happening around them was accelerating, and every instinct within her warned that time was becoming increasingly precious.

Without allowing herself the opportunity to hesitate, she seized Galilhai's arm and pulled her forward.

"Run. Now."

The young girl obeyed immediately. Together they hurried through the forest, weaving between roots and low branches while the distant eyes continued watching from the darkness. Sam focused entirely on the presence she hoped to find ahead of them. The plan had been simple. Find Esa. Find Pamahas. Stay together. Yet the deeper they ventured into the woods, the more uncertain she became. The forest seemed determined to distort distance itself. Every path appeared capable of leading somewhere else.

Please be there, she thought. Please.

Then, suddenly, a familiar presence entered her mind.

There is no longer any danger. Feel my presence. I am here.

Relief flooded through her so quickly that it nearly overwhelmed her. The voice carried the unmistakable calm that always accompanied Esa, a calm so profound that it seemed capable of existing independently from circumstance. Even surrounded by darkness, confusion, and fear, the wolf god's presence remained untouched by any of it.

Guided by that sensation, Sam continued forward until the forest gradually opened into a small clearing. The moment she stepped into it, her heart sank.

Esa was lying upon the ground beside Pamahas.

The wolf god's massive form remained still and attentive, one paw resting gently upon the woman's forehead. Around them, the ada'a occupied the surrounding trees. Their yellow eyes glimmered between branches and leaves, yet none approached the clearing itself. They watched in silence, waiting with the patience of predators who sensed that something important was unfolding before them.

"Pamahas!" Sam cried, rushing forward.

She dropped to her knees beside the red-haired woman and immediately understood that something was terribly wrong. The vibrant warmth that always seemed to radiate naturally from Pamahas had diminished almost entirely, leaving behind a stillness that felt profoundly unnatural. Her sun-kissed skin had become pale and fragile. Her lips remained slightly parted. Her eyes, still open, stared beyond the canopy toward a sky they no longer seemed capable of seeing. For a moment Sam simply looked at her, unable to reconcile the woman before her with the guide who had led them through the wonders and dangers of the Other World.

"What happened to her?"

Esa lowered his gaze toward Pamahas.

"A stingray wounded her. Her life is now slipping back toward Puha."

The words struck Sam with astonishing force. She stared at the wolf god, waiting for him to say something more, waiting for some explanation that would transform the sentence into something less final. None came. Pamahas had always seemed inseparable from the Other World itself. She belonged to this place in the same way the forests, rivers, mountains, and luminous skies belonged to it. The possibility that she could simply disappear felt absurd, as though someone had announced that the moon had decided to abandon the heavens.

"We need her, Esa," she said, her voice trembling despite every attempt to control it. "You are an almighty creature. Please, do something."

The great wolf remained silent for several moments, not because he was considering her request, but because he already understood the pain that had produced it. When he finally spoke, his voice carried neither indifference nor resignation. It carried acceptance.

"It is not my inability to change this moment that concerns me. It is my willingness to accept it."

Sam stared at him in disbelief.

"There must be an explanation. This is a mistake. Pamahas cannot die."

A deep sadness entered Esa's eyes, though it seemed directed toward something larger than Pamahas alone. It was the sadness of witnessing a truth that every living thing eventually encounters and almost none welcome when it arrives.

"When rain falls upon the desert, it does not ask whether the earth is prepared to receive it. When winter arrives upon the mountains, it does not seek permission from the trees. The movements of Puha do not become less sacred simply because they bring pain."

Sam lowered her gaze. The explanation offered no comfort. It felt beautiful and unbearable at the same time.

"That is not enough."

"It never is," Esa replied softly. "Not while the heart is still negotiating with reality."

The words settled heavily over the clearing. Galilhai had remained silent throughout the exchange, tears streaming down her face as she stood with both hands covering her mouth. The young girl looked as though she were witnessing the collapse of something she had believed would endure forever. Around them, the forest itself seemed to reflect that sorrow. The luminous flowers growing beneath the trees gradually folded inward. The strange colors illuminating the undergrowth dimmed. Even the wind appeared reluctant to disturb the clearing. An immense stillness settled across the Dark Woods, transforming the place into something solemn and sacred, as though the forest had gathered to witness a farewell.

Sam looked down at Pamahas once more and felt a pain she had not expected. Memories surfaced without invitation. Pamahas welcoming them into the Other World. Pamahas guiding them through impossible landscapes. Pamahas speaking with quiet certainty whenever confusion threatened to overwhelm them. Until that moment, Sam had never realized how naturally she had assumed those experiences would continue. There would always be another question to ask. Another lesson to learn. Another journey to take. The future had seemed so abundant that she had never considered the possibility of its sudden absence.

Now, for the first time, she understood how fragile those assumptions had been.

A sob escaped her despite her efforts to suppress it. Then another followed, and soon the grief she had been resisting broke through completely. It expanded until it occupied every corner of her awareness, leaving room for nothing else. The forest disappeared. The watching ada'a disappeared. Even the danger that had driven them there seemed distant and irrelevant. There was only loss and the terrible certainty that nothing she said or did could prevent it.

Yet grief, like every storm, eventually exhausted itself.

The struggle slowly began to loosen its hold upon her. Her desperate need for reality to become something other than what it was gradually faded. Not because she approved of the moment. Not because she understood it. Simply because she no longer possessed the strength to oppose it. For the first time since arriving in the clearing, she stopped arguing with what was happening. The sorrow remained. The pain remained. Yet beneath both she discovered something deeper and quieter, a stillness that accepted the moment exactly as it was.

A single tear escaped from the corner of her eye and fell upon Pamahas's forehead.

For several seconds nothing happened. The clearing remained silent. The forest remained still. Sam almost lowered her gaze again, convinced that the moment had passed, when she noticed something so subtle she initially wondered whether grief had distorted her perception. A faint warmth appeared beneath Pamahas's skin. It spread slowly at first, carrying with it the gentlest trace of golden light, like the first hint of dawn emerging beyond a distant horizon. The radiance continued expanding through invisible pathways beneath the surface, growing brighter with each passing moment as the pallor that had settled upon her face gradually surrendered to color.

The transformation unfolded with such quiet certainty that no one spoke.

Warmth returned. Color returned. Life itself seemed to be retracing its steps.

Nor was the change confined to Pamahas alone. The oppressive heaviness lingering throughout the clearing began to weaken. The luminous vegetation brightened. The strange flowers slowly reopened. The darkness between the trees retreated. Even the ada'a shifted uneasily among the branches, their glowing eyes filled with something that resembled confusion. They behaved like creatures witnessing an event that contradicted the rules by which they understood the world.

Esa slowly rose to his feet.

His gaze remained fixed upon Pamahas, yet something within his expression had changed. For the first time since Sam had met him, uncertainty appeared within the ancient wolf god's eyes. It was not fear. It was not disbelief. It was recognition struggling to understand itself.

The golden radiance continued flowing through Pamahas until her chest expanded sharply with a sudden breath. Air rushed into her lungs. Her eyes focused. The distant emptiness that had occupied them vanished, replaced once more by the vitality that had seemed lost only moments earlier. She blinked several times as though returning from an immense distance before slowly turning her head toward the faces surrounding her.

"I am alive."

The words barely rose above a whisper, yet they carried through the clearing with the force of a revelation.

Galilhai's tears became tears of relief. Sam could do nothing except stare. Her mind searched desperately for an explanation, yet every explanation dissolved before it could fully form. Only Esa remained silent. While the others focused upon Pamahas, his attention had settled entirely upon Sam.

The miracle had restored the woman.

The mystery remained with the girl.

CHAPTER XXII

Unexpected Divergence

It's not so much about going left or right as it's about being centered in the present moment. Then, we are on the right path since it's the only real path there is.

Alejandra moved slowly through the chamber, careful not to disturb the silence that had settled over the room like another layer of dust. The hidden space beneath Vikingsholm did not feel abandoned in the ordinary sense. Abandoned places usually carried the sadness of neglect, of something once useful surrendered to time. This chamber felt different. It felt concealed. Preserved. Protected from accidental discovery by the same darkness that had gathered in its corners for decades. The cold stone walls were mottled with moss and mineral stains, and the air held the damp odor of lake water, old wood, and paper slowly surrendering itself to age.

Paintings covered most of the walls.

They were all the same size and shape, framed in dark wood whose varnish had cracked into fine irregular lines. Yet none of them hung perfectly straight. Some leaned slightly to the left. Others had sagged against their wires. A few rested so crookedly that Ale wondered whether they had been disturbed by the shifting of the earth, the settling of the estate, or by hands searching for something they were not meant to find.

Most depicted Lake Tahoe.

At first, that seemed natural enough. Mrs. Annika Petersen had lived near these waters. A woman of wealth and leisure might easily spend years painting the same landscape from different moods and distances. Yet the longer Ale studied the images, the less ordinary they became. In one, Emerald Bay appeared beneath a sky bruised purple by storm clouds, though the lake itself reflected no storm at all. In another, Fannette Island rose from a sheet of mist while the Tea House at its summit seemed to lean impossibly forward, as though listening. A third painting showed the lake at night, but beneath the surface, hidden among the dark blue strokes, pale shapes hovered like faces glimpsed through water.

Ale stopped before a painting near the far wall.

This one was different.

The oil strokes were thicker, more urgent, and less controlled than the others. Shades of blue, green, gray, and black had been layered into a violent gradient that transformed Lake Tahoe into something almost alive. Waves struck a small fishing boat beneath a collapsing sky. The boat had been painted at an angle that made it appear moments away from breaking apart. Rain slashed across the scene in silver lines, and in the center of the vessel a young man lay motionless upon the deck with his eyes closed while a young woman knelt beside him, holding his hand with both of hers.

Ale stepped closer.

The impasto texture made the figures difficult to discern clearly. Their faces were suggested more than rendered, shaped by raised strokes and shadows rather than careful detail. Even so, something about them disturbed her. The young woman's posture. The curve of the man's jaw. The way the two figures seemed both unfamiliar and impossibly known.

She lifted her hand and stopped just before touching the dried paint.

A strange pressure moved through her chest.

I have seen them before.

The thought came with such certainty that she immediately looked over her shoulder, half expecting someone else in the room to have heard it. Noah and Maia were near the glass exhibitor, examining the objects inside while Honi stood a few steps behind them, watching the chamber with an expression that suggested he had entered it many times and understood it less with each visit.

Ale turned back to the painting.

In the lower corner, beneath a smear of foam breaking against the boat, white letters marked the artist's initials.

A.P.

"Honi," she said quietly.

The old caretaker approached with measured steps, his eyes following hers to the painting. For several seconds he said nothing.

"Did Mrs. Petersen paint these?" Ale asked.

Honi nodded, though his answer did not come immediately. "Every one I know of."

Ale looked at the storm again. "This one feels different."

"It always did," Honi said.

The admission made her turn toward him.

"You noticed it too?"

"I noticed many things in this room," he replied. "Understanding them was another matter."

That answer unsettled her more than certainty would have. "Who are they?"

Honi studied the couple in the boat, then shook his head. "I don't know. Mrs. Annika never told me. She rarely explained what she painted, and when she did, her explanations were stranger than the paintings themselves."

"What do you mean?"

He glanced at the other walls, as though the images might object to being discussed in their presence. "After the attack, she changed. People around the estate said grief had altered her, but grief does not usually teach a person to paint places they have never visited. She began waking in the middle of the night and covering canvases before sunrise. Lakes under impossible moons. Stone formations she called gates. Forests made of gold. A pyramid-shaped rock rising from water that was not water."

Ale felt a chill descend along her spine.

"Wono," she whispered.

Honi looked at her carefully. "Maybe."

Noah, who had been listening from near the exhibitor, turned toward them. "She dreamed about the Other World?"

"I believe she dreamed about something," Honi said. "Whether it was the Other World, I cannot say. Mrs. Annika had many secrets, and she did not trust most people with them."

Maia gave a quiet laugh without humor. "That seems to be a theme around here."

Ale kept her eyes on the painting. The storm, the boat, the unconscious young man, the woman gripping his hand. The scene seemed less like memory than warning. "Did she ever mention this painting specifically?"

"No," Honi said. "But she kept it covered for years."

Ale looked at him. "Covered?"

"With a dark cloth," he answered. "I only saw it after she died, when the family hired conservators to catalog the room. Even then, one of them said the canvas seemed newer than the others, as though she had returned to it again and again."

Of all the mysteries hidden inside the chamber, the painting disturbed her the most. The cube raised questions. The key suggested answers. The painting did neither. It simply waited.

Noah walked closer, his face tense. "Why would she hide a painting in a secret room and then cover it inside the secret room?"

No one answered.

The question remained in the chamber, joining the dampness and the dust.

Near the glass exhibitor, Maia had grown unusually still. She was no longer looking at the artifacts displayed beneath the glass, but at the side of the wooden base supporting it. Her fingers traced the carved edge slowly, following a line so faint that Ale would not have noticed it from where she stood.

“What is it?” Noah asked.

Maia brushed a thin layer of dust away with her thumb.

"Someone kept coming back to this spot."

"How can you tell?"

"Because everything around it was left alone."

The exhibitor was old, heavy, and beautifully constructed, its wood darkened by age and polished by years of careful handling. Along one side, near the lower corner, a carved border repeated a pattern of waves, pine branches, and small geometric symbols. At first, the design appeared purely decorative, but Maia had found a narrow interruption where the pattern did not align. A pyramid shape, no larger than a thumbnail, sat at the center of the irregularity.

“That looks intentional,” Ale said.

Maia pressed gently against the pyramid.

Nothing happened.

She frowned and pressed again, this time lower, then higher. The wood gave a faint click, but the panel did not open.

“It’s stuck,” she said.

“Or locked,” Noah replied.

Maia looked across the surface, thinking. “No, not locked. Listen.”

She pressed the pyramid again.

This time they all heard it: a small metallic sound from within the base, like something shifting and failing to release.

Honi moved closer. "I never noticed that."

Maia gave him a quick look. "You maintained this place and never noticed a hidden drawer?"

"I maintained what I was permitted to maintain," he said. "Mrs. Annika made certain no one touched what she wished to keep hidden."

Ale studied the carved pattern, then noticed a second symbol near the opposite side of the panel. It was not a pyramid but a small circle crossed by a vertical line, almost swallowed by the decorative waves.

"Try pressing both," she said.

Maia placed one finger on the pyramid while Ale pressed the circle.

The mechanism released with a sharper click.

A narrow drawer slid outward less than an inch.

Noah exhaled. "Okay. That's not suspicious at all."

Maia carefully pulled the drawer open.

The smell of old cedar rose from within.

Several objects rested inside, arranged with the precision of things deliberately preserved rather than forgotten. There was a small wood-carving knife with a darkened handle, a brittle black-and-white photograph, a folded piece of yellowed paper bound with string, and a cube-shaped artifact that seemed at first to be made of pinewood.

Maia reached for the cube.

The moment she lifted it, her expression changed.

"What?" Ale asked.

Maia raised it slightly in her palm. "This is heavier than it should be."

The weight alone unsettled Maia, but the longer she held the cube, the more certain she became that something inside it was not still, as though its center of gravity belonged to a hidden movement her eyes could not detect. For a brief instant, she had the distinct sensation that the cube had shifted in her hand. Not physically. Not enough to be seen. More like the subtle feeling of balance changing inside an object that should have been perfectly still.

Noah stepped forward.

The cube was no larger than a few inches on each side, yet Maia held it with the care one would give to a stone rather than a piece of wood. Each face had been marked with a different symbol burned into the surface with remarkable precision. The dark pyrography lines had a cedar-like color that stood out against the lighter grain, forming shapes that looked ancient without appearing random.

Noah's face paled.

"No," he said.

Ale looked at him. "What?"

He extended his hand but did not take the cube immediately. "That looks like one of the Destiny Dice."

Silence moved through the room.

Even Honi seemed to stop breathing for a moment.

Maia stared at the object in her palm. "You're sure?"

"No," Noah said, though the uncertainty in his voice sounded more like fear than doubt. "I'm not sure. I can't be sure. Esa and Pamahas talked about the Destiny Dice like they were in the Other World. If one of them was here, they would have told us."

"Unless they didn't know," Ale said.

Noah shook his head. "How could they not know?"

Ale did not answer, because the question troubled her as much as it troubled him. She took the cube from Maia and immediately understood why the weight had startled her. It looked like pinewood, yet its density felt wrong, as though something concealed inside the wooden shell pulled against her palm.

"It has a core," she said.

"Metal?" Maia asked.

"Maybe."

Honi leaned closer without touching it. His expression had shifted from curiosity to unease. "Mrs. Annika kept many strange objects in this chamber, but I have never seen that before."

Noah looked at him sharply. "You're sure?"

"I would remember."

That answer carried weight.

Ale turned the cube slowly, studying each burned symbol. One face bore a pyramid. Another, a spiral. Another, a fish. Another, a shape resembling a door or gate. The markings did not feel decorative. They felt purposeful. Like instructions written in a language none of them could read.

"If this is a replica," Maia said, "it is a very strange replica."

"And if it isn't?" Ale asked.

Noah rubbed his forehead. "Then Mrs. Petersen was involved in this much deeper than we thought."

Ale placed the cube carefully on top of the exhibitor and reached into the drawer for the photograph.

The paper was brittle and slightly curled at the edges. In the image, Mrs. Annika Petersen sat alone at a dining table aboard what appeared to be a luxurious train. The table had been arranged with fine china, polished silverware, crystal glass, and a bottle of wine whose label was too blurred to read. Patterned curtains framed the windows behind her, matching the linen tablecloth with an elegance that felt almost theatrical. She wore a long dress with padded shoulders, white gloves, and a flowered hat resting above her light hair. Everything about her posture seemed composed. Dignified. Controlled.

Yet her face contradicted the rest of the image.

The camera had captured her looking slightly away from the lens, and in that accidental turn of the head Ale saw something she had not expected.

Fear.

Not the fear of someone in immediate danger, but the quieter and more enduring fear of someone who had learned something she could no longer unknow.

Ale turned the photograph over.

On the back, written in dark ink with careful, deliberate letters, was a verse.

THEREFORE, I RETRACT, AND I REPENT IN DUST AND ASHES.

JOB 42:6

Ale read the words aloud.

Maia's expression softened into confusion. "That's biblical, right?"

"The Book of Job," Ale said.

"So she learned something?" Maia asked.

Ale studied the photograph.

"No. I think she learned she was wrong."

Ale stared at the handwriting. "Job suffers without understanding why. He questions God. He demands answers. And when he finally encounters the divine, he realizes the mystery is larger than his ability to judge it."

Honi crossed himself quietly, almost unconsciously.

Maia noticed. "You knew she was religious?"

"I knew she attended church when she was young," Honi said. "But later in life, she spoke less of religion and more of judgment. Repentance. Consequence. She once told me that some doors should remain closed because not everyone who opens them is prepared to face what looks back."

Ale turned the photograph over again and studied Annika's face. "What did she do?"

Honi did not respond immediately.

When he finally spoke, his voice had lowered. "I don't know."

This time Ale believed him.

Maia returned her attention to the drawer. "There's more."

She reached inside and removed the folded paper. The string binding it had become brittle with age, and when she placed it on the exhibitor, the knot loosened almost by itself. Noah unfolded it carefully.

It was a sketch.

The drawing appeared to show Fannette Island, though not as it looked from the shore. The island had been rendered from above, its rocky outline surrounded by dark water. At the top of the hill, the small stone Tea House had been marked with a circle. Beneath the sketch, written in the same careful hand as the biblical quotation, were three words.

NOT THERE.

BELOW.

Noah frowned and turned the sketch slowly beneath the light.

"Wait," he said. "This isn't only showing the island from above. Look at the lines here. They're not shoreline marks. They're elevation."

Ale felt the chamber grow colder.

Noah looked toward Honi. "Below what?"

Honi's face had gone pale.

"The Tea House," he said.

Maia glanced at him. "You know something."

"I know only a story," Honi replied.

"Then tell us the story," Ale said.

Honi looked toward the chamber door, as though suddenly aware of the weight of the estate above them. "Mrs. Annika had the Tea House built on Fannette Island, but she almost never used it for tea. The staff joked about that. They thought it was another eccentricity of a wealthy woman. But a few of the older workers said she visited the island alone, always near dusk, and always returned before full darkness. Once, years before I worked here, one of the groundsmen claimed he heard hammering beneath the stones after midnight."

"Beneath the Tea House?" Noah asked.

Honi nodded. "That was what he said. No one believed him. Or perhaps no one wanted to."

Maia reached once more into the drawer, feeling along the back with her fingertips. Her hand paused.

"I think there's another compartment."

She pressed against the rear panel. It resisted, then gave way with a small scraping sound.

Inside lay a skeleton key.

The key was narrow and antique, its metal darkened by rust. The elaborate bow had cracked in one place where corrosion had eaten into the design. A small tag hung from it by a tarnished ring.

TEA HOUSE

Ale looked at Noah.

Noah looked at the cube.

The chamber seemed to hold its breath around them.

"What are the odds," Maia said quietly, "that we find something that looks like a Destiny Die, a repentance verse, a drawing of Fannette Island, and the Tea House key in the same hidden drawer?"

"None," Noah said.

Ale picked up the key. It felt cold against her skin, colder than the room itself. "Then we go to Fannette Island."

Noah's reaction was immediate. "We are running out of time."

"I know."

"We don't even know if that thing is one of the Destiny Dice."

"That is exactly why we have to go."

Noah looked frustrated, but not because he disagreed. The fear in his face came from knowing she might be right.

Ale softened her voice. "Listen to me. Mrs. Petersen painted Wono. She dreamed about the Other World. She hid something that may be one of the Destiny Dice. She left a verse about repentance and a map pointing to the Tea House. Whatever she was involved in, it did not end with her. It is still here, waiting for someone to understand it."

Maia nodded slowly. "And Fannette Island is on the way out of Emerald Bay anyway."

Honi looked toward the cube with visible reluctance. "I had already planned for us to stop there."

All three turned toward him.

"Why?" Noah asked.

"There is a small shed on the island," Honi said. "Not the Tea House itself, but a separate storage structure used by the estate. It contains equipment we may need before entering open water. Rope, lamps, tools, and a few hunting rifles from the old days. I have the key to the shed."

"Rifles?" Ale asked.

"Hunting rifles," Honi clarified. "Old ones. I do not know whether they still function."

Noah looked toward the hidden drawer. "And you did not think the Tea House mattered before now?"

"I thought it was a stone shell built for appearances," Honi said. "Mrs. Annika made many things appear harmless."

"The older staff used to joke that she was building a fairy tale on the shore of the lake," Honi said, his gaze returning to the hidden drawer. "Eventually, they stopped joking."

That answer settled over them with uncomfortable force.

Ale wrapped the Tea House key carefully in a cloth and placed it in her pocket. Noah took the cube, though he did so reluctantly, as if accepting possession of the object made its significance harder to deny. Maia folded the sketch again and carried the photograph with the Job verse facing inward, preserving Annika's face from the room that had kept her secrets for so long.

They left the chamber in silence.

By the time they emerged from Vikingsholm, the air outside felt impossibly open. The estate stood behind them with its carved wood, steep roofs, and old grandeur, but Ale could no longer see it as a historic mansion visited by tourists and maintained by caretakers. It felt instead like the visible portion of something much larger, a beautiful mask placed over an old wound.

They descended toward the water behind the estate.

The private wooden pier extended into Emerald Bay, where a white fishing boat waited against the gentle movement of the lake. Honi boarded first and entered the cabin, checking the controls with the practiced movements of someone who had repeated the task many times. Noah helped Maia step aboard, then turned to Ale.

For a moment she paused at the edge of the pier.

The lake stretched before them with deceptive calm. Its surface held the afternoon light in rippling fragments, while beyond the mouth of the bay the greater body of Lake Tahoe expanded toward the distant mountains. Somewhere beneath that beauty, something ancient and violent had awakened. Somewhere beyond the boundaries of their understanding, Sam was searching for answers in a world that should not exist.

Ale stepped onto the boat.

The engine started with a low vibration that traveled through the deck beneath their feet. As the vessel pulled away from the pier, Vikingsholm gradually receded behind them, its hidden chamber and unanswered questions sinking back into the trees and stone.

Fannette Island rose ahead.

Its granite slopes emerged from the water like the back of some ancient creature resting beneath the lake. Pines and shrubs clung to its rocky surface, their green forms gathered between cracks and ledges carved by time. At the summit, small and solitary against the sky, stood the Tea House.

From a distance, it did not look like much.

A stone building. A ruin.

A curiosity left behind by wealth and eccentricity.

Yet as the boat crossed the water toward it, Ale felt the key resting heavily in her pocket and understood that the little structure at the top of the island had never been merely a place for tea.

It had been waiting.

CHAPTER XXIII

Goodbye for Now

Don't be sad to say goodbye; be grateful that you had the chance to say hello. Separation belongs to the World of Form. In truth, all things remain connected and will become whole once again.

Shilah left Wovoka's hut after the wind had calmed and walked alone through the sleeping settlement. The fires that had burned earlier in the evening were now low and scattered, their embers breathing softly beneath layers of ash while small sparks lifted occasionally into the darkness before vanishing among the stars. Beyond the outer huts, Pyramid Lake rested beneath the moonlight with a stillness that made the world appear older than memory. Its dark surface held the heavens in broken fragments, and for a moment Shilah had the strange impression that the stars above him and the stars below him were equally distant.

He followed a narrow path toward a dwelling near the edge of a slope facing the lake. The roof had been dyed a deep purple that appeared almost black beneath the night sky, a color difficult to achieve and therefore never used without meaning. It required patience, knowledge, and careful gathering of rare pigments from plants and other living things, and those who passed the hut understood without being told that someone of spiritual importance lived there. Yet Shilah had never thought of the dwelling in that way. To him, it was not a house of honor, nor the home of the nameless elder's grandson, nor the place where certain people came when disputes required a calm mind and a truthful heart. It was simply the place where Alo waited.

A faint glow moved behind the leather covering at the entrance.

Shilah paused before entering.

He had faced animals larger than himself without hesitation. He had crossed ridges at night, climbed stone under moonlight, and drawn his bow against men whose eyes carried violence. Yet the thought of stepping into that hut with the foreign banner still burning in his mind filled him with a fear he did not wish to name.

When he finally entered, the smell of sage, pine smoke, and warm earth received him.

Alo was awake.

He sat near a small lamp with his legs folded beneath him, his body wrapped loosely in a woven blanket dyed with pale geometric patterns. The light touched his face gently, revealing the quiet asymmetry that always made strangers look twice and made Shilah feel, each time, as though Puha had placed two different skies inside one person. One of Alo's eyes carried the deep brown of wet bark after rain. The other held the blue-green clarity of shallow water over stone. Between them rested no conflict. Only balance.

Alo did not ask why he had come.

He only watched him.

That was often enough.

Shilah crossed the hut and sat beside him. For a while, they listened to the silence together. Outside, the lake moved faintly against the shore. Somewhere in the settlement, a child murmured in sleep before settling again. The night seemed peaceful, but Shilah knew now that peace could exist at the edge of terrible things.

"You went far tonight," Alo said at last.

Shilah looked toward the lamp flame.

"Far enough."

"And you returned carrying something heavier than your bow."

The warrior almost smiled, but the expression failed before it reached his mouth. Alo had always possessed that strange ability to touch the truth without forcing it open. His grandmother called it attention. Others called it wisdom. Shilah had no name for it. He only knew that lies became useless in Alo's presence.

"I saw men," Shilah said. "Foreign men."

Alo's gaze did not change, though the stillness around him deepened.

"They had horses, weapons, and a banner raised above their camp. The cloth moved like something alive. Red, white, and blue, with white stars inside a dark corner. I did not understand its meaning, but I could feel that it belonged to many people, not only to the two men sitting beneath it."

Alo listened without interruption.

"Their weapons were unlike ours," Shilah continued. "I do not know their power, but Wovoka knows enough to be troubled by them. He says more will come."

Outside, the lake released a small sound against the stones, then withdrew into silence.

Alo lowered his eyes briefly. "Then the first wave has touched the shore."

Shilah looked at him.

"That is what Wovoka would say."

"My grandmother would say the wave was already traveling before any shore received it."

The words entered Shilah quietly, though they did not comfort him. He had not come searching for explanations of history or the hidden movement of destiny. He had heard enough of those from Wovoka, and he believed them as much as he was able. Yet belief did not quiet the body. It did not remove the image of metal weapons glinting beside the fire. It did not loosen the tightening in his chest whenever he imagined those foreign men walking closer to the settlement, closer to the lake, closer to this hut.

Alo reached for his hand.

Shilah allowed it.

The contrast between them had always seemed meaningful to others. Shilah's strength lived openly in his body, in the width of his shoulders, in the hard discipline of muscle shaped by hunting, climbing, and war. Alo's strength lived differently. It did not announce itself through force. It moved through patience, through listening, through the rare ability to remain centered while others were pulled apart by fear. Yet when Alo's fingers closed around his, Shilah felt no weakness in him. Only another kind of power.

"The body is loud," Alo said, as though following a thought Shilah had not spoken.

Shilah turned toward him.

"It tells us when it hungers, when it bleeds, when it desires, when it fears. Because it speaks so loudly, we sometimes believe it is the whole of who we are."

"And it is not?"

Alo's thumb moved slowly across the back of his hand.

"You know it is not."

Shilah wanted to answer immediately, but could not. He had spent his life training the body, sharpening it, trusting it, preparing it to protect what he loved. His body knew how to run without tiring, how to draw a bow without shaking, how to stand between danger and the people behind him. But now, for the first time, he had encountered a danger his body could not fully answer.

"I can fight men," he said. "I can fight hunger. I can fight heat, cold, pain, exhaustion. I can fight anything that stands before me in the World of Form."

Alo looked at him with tenderness.

"But not what might be taken from you."

Shilah's throat tightened.

The words were not accusation. They were not pity. They were simply true.

He looked toward the doorway, where the lake could be seen through the narrow opening in the leather. Moonlight moved over the water in pale bands, and he remembered the banner rising and falling above the foreign camp, how its colors had remained in his mind long after the voices faded. He had thought at first that the banner frightened him. Then the weapons. Then the number of men who might follow. Only now, sitting beside Alo in the lamp's quiet glow, did he understand that those things had merely pointed toward the deeper fear beneath them.

"When I saw them," Shilah said, "I did not think of myself."

Alo's hand remained steady in his.

"I know."

"I thought of the settlement. The children. The elders. The lake."

"Yes."

Shilah closed his eyes.

"And then I thought of this hut."

The lamp flame bent slightly as a faint draft moved through the room.

Alo leaned closer, resting his forehead against Shilah's shoulder. He did not tell him not to fear. He did not shame the fear or call it an illusion too quickly. Instead he allowed it to exist between them, visible and unhidden, until it no longer needed to disguise itself as anger or courage.

"My grandmother once told me that people suffer because they try to hold water with closed fists," Alo said softly. "The tighter they grip, the faster it leaves them. But when the hand opens, the water touches the skin before returning to where it belongs."

Shilah listened.

"I hated that teaching when I was a child," Alo continued. "It sounded like surrender."

"And now?"

"Now I know surrender is not always weakness. Sometimes it is the moment we stop fighting the shape of truth."

Shilah looked down at him. "If war comes, truth may take many things."

"Yes."

"It may take me."

Alo lifted his head.

"It may."

"It may take you."

A sadness entered Alo's face then, but not despair. The difference mattered. His eyes glistened beneath the lamplight, and in them Shilah saw not indifference to loss, but a love vast enough to face it without turning away.

"It may," Alo said again.

The answer hurt because it did not hide from anything.

Shilah drew a slow breath.

"How can you say that with peace?"

Alo touched his chest lightly, then touched Shilah's.

"Because this is not the final place where we meet."

For a long moment, the words rested between them with the quiet force of something already known before it was spoken. Outside, the lake continued its ancient breathing. Beyond the ridge, beyond the desert, beyond every visible thing, Puha moved through forms that appeared, vanished, and appeared again. Shilah had heard such teachings since childhood. He had repeated them beside fires, listened to them during ceremonies, accepted them in the way one accepts the sunrise. Yet hearing them now, with Alo's hand against his chest and the possibility of loss standing so near, changed them. They were no longer teachings. They were demands.

Alo seemed to understand this.

"The body is a doorway," he said. "Beautiful, sacred, temporary. We honor it because Puha moves through it, but we do not mistake it for the whole house."

Shilah lowered his gaze.

"And if I cannot remember that when the weapons come?"

"Then remember this."

Alo leaned forward and kissed him, not with urgency, not with fear, but with a gentleness that made the moment feel larger than desire. Shilah received the kiss as one receives water after a long crossing. When Alo pulled away, the warrior remained still, carrying the warmth of it like a small flame protected between both hands.

"You are afraid because you love," Alo whispered. "Do not be ashamed of that. A warrior who pretends love has not made him vulnerable does not yet understand what he is protecting."

The words entered Shilah more deeply than any warning about war.

He had imagined courage as firmness, as readiness, as the refusal to bend before danger. Alo reminded him that courage could also be tenderness kept alive inside fear. It could be the willingness to protect without believing protection granted ownership. It could be loving someone fully while knowing that the World of Form made no promise to preserve any shape forever.

Shilah reached for him and held him close.

Alo rested against his chest, and for a while neither spoke. The hut became quiet around them. The lamp burned steadily. The lake reflected the moon. The settlement slept, unaware that the first sign of a different future had already appeared beyond the mountains.

War was coming.

Yet in that moment, beneath the purple roof and the breathing silence of the lake, Shilah felt something steadier than the fear. The enemy might come with banners, weapons, hunger, and the certainty of men who believed the world became theirs because they named it. They might wound the land. They might scatter families. They might force the World of Form into shapes no one among the Nu-Mu had chosen.

But they could not enter the place where Puha held what was true.

They could not conquer what had no boundary.

They could not sever what had never belonged only to the body.

Shilah closed his eyes and pressed his lips gently against Alo's hair. The fear remained, but it no longer stood alone. Love stood with it. Acceptance stood with it. Somewhere beyond both, quiet and immeasurable, Puha remained.

For the first time since seeing the foreign banner, Shilah allowed himself to breathe.

Pamahas rose slowly, leaning against Esa as though the act of standing required her to remember the body she had nearly abandoned.

The yellow eyes surrounding the clearing withdrew into the trees. The ada'a did not flee at once, but their hunger seemed to lose its certainty. One by one, their shapes dissolved behind bark, mist, and shadow until only the faintest movement among the branches suggested they had ever been there. The creek that had raged through the Dark Woods quieted into a low, silver murmur, and the black fog that had gathered over the ground began to loosen beneath the soft radiance moving from Pamahas's skin.

Galilhai ran to her first.

She crossed the clearing without hesitation and threw her arms around Pamahas with the desperate tenderness of a child who had seen something beautiful taken away and returned before her heart knew how to survive either event. Pamahas lowered one hand to the back of Galilhai's head and held her close. For several moments, neither spoke. Galilhai wept against her, and Pamahas closed her eyes, receiving the girl's grief with a solemn gentleness that made the clearing feel less like a place of danger and more like a threshold where sorrow had been permitted to become holy.

"You are alive," Galilhai whispered.

Pamahas opened her eyes.

"Yes," she said softly. "For now."

The answer quieted the child.

Sam stood a few steps away, unable to move closer and unable to look away. She could still feel the strange calm that had passed through her before the tear fell. It had not felt like power. That was the part she could not understand. Power, as she had imagined it, should have felt forceful, urgent, overwhelming. What had moved through her had been the opposite. It had arrived only when she stopped demanding, stopped fighting, stopped trying to bend the moment into another shape. Even now, with Pamahas breathing before her, Sam did not feel victorious. She felt exposed, as though something hidden inside her had opened before she was ready to know its name.

Esa watched her from beside Pamahas.

The wolf god's golden eyes carried an expression Sam had never seen in him before. Not fear. Not surprise exactly. Something deeper and quieter, as though he had witnessed an ancient door move upon its hinges after ages of silence.

"What happened?" Sam asked.

Her voice sounded smaller than she expected.

Pamahas turned toward her. The glow that surrounded her body remained faint but steady, no longer the radiance of effortless beauty Sam had first noticed upon meeting her, but something more fragile and more profound. She looked alive, unmistakably alive, yet part of her seemed to be listening to a distance no one else could hear.

"You accepted," Esa said.

Sam shook her head slightly. "I don't know what that means."

"That is better than pretending you do."

The answer did not comfort her, but it felt true.

Pamahas released Galilhai gently and stepped toward Sam. "You did not command Puha. You did not force it to obey you. For one moment, your fear became silent enough for something greater to pass through."

Sam looked at her hands as though they belonged to someone else. "I brought you back."

"No," Pamahas said, not unkindly. "Puha returned me through you."

The distinction settled over Sam with unexpected weight. She wanted to ask why. She wanted to ask how. She wanted Esa or Pamahas to explain the boundaries of what had happened, to tell her whether she could do it again, whether she was supposed to do it again, whether the ability was a gift or a burden or both. Yet each question seemed too small for the moment. They would have turned the miracle into a problem her mind could examine from a safe distance, and nothing about what had happened felt safe.

"I felt peace," Sam said at last. "Not happiness. Not relief. Just peace."

Pamahas smiled faintly. "Then remember that feeling. Not as something to possess, but as a place within you where Puha can be heard."

Around them, the Dark Woods began to change.

At first the transformation was so delicate that Sam thought the clearing itself had merely brightened. Then color emerged from places that had seemed incapable of holding it. Gray bark revealed hidden undertones of copper, green, and deep violet. The blackened moss along the stones softened into blue and gold. Flowers that had remained closed beneath the fog opened slowly, petal by petal, releasing points of color that gathered across the forest floor like fallen pieces of sunrise. The creek cleared as it moved, carrying threads of silver light over smooth stones that had been invisible beneath the murk only moments earlier.

The change continued outward.

Branches that had twisted toward the path like warning hands gradually loosened. Leaves unfolded from dark knots along the trees. Small red beetles emerged from beneath pieces of bark and began moving across the newly brightened roots. Lavender butterflies rose from the undergrowth, their wings trembling as though they had been waiting for permission to remember flight. Far above, somewhere beyond the canopy, a bird sang one tentative note, then another, and the sound passed through the forest with the astonishment of first music.

Galilhai turned in a slow circle, her tears drying on her cheeks.

"The woods were not dead," she said.

"No," Esa replied. "Only forgotten by themselves."

Sam watched the darkness withdraw into the distance. It did not vanish entirely. It remained between certain trunks and beneath certain stones, but it no longer ruled the place. Light had not destroyed it. Light had given it proportion.

Pamahas stood beside her, one hand resting lightly against Galilhai's shoulder.

"This forest has carried fear for a long time," she said. "Fear changes what it touches. So does love. So does attention. Today it remembered another shape."

Sam looked at her. "Because of me?"

Pamahas's gaze softened. "Because of what moved through you."

Before Sam could answer, a narrow radiance appeared among the trees at the far edge of the clearing. It began as a thin line of gold along the forest floor, then widened gradually into a path. Roots pulled back from it. Branches lifted. The bushes unfolded away from one another, revealing a passage that extended through the revived woods toward a pale brightness in the distance.

The desert waited beyond it.

Sam understood before anyone spoke.

“No,” Galilhai said quietly.

Pamahas looked down at her.

The little girl’s face had changed. The joy of seeing Pamahas alive had not disappeared, but something heavier had entered it, the first recognition that receiving someone back did not mean keeping them.

“You are not coming with us,” Galilhai said.

Pamahas knelt before her. “No.”

“But you just came back.”

“Yes.”

Galilhai’s mouth trembled. “Then why?”

Pamahas reached for both of her hands. “Because every path has a place where even those who love you must stop walking beside you. If they continued beyond that place, the path would no longer belong to you.”

The child lowered her eyes.

“I don’t want it to belong to me.”

“I know.”

Pamahas pulled her into another embrace, and this time the farewell inside it was unmistakable. Galilhai held on with both arms, pressing her face against Pamahas as though she could delay the moment through the force of her love. Pamahas did not hurry her. She let the child cling to her, let her cry, let her resist the shape of what had to be, because acceptance did not always arrive as quickly as wisdom described it. Sometimes it had to pass through the body first.

When Galilhai finally stepped back, Pamahas touched the girl's cheek.

"You crossed Wono when you were afraid," she said. "You witnessed sorrow when you were too young for sorrow. You saw beauty turn dangerous and darkness reveal its hunger. Yet you are still here. Do not believe courage means the absence of fear. Courage is the part of you that keeps listening when fear becomes loud."

Galilhai nodded, though her tears continued falling.

Esa approached then, lowering his great head until his eyes were level with hers.

"And remember this," he said. "Attention is a doorway. Wherever you place it, something in you travels there first. Guard it carefully."

Galilhai looked at him with solemn concentration, as though she understood enough to know she would understand more later.

Then Pamahas turned to Sam.

For some reason, facing her felt harder.

Sam had not expected to need Pamahas so much. She had not expected to trust her voice, her steadiness, her strange certainty. Yet standing before her now, Sam understood that the Other World had become less impossible because Pamahas had been there to interpret its wonder. Without her, the path ahead felt suddenly vast.

"I don't know what I'm doing," Sam said.

"No one does at the beginning of a true path."

"That isn't reassuring."

Pamahas smiled, and for a moment the familiar warmth returned to her face. "It is not meant to reassure you. It is meant to free you from pretending."

Sam looked toward the bright path opening through the woods. "What if I can't do it again?"

"Healing?"

Sam nodded.

Pamahas considered this with the seriousness the question deserved. "Then you will not do it again until you can. Gifts are not servants. They are relationships. You do not own what moved through you today. You learn how to become worthy of its trust."

The words entered Sam slowly.

"What am I supposed to do?"

"Stay awake inside yourself. When fear rises, do not worship it. When grief arrives, do not flee from it. When power comes, do not mistake it for yourself."

Sam swallowed.

"And if I fail?"

"Then learn."

The simplicity of the answer nearly broke her.

Pamahas stepped closer and placed both hands over Sam's hands. Her touch was warm, but beneath the warmth was something else, something that felt like distance, as though part of her still remembered the place from which she had been returned.

"You brought me back," Pamahas said softly. "But do not carry that as pride. Carry it as responsibility."

Sam nodded.

"I'll try."

"That is enough for now."

Esa moved beside Pamahas, his large form outlined by the renewed light of the forest. "The desert beyond these woods will not welcome you or oppose you. It will reveal what you bring into it."

Sam looked at the pale opening ahead.

"What are we looking for?"

"The same thing all beings seek, whether they know it or not," Esa said. "The way through."

The answer gave her direction without giving her certainty, which seemed to be the only kind of answer Esa ever offered.

Pamahas looked from Sam to Galilhai, and the softness in her expression deepened. "This is goodbye for now."

Galilhai began crying again, but this time she did not step forward. She remained where she was, struggling to let the words exist.

"For now?" she asked.

Pamahas nodded. "All true meetings continue beyond the moment when form separates."

Sam felt the truth of those words before she could have expressed it. Goodbye did not mean absence. Not here. Not entirely. It meant a change in form, a movement from visible companionship into something quieter and more difficult to trust.

Pamahas and Esa stepped aside.

The path brightened.

Sam took Galilhai's hand.

Together they entered the passage through the restored woods. On either side of them, flowers leaned toward the light. Butterflies crossed the air in lavender flashes. The creek followed briefly beside the path before disappearing beneath smooth stones, its song fading behind them as they walked.

Neither girl spoke. There was too much to carry and no language wide enough to hold it.

Near the end of the forest, Sam looked back.

Pamahas stood beside Esa at the edge of the clearing. The red-haired woman lifted one hand in farewell. The wolf god remained still, watching with the patience of mountains and stars.

Then the trees shifted gently between them.

The clearing disappeared.

Sam held Galilhai's hand more tightly and continued forward until the final branches thinned and the last leaves gave way to open air. The revived colors of the Dark Woods ended behind them, and ahead stretched a vast desert of pale sand beneath an immense sky.

For a moment, both girls stood at the threshold.

Behind them waited the forest, transformed by a miracle neither of them fully understood. Before them waited the desert, silent and immeasurable, offering no promise except distance.

Sam drew a slow breath.

Then, still holding Galilhai's hand, she stepped into the open sand.

CHAPTER XXIV

Let There Be Light

Let our souls shine through our words and actions, and we'll witness that there is no such thing as darkness. Shadows are nowhere to be found when the light stops being obstructed by useless layers.

Noah watched Fannette Island rise from the water ahead of them. From the boat, the island appeared smaller than it had from the shore, yet somehow more imposing. Granite slopes broke through the surface of Emerald Bay like the exposed back of something ancient resting beneath the lake, while pines and shrubs clung to the stone with a stubbornness that made the place seem both fragile and unwilling to disappear. At the summit, the Tea House stood beneath the noon sun, solitary and pale against the wide blue sky.

Noah felt the miniature Wono inside his pocket.

The artifact rested there with a weight that had begun to feel less physical than moral. Since morning, every decision had seemed to gather around it. Every movement toward the lake, every unanswered question, every strange discovery hidden inside Annika Petersen's world had drawn them closer to this moment. The sunlight reflected from the turquoise water and moved across his face in trembling patterns. Ale had joked earlier that his gray eyes looked almost blue now, but Noah felt the change as something deeper than light playing tricks upon the surface. Something inside him had shifted. He could not have explained it, and he did not try.

He was thinking of Sam.

Not as she was now, lost somewhere beyond the World of Form, but as she had been years ago, before grief, before Tahoe, before any of them had known enough to be afraid of lakes, dreams, or impossible things.

The memory returned with such clarity that for a few moments the boat, the island, and the shining water around him seemed to recede.

He was eight years old again, standing in the backyard of a neighbor's house during a birthday party where the adults had gathered under a white canopy and the children had been left to invent a world among trees, lawn chairs, flowerpots, and a wagon-style planter overflowing with bright summer blooms. They had been playing hide-and-seek. Noah had been the seeker, and he had already found everyone except Sam.

At first he believed she had found the best hiding place.

Then he heard a small sound behind the planter.

It was not laughter, nor the contained excitement of a child trying not to be discovered, but something softer.

He moved closer and saw her crouched behind the wooden wheel of the planter with both hands cupped near the ground. A clay pot had fallen beside her and broken into several pieces, spilling dark soil across the grass. Noah could see her feet beneath the planter, and by the rules of the game he should have called out that he had found her. Instead he watched in silence.

Sam was not hiding.

A small bird lay in the soil where the pot had shattered, one wing trembling against the grass. Sam had removed one of the paper napkins from the party table and was trying to gather the creature into it without hurting it. Her eyes were wide with worry, but she was not crying. She was speaking to the bird in a voice so low that Noah could not hear the words. He remembered thinking, even then, that she sounded less like a child playing pretend and more like someone making a promise.

When she finally noticed him, she did not ask him not to tell the others where she was.

She only said, "Help me."

So he did.

That was the first thing Noah remembered clearly about loving Sam, though at eight years old he had not known the word for it. He remembered the feeling instead. The strange certainty that some people noticed suffering before they noticed winning. The knowledge, quiet and immediate, that Sam belonged to that rare kind of person.

Ale's voice returned him to the boat.

"You're thinking about her."

Noah looked away from the island.

Ale stood beside him near the taffrail, her hair moving softly in the wind. She did not say Sam's name. She did not need to.

"I keep thinking about the first time I saw her," Noah said.

Ale's expression softened.

"She was trying to save an injured bird at a birthday party," he continued. "Everyone else was playing. She stopped."

"That sounds like Sam."

Noah nodded, but the movement felt heavy. "I should have told her."

"That you love her?"

He looked toward the water again. "Yes. But not only that."

Ale waited.

"I should have told her what she was. What she is. I think part of me always assumed there would be time."

The boat moved steadily toward the island.

Ale leaned against the railing beside him. "After her mom died, Sam could barely survive anyone looking at her too directly. You were there in the only way she could accept. You didn't force her to speak. You didn't try to fix what couldn't be fixed. You stayed."

"I stayed too quietly."

"Maybe," Ale said. "But quiet was all she could bear then."

Maia approached from behind them, holding the folded sketch they had found in the hidden drawer beneath Vikingsholm. She had been studying it since they left the estate, turning it occasionally as if the paper might reveal another message if viewed from the correct angle.

"For what it's worth," Maia said, "I think Sam knows more than she admits."

Noah gave her a faint smile. "About what?"

"Everything." She folded the sketch carefully. "She's the kind of person who pretends not to know what people feel because admitting it would make her responsible for answering."

Ale glanced at Maia with mild surprise. "That is the most emotionally observant thing you've said all week."

Maia shrugged. "I observe things. Sometimes those things are people."

The three of them stood together in silence for a moment.

Inside the cabin, Honi guided the boat toward the island with steady concentration. He had said little since they left Vikingsholm. Every now and then he glanced toward the water ahead, his face unreadable behind the reflection on the glass.

Ale lowered her voice.

"I still don't trust him."

Noah followed her gaze toward the cabin. "Because of what he knows?"

"Because of what he chooses not to know."

Maia looked toward Honi as well. "That's actually worse."

Ale nodded. "He has answers when they make him necessary and uncertainty when they protect him. I don't like that."

Noah considered this. He had wanted to believe Honi because they needed him, because Honi knew the lake, because Honi had guided them to places they never would have found alone. Yet need had a way of dressing suspicion in patience. He knew that too.

"He could have left us lost in Vikingsholm," Noah said. "He didn't."

"People can help you toward the place where they intend to betray you," Ale replied.

Maia looked at her. "That is deeply unsettling."

"It's also true."

Noah said nothing.

In his pocket, Wono seemed to press more heavily against him.

The boat reached the island a few minutes later.

Honi brought it close to a small stretch of rocky shore where the water lapped quietly against stone. One by one, they stepped from the vessel onto Fannette Island. The place felt different beneath their feet than it had appeared from a distance. The vegetation was thicker, almost excessive in places, pushing through cracks in the granite and crowding the narrow path that climbed toward the summit. Shrubs leaned across the old cobblestone road as though attempting to reclaim it, and the stones themselves had shifted out of alignment after years of weather, roots, and neglect.

A small wooden sign stood near the path, half swallowed by brush.

An arrow had been carved deeply into its surface.

TEA HOUSE

The letters had faded, but the cuts remained.

They climbed slowly beneath the noon sun. Heat settled over the island in shimmering waves, though the breeze from Emerald Bay moved between the rocks often enough to keep the ascent bearable. Through gaps in the shrubs, the lake appeared in sudden flashes of blue so intense that the color seemed unreal. Behind them, Vikingsholm had already begun to look distant, almost innocent, its secrets hidden once more beneath trees and stone.

"It's strange," Maia said, pausing to catch her breath. "From the shore, this place looks decorative. Like a postcard."

Ale looked up the steepening path. "That's probably what it was supposed to look like."

"And beneath that?"

Ale touched the key in her pocket. "That's what we're here to find out."

Honi climbed ahead of them with his cane, though he moved more steadily than his age and posture suggested. Every so often he stopped, not only to rest but to look toward the Tea House. Noah noticed this and said nothing.

The path turned sharply near a drop in the rock, then straightened toward the summit.

The Tea House appeared fully before them.

It was smaller than Noah expected.

The one-story stone building sat upon rough ground where large granite rocks lifted it above the rest of the island. Its cubic shape made it appear less like a cottage than a sealed box. Large windows occupied each side, though their glass had clouded with age, dust, and scratches left by branches. The wooden door at the entrance had rotted badly, barely held in place by rusted hinges. Nearby stood a small shed with a tarnished zinc roof, its walls warped and leaning toward the Tea House as if the structure had grown tired and chosen the stone building as its final support.

For several seconds, none of them moved.

The Tea House did not look haunted. That would have been easier to understand. Instead, it carried the unsettling impression of a place emptied deliberately, as though its true purpose had been removed while the shell remained behind.

"What are we looking for?" Noah asked.

Ale removed the rusted key from her pocket. "Anything that was meant to stay hidden."

Noah approached the door and placed one hand against the wood. It shifted immediately beneath his touch. A brittle crack traveled down the frame. He stepped back just as the hinges gave way and the door collapsed inward, striking the floor with a dull, exhausted sound.

Dust rose into the sunlight.

Maia coughed and waved a hand in front of her face. "Well. That answers the question of whether the key opens the front door."

They entered carefully.

The interior consisted of a single room, though the word room felt generous. The place was little more than stone, light, and the remains of an intention no one had fulfilled in decades. The wallpaper had peeled away in long strips, exposing portions of cold wall beneath it. Curtains had fallen below the windows and lay stiff with dust and sand. At the center of the room stood a long dining table, though no chairs surrounded it. That absence bothered Ale immediately.

"Where are the chairs?" she asked.

Honi stood near the doorway. "There used to be four."

"Used to be?"

"I have seen old photographs."

Maia moved toward the table, her eyes already searching. "Four chairs, no tea service, no cabinet, no stove, no shelves. For a Tea House, this place had very little interest in tea."

Noah looked around.

The more he studied the room, the more he understood what she meant. Nothing about the arrangement suggested leisure. There were no signs of comfort, no lingering elegance, no trace of the casual luxury one might expect from a wealthy woman's island retreat. The table faced the western window, but the center of its surface bore faint scratches that seemed too deliberate to be accidental. Lines intersected there in a worn circular pattern, as though something had repeatedly been placed upon the same spot and turned by careful hands.

Ale noticed it too.

"Annika came here often."

Maia bent closer to the tabletop. "And she kept using this."

Noah looked toward Honi. "You said she rarely spent time here."

"That is what the family said."

"And what do you say?"

Honi's expression remained difficult to read. "I say families often preserve the version of a person they can explain."

Maia circled the table, running her fingers near the carved border without touching it too firmly. "There are marks here."

Ale joined her. "Like the exhibitor."

"Similar, but not identical."

Near the table's edge, beneath a layer of dust, a small pyramid had been carved into the wood. It was almost hidden among a pattern of waves and branches, but Maia found it quickly. This time she did not press it immediately. Instead she leaned down and studied the design surrounding it.

"There should be another symbol," she said.

Ale looked across the table. "Circle with a line?"

"Maybe."

Noah walked to the opposite side. "Here."

He brushed dust aside and revealed a small fish burned into the wood near one of the table legs.

Maia frowned. "That's different."

"Try them together," Ale said.

Maia placed one finger on the pyramid. Noah pressed the fish.

Nothing happened.

Maia glanced at the scratched circle in the center of the table. "Wait."

She moved to the worn pattern and placed her palm over it. The wood felt smooth there, almost polished by repeated contact. Noah kept his finger on the fish while Ale pressed the pyramid.

A mechanism shifted beneath the table.

The sound was low, metallic, and much deeper than any of them expected.

A hidden drawer slid open from the side facing the western window.

Noah stared at it.

Maia gave a small nod. "That's more like it."

The smell that emerged was not cedar this time.

It was smoke.

Old smoke.

Ale slowly opened the drawer the rest of the way.

Inside lay a black-and-white photograph, a small ceramic bowl with a matching lid, a sealed glass bottle filled with clear liquid, and another cube-shaped artifact wrapped in brittle cloth.

No one reached for anything at first.

The hidden drawer did not feel like storage.

It felt like instruction.

Ale lifted the photograph first.

It showed a fisherman standing barefoot on a boat, holding up an enormous trout with both hands. He wore faded jeans and a flannel shirt. His smile had the proud exhaustion of someone who had struggled against the lake and won, at least for a moment. Beside him rested a woman's suitcase with a delicate floral print. On top of it sat the same hat Mrs. Petersen had worn in the train photograph.

Maia leaned closer. "Why would her hat be on a fisherman's boat?"

Noah looked at the image carefully. "Maybe she was there."

"Then why isn't she in the picture?"

Ale turned the photograph over.

A message had been written across the back in Annika Petersen's careful hand.

AND GOD SAID, LET THERE BE LIGHT, AND THERE WAS LIGHT.

GENESIS 1:3

The words seemed to brighten the room and darken it at the same time.

Maia read them silently, her lips barely moving.

"Job in the first drawer," she said. "Genesis in the second."

Ale nodded. "First repentance. Then creation."

Noah looked toward the covered cube. "Or revelation."

Honi remained near the doorway, watching them.

Ale noticed but said nothing.

Maia unwrapped the cloth from the cube. Like the first, it appeared to be made of pinewood. The faces were marked with different burned symbols, though one side bore a single letter carved deeper than the rest.

R.

Noah removed the first cube from his bag and placed it beside the second.

The first bore the letter A.

A and R.

Maia pushed her glasses up the bridge of her nose. "They were meant to be found together."

"Or used together," Ale said.

Noah touched one cube, then the other. Both carried the same impossible density, the same strange sense that something within them possessed weight without stillness. The longer they rested beside each other, the more the air around them seemed to tighten, not visibly, but in the body, the way pressure changes before a storm.

"What do we do with them?" Noah asked.

No one answered.

Then Ale looked toward the ceramic bowl.

The lid had been placed upside down, and inside it rested three old matches, preserved in a strip of folded paper. Beside the bowl, the glass bottle remained sealed with wax.

Maia read the faded label. "Benzene."

Ale's eyes moved from the bottle to the bowl, then to the two wooden cubes.

Noah understood at the same moment she did.

"No," he said. "We are not setting mysterious artifacts on fire simply because Mrs. Petersen left us matches and a bottle of benzene."

Maia adjusted her glasses.

"I have to admit that's a reasonable concern."

Ale did not smile. "She left Job. Then Genesis. Repentance. Then light."

"Light does not always mean fire," Noah said.

"In this drawer, it might."

Honi finally spoke from the doorway.

"Mrs. Annika believed some things had to lose their outer form before their purpose could be seen."

All three turned toward him.

"You knew that?" Ale asked.

"I knew she said it," Honi replied. "I did not know what she meant."

Noah looked at the cubes again. The wood seemed ordinary and impossible at once. He thought of Sam holding an injured bird in a paper napkin, of her hands trying to save something fragile. Then he thought of the miniature Wono in his pocket, and of the lake waiting beyond the island.

"We don't have time to be wrong," he said.

Ale met his eyes. "We also don't have time to ignore the only instructions Annika left us."

No one argued further.

Ale poured the clear liquid into the ceramic bowl. The sharp chemical smell spread immediately through the room. Maia placed both cubes inside with visible reluctance, arranging them so the carved letters faced upward. A. R. For a moment the symbols looked meaningless. Then the liquid moved around them, and the burned markings across the wood darkened as though waking.

Ale struck a match.

The flame trembled in the draft from the broken doorway.

She dropped it into the bowl.

Fire rose instantly.

Not wildly.

Not like ordinary fuel catching.

The flame gathered itself around the cubes in a clean, narrow column of pale gold, burning upward without smoke. Noah stepped back. Maia covered her mouth. Ale watched without blinking.

The wood did not burn from the outside inward.

It split.

Fine cracks opened across the surface of both cubes, tracing the burned symbols as though the markings had been seams all along. Light escaped through them. The letters A and R glowed briefly, then vanished beneath the fire as the pinewood peeled away in curling black layers.

Inside each cube, something metallic appeared.

Gold.

When the flames began to weaken, Ale placed the lid over the bowl. The room fell into sudden quiet. They waited until the heat diminished, then Noah removed the lid with the edge of his sleeve.

Two golden cartridges rested in the ash.

They were rifle rounds, but unlike any Noah had ever seen. The casings gleamed with a dull, ancient luster, and each bullet bore a small engraved symbol near its base. One carried the pyramid. The other carried the fish.

Noah turned the cartridges beneath the light.

The symbols had not merely been engraved.

They appeared worn, as though countless hands had touched them before the bullets were hidden inside the wooden shells.

"Look at this."

Maia leaned closer.

Around the pyramid was a second marking, nearly invisible beneath the gold.

Three small lines.

Not scratches.

Deliberate.

The same three lines appeared beneath the fish.

Noah frowned.

"I've seen this before."

"Where?"

He shook his head.

"I don't know."

The certainty remained nonetheless.

Somewhere in the growing maze of mysteries surrounding Wono, Lake Tahoe, and the Other World, those symbols already existed.

Maia whispered, "They were never dice."

Ale stared at them. "They were hiding what the dice were protecting."

Noah reached into the bowl and lifted one carefully. It was warm but not burning. As he wiped ash from the casing, the engraved pyramid caught the light from the window.

"It's a bullet," he said.

Honi approached for the first time since they entered the room. "May I?"

Noah hesitated, then handed it to him.

Honi examined the cartridge closely. His face remained calm, but something in his eyes changed with terrible subtlety. It was gone almost as soon as Noah noticed it.

"Old," Honi said. "And unusual. Not for the rifles in the shed."

Maia looked toward the second cartridge. "Then what are they for?"

Honi returned the bullet to Noah.

"For the weapon that was meant to use them."

The answer chilled the room.

"Where is that weapon?" Ale asked.

"I do not know."

Noah put both cartridges into his pocket. He did not like the feel of them resting near Wono.

"We can search later," he said. "Right now we need to get back to the boat."

They left the Tea House with the photograph, the empty bottle, and the two golden cartridges. Honi crossed to the shed and unlocked it with the key he had brought. Inside, he found an old hunting rifle wrapped in cloth, a small box of ammunition, rope, lamps, and other equipment from another era of the estate. He moved slowly, almost ceremonially, as though each object required recognition before being taken.

Noah waited near the Tea House with Ale and Maia.

"There has to be a reason Annika hid bullets inside those cubes," Ale said.

"There is," Noah replied. "We just don't know it yet."

Maia looked toward the shed. "If they don't fit that rifle, then either the correct weapon is somewhere else, or the bullets are not meant to be fired in the ordinary way."

Ale turned to her. "What does that mean?"

"I have no idea," Maia admitted. "But nothing about this has behaved normally so far."

Noah looked toward the lake. "We can figure it out after we release Wono."

Behind them, Honi emerged from the shed carrying the rifle.

He no longer used his cane.

At first, Noah noticed only the absence of the tapping sound.

Then he turned.

Honi stood several feet away, holding the rifle with both hands. His posture had changed completely. The stoop had vanished. The hesitation in his movements was gone. He did not look younger exactly, but the weakness he had worn since they met him had fallen away like a discarded garment.

The rifle was pointed at Noah's chest.

Ale went still.

Maia stopped breathing.

Noah slowly raised his hands.

Honi's expression was calm.

That was what frightened Noah most.

"Honi," he said carefully.

The old man looked almost sorrowful. "I wish there had been another way."

Ale's voice hardened. "There was. You could have told the truth."

"If I had told you the truth, you would have refused to come."

"Because you were planning to betray us."

"No," Honi said. "Because you still believe survival is the highest good."

The wind moved across the island, carrying the scent of pine and heated stone.

Noah kept his hands raised. "What do you want?"

"The miniature Wono."

Noah's jaw tightened.

Honi shifted the rifle slightly, not enough to fire, but enough to remind them that argument had limits.

"Place it on the ground and step away."

Noah did not move.

Honi's eyes softened with something that almost resembled pity. "You think I am destroying your chance to save the world."

"Aren't you?"

"I am refusing to postpone what must happen."

Ale stared at him. "You're helping the monster."

"I am helping the circle close."

The words landed with terrible quiet.

Noah slowly removed Wono from his pocket. The miniature pyramid rested in his palm, impossibly small for what it carried.

"You said you wanted to release it into the lake."

"I said what you needed to hear."

Maia's voice trembled.

"Why?"

Honi looked toward Lake Tahoe.

For the first time, his calmness seemed to reveal the ruin beneath it.

"Because everything separated suffers," he said quietly. "Every body. Every name. Every memory."

"Children suffer too," Maia said.

Honi nodded.

"Yes."

The answer struck them harder than denial would have.

Maia stared at him.

"And you're willing to accept that?"

"I am willing to accept what already exists."

"That's not acceptance."

Her voice had sharpened unexpectedly.

"That's choosing not to care."

For the first time, something flickered behind Honi's eyes.

Not anger.

Weariness.

"You believe compassion means preventing suffering," he said.

"Doesn't it?"

"No."

His gaze drifted toward the water.

"Compassion is seeing suffering clearly enough that you stop lying about what causes it."

"No," Noah said. "We call it life because people matter."

"They matter because they are Puha," Honi replied. "And because they are Puha, they do not need to remain trapped in pieces."

Ale shook her head. "That is not compassion. That is surrender dressed as wisdom."

Honi looked at her, and for one brief moment anger flickered behind his composure before vanishing again.

"You speak from the privilege of wanting more time."

"I speak from the privilege of not wanting everyone dead."

"Death is a word the body invented."

"And pain?" Maia asked quietly. "Did the body invent that too?"

Honi's gaze moved to her.

Maia did not look away, though her face had gone pale.

"No," he said. "Pain is the sound of separation."

"Then why would you choose more of it?"

The question reached him. Noah saw it. For a moment Honi's certainty faltered, not because he did not have an answer, but because the answer cost him something to speak.

"Because a wound cannot heal while the knife remains inside."

Ale's voice lowered. "And you think the World of Form is the knife."

"I know it is."

Noah felt the miniature Wono growing heavier in his hand.

"What happened to you?"

Honi stared at him.

For a long moment, the wind was the only sound between them.

"I once believed my people would listen," Honi said. "I studied every story they had preserved. Every ceremony. Every warning. Every fragment that remained after the old knowledge was broken by time, conquest, shame, and survival. I believed understanding would make me useful. I believed usefulness would become trust. I believed trust would become leadership."

His eyes did not leave Noah's.

"But the tribe did not need a leader who wanted to be chosen. It needed servants. I did not understand the difference until it was too late."

Honi continued.

"When the dreams began, I thought Puha had finally answered me. I saw the lake open. I saw Wono sink. I saw the boundaries dissolve. For the first time, I understood that all suffering came from division. I went back to them with the truth."

"And they rejected it," Ale said.

"They recognized the hunger inside it before I did."

Ale had been staring at him for several seconds.

"No," she said quietly.

Honi looked at her.

"That's not what they saw."

The old man's expression hardened slightly.

"And what do you believe they saw?"

Ale did not hesitate.

"You keep talking about humanity."

She stepped forward.

"Humanity. Creation. The world. Puha."

Her eyes never left his.

"But every time someone mentions an actual person, you stop talking."

Silence settled between them.

"Sam."

Ale pointed toward Noah.

"His grandmother."

She pointed toward Maia.

"The people in Tahoe."

Her voice softened.

"You don't hate humanity, Honi."

The words landed with startling precision.

"You've simply stopped loving people."

The sentence silenced everyone.

Honi's face hardened again, though sadness remained beneath it.

"They called me dangerous. Perhaps they were right. But danger does not make truth untrue."

Noah stared at him. "You know what you are doing will hurt people."

"Yes."

"Children."

"Yes."

"Sam."

Honi's expression shifted faintly.

Noah stepped forward despite the rifle.

"She is trapped because of this. Because of the monster. Because of whatever is happening between the lake and Wono. And you're willing to let her die for an idea."

Honi tightened his grip on the rifle. "Do not mistake my willingness to sacrifice for indifference."

"That is exactly what indifference sounds like when it learns sacred words."

For the first time, Honi looked wounded.

Then the wound closed.

"Place Wono on the ground."

Noah held the artifact a moment longer.

Ale's eyes flicked toward him, warning him not to try anything. Maia stood frozen beside her, watching the rifle with the stillness of someone calculating and finding no path that did not end in blood.

Noah lowered himself slowly and placed Wono on the stone.

"Step back."

He did.

Honi approached without lowering the rifle. He crouched with surprising ease, picked up the miniature pyramid, and placed it inside his coat pocket. The movement was gentle, almost reverent.

"You do not have to do this," Noah said.

Honi looked toward the lake. "I have been doing this for years."

The words chilled Noah more than the weapon.

Honi gestured toward the path with the rifle.

"Down to the shore."

No one moved.

"Please," Honi said.

The softness made the command worse.

They obeyed.

The descent felt different from the climb. Earlier, Honi had leaned on his cane and allowed them to believe age had made him fragile. Now he walked behind them with steady steps, the rifle aimed without trembling. The island that had seemed lush and mysterious on the way up now felt like a trap closing around them. Every stone shifted beneath their feet. Every bush seemed too dense. Every glimpse of blue water looked impossibly far away.

They reached the rocky shore within minutes.

The boat moved gently beside the stones.

Honi stopped several yards away and motioned for them to remain where they were.

"You are leaving us here?" Ale asked.

"For now."

Maia's voice sharpened. "Without food? Without water?"

"You will find shelter."

Noah stared at him. "Where are you going?"

Honi looked toward the open lake.

"To stop you from wasting the last mercy this world will ever receive."

He boarded the boat alone.

Noah took a step forward.

Honi raised the rifle.

Noah stopped.

The engine started.

The boat pulled away from Fannette Island, first slowly, then with gathering speed. Honi did not look back. He stood at the helm with Wono in his possession, moving across the blue surface of Lake Tahoe toward a destination none of them could name.

For several moments, none of the friends spoke.

They had been deceived. Used by a man they had chosen to trust and stranded upon an island that suddenly felt far smaller than before.

The realization settled over them with a humiliation more painful than fear. They had believed themselves cautious. They had questioned him. They had suspected him. And still he had guided them exactly where he wanted them to go.

Ale turned away first, cursing under her breath.

Maia sank onto a rock, her hands trembling.

Noah remained standing.

His pocket felt wrong without Wono.

Then the light changed.

It did not dim gradually.

It withdrew.

The noon sun remained overhead, yet the island seemed to fall beneath a shadow that did not belong to any cloud. The water beyond the shore lost its turquoise brilliance and turned gray from within, as though color had been drained out of it. Across the lake, a vast bank of fog advanced with unnatural speed, swallowing the horizon, the mountains, and the sky behind it.

Ale looked up.

"What is that?"

Noah knew before he answered.

The memory of Lake Tahoe's earlier warning returned with terrible clarity: fog moving where fog should not move, water changing color, the world becoming unsafe around something unseen.

"We need shelter," he said.

The wind struck them hard enough to bend the shrubs along the shore.

Maia stood slowly, her eyes fixed on the approaching fog. "That is not weather."

Noah grabbed her arm. "Tea House. Now."

They ran.

The fog rolled across the lake like a living wall. Its surface twisted and folded into shapes that refused to remain shapes for long. For an instant, Noah thought he saw faces within it, enormous and stretched, mouths opening wider than any human mouth could open. Then they dissolved into spirals, then into hollow sockets, then into darkness moving inside whiteness. The mind wanted to make symbols from what it saw, but the fog changed too quickly, devouring interpretation before it could become thought.

The wind carried a sound with it.

Not thunder.

Not voices.

Something between breath and hunger.

They climbed the path as fast as they could. Loose stones shifted beneath their shoes. Branches lashed against their arms and faces. The air thickened around them with each step, damp and metallic, filling their mouths with the taste of old water.

The Tea House appeared above them through the moving haze.

Almost there.

Then Maia stopped.

She stood near the edge of the path, staring out across the lake from the cliffside.

Noah turned back. "Maia!"

She did not move.

The fog had reached the lower rocks of the island. It climbed upward in long, reaching strands, swallowing trees, stones, and sunlight. Within it, the impossible faces appeared again, not fully formed, but suggested by shadow and absence. Long mouths opened in silence. Empty eyes stretched across the gray.

Maia's voice was barely audible over the wind.

"This is it."

Ale grabbed her hand. "Move."

Maia looked at her, and the rational steadiness that usually anchored her had vanished.

"This is the end."

Noah took her other arm.

"No," he said, though he did not know whether he believed it. "Not yet."

Together, they pulled Maia away from the cliff and ran toward the Tea House.

Behind them, the fog climbed the island with impossible speed.

Trees disappeared inside it. Then rocks.

Then, entire sections of shoreline vanished as though they had never existed.

Noah glanced back once.

Far out upon the water, where sunlight still survived, he could see Honi's boat racing toward the center of the lake.

The vessel looked impossibly small against the advancing wall of gray.

For a brief instant, a shaft of sunlight pierced the fog and illuminated the miniature silhouette.

Then the light disappeared. The boat vanished. The fog continued advancing.

And for the first time since arriving at Lake Tahoe, Noah wondered whether darkness was not the absence of light, but the memory of a light that had already withdrawn.

CHAPTER XXV
The Hollow Beyond Wono

You don't need to pursue anything in this life. It's not that you will become this or that. You already are. And if you realize this fact, you will live a life with purpose and endless possibilities.

The settlement had fallen into a silence that did not belong to fear. It was older than fear, deeper than uncertainty, the kind of silence that settled over the earth when words had already done what they could and the spirit was asked to listen without reaching for explanation.

Dozens of Nu-Mu sat facing Pyramid Lake. Elders, hunters, artisans, healers, and warriors formed wide circles around a small fire whose smoke rose without wandering, as if the morning itself had chosen not to disturb it. Beyond them, the lake stretched beneath the paling sky, holding the first bands of dawn in long, trembling reflections of silver and gold.

At the center of the gathering, Alo sat with his eyes closed.

The wooden striker moved slowly along the inner rim of the singing bowl he had shaped many winters before, and from that gentle movement came a sound so delicate at first that it seemed less created than discovered. It rose from the bronze in a patient vibration, widening through the settlement, passing over the knees of the seated people, through the breath of the horses, across the dry grasses, and outward toward the listening water.

No one spoke. The sound entered them quietly. It did not command or instruct. It gathered.

For a while, even the wind seemed to lower itself before passing through the field. The lake answered with a small movement along the shore, and the reeds bent together as if they too had heard something beneath the note, something older than music and nearer to prayer.

Then Alo lifted the striker.

The bowl became silent.

Still, the sound remained.

Wovoka stepped forward from the edge of the circle.

The old medicine man stood with Pyramid Lake behind him and the morning light touching the silver strands in his hair. He looked upon his people slowly, not as a leader counting those who would fight, but as a father recognizing every face before him. Children sat close to their mothers. Elders watched with clear, solemn eyes. Warriors rested their hands near spears whose tips waited to be marked with the glowing clay prepared by the older woman.

For several breaths, Wovoka said nothing.

Then he spoke.

"Many believe darkness is the enemy of light."

His voice carried gently across the gathering.

"But darkness is not strong because it is dark. It is strong only where nothing has remembered itself."

The people listened without moving.

"A shadow cannot bear the flame, not because the flame wounds it, but because the flame reveals it. And what has spent its life hiding from truth will call revelation pain."

The old woman lowered her fingers into the dark clay basin. The liquid inside it glowed faintly green, as though some hidden life had awakened beneath its surface.

Wovoka turned his gaze toward the lake.

"Water does not fear its own reflection. It receives what is shown. It trembles, it breaks, it gathers itself again, and still it remains water."

The first sunlight touched the edge of Wono in the distance.

"The enemy approaching our land has forgotten this. It has forgotten the beginning from which all things come. It has forgotten that even power without Puha becomes hunger, and hunger without remembrance becomes ruin."

A faint movement passed through the warriors, but none interrupted him.

"We do not rise today because we desire war. We rise because life has asked us to remember who we are when death stands before us wearing the shape of certainty."

He placed one hand over his chest.

"The coyote must remember."

His eyes moved toward the hills.

"The eagle must remember."

Then his gaze returned to the gathered people.

"The Nu-Mu must remember."

The old woman began moving among the warriors. One by one, she touched the glowing clay to the tips of their spears, and each weapon received the mark in silence. When she came to Shilah, she paused before him and studied the young warrior's face.

He stood still beneath her gaze.

No fear showed in him, though fear was present. No pride lifted his chin, though the burden placed upon him was greater than any praise could carry.

The old woman touched the clay to his spear.

"May Puha move through your hands before anger can reach them," she said.

Shilah bowed his head.

The blessing passed through the formation until every spear carried the same green radiance, small flames of color against the widening morning.

Wovoka watched the warriors mount their horses. The animals shifted beneath them, restless but obedient, their bodies gleaming with the first warmth of the sun. Behind them, the settlement remained seated. No one cheered. No one cried out. To do so would have made the moment smaller than it was.

The warriors turned east.

For a breath, they were still.

Then Shilah lifted his spear, and the line began to move.

Across the open field, the Nu-Mu rode toward the rising sun, carrying with them the sound of Alo's bowl, the blessing of the old woman, the silence of their people, and the ancient knowledge that a shadow cannot enter a place where the soul has already awakened.

The stars continued their slow migration across the aqueous sky.

Far above the desert, they drifted through currents of luminous blue as though the heavens themselves had become a great celestial river. Their reflections shimmered faintly upon the dunes below, transforming the endless sand into a landscape suspended between earth and water, memory and dream.

Sam and Galilhai followed their passage.

The desert stretched in every direction. No mountains interrupted the horizon. No trees marked the distance. Only dunes rose and fell beneath the strange light of the Other World, their pale slopes shaped by winds that seemed older than time itself.

For a long while, neither spoke.

The silence did not feel empty.

It belonged to the desert.

The farther they walked, the more Sam sensed that this place existed beyond ordinary measures of distance and time. The stars moved. The dunes shifted. Yet the horizon never appeared closer. It was as if the landscape cared little for destinations and far more for the act of crossing.

Galilhai walked several paces ahead, occasionally stopping to watch the drifting constellations before continuing onward. There remained something profoundly childlike in her movements. Wonder reached her before fear. Curiosity arrived before doubt.

Sam found herself admiring that.

The child had crossed into another world, witnessed ancient visions, spoken with beings that defied reason, and still carried herself with the uncomplicated sincerity of someone who had not yet learned to fear every uncertainty.

The same could not be said for Sam.

Her thoughts wandered increasingly toward the World of Form, toward Noah, Maia, and Alejandra, toward the life she had left behind and the people who still inhabited it.

Most often, however, her thoughts returned to her mother.

The memory emerged gradually, not as a single image but as scattered fragments: a gentle voice speaking to a frightened patient, a hand resting upon another hand, the quiet patience with which her mother listened when listening alone seemed capable of easing another person's suffering.

As a child, Sam had never fully understood it.

She understood it a little better now.

Some people spent their lives accumulating things. Others accumulated accomplishments. Yet the individuals she admired most always seemed to be searching for something else entirely.

Something larger than themselves.

Something that connected one life to another.

The thought lingered.

Eventually she looked toward Galilhai.

"Do you ever wonder why all of this happened to us?"

The child turned.

The question seemed to surprise her.

She considered it seriously for several moments before looking toward the stars.

"I don't know."

The answer made Sam smile.

Galilhai continued walking.

"My father says that sometimes people become so busy looking for answers that they stop paying attention to what is already in front of them."

Sam recognized Wovoka immediately.

A faint laugh escaped her.

"That sounds like him."

Galilhai nodded.

"He says it all the time."

The desert wind crossed softly between them.

For a while neither spoke again.

Then the child glanced back.

"When I was little, I asked him why birds fly."

Sam waited.

"He told me the question wasn't why birds fly."

The dunes rolled endlessly around them.

"He said the real question is why people keep forgetting they can."

Sam lowered her gaze.

Something about the simplicity of the statement settled deeply within her.

Not because she fully understood it.

Because she felt that she almost did.

The journey continued.

Time loosened its grip.

The stars drifted.

The dunes changed.

Eventually exhaustion settled into their bodies.

The endless landscape seemed determined to test every remaining reserve of strength.

Without discussing it, both stopped near the crest of a dune and sat upon the warm sand.

For several moments neither moved.

Sam lowered her hand beside her.

The instant her fingers touched the ground, a subtle vibration passed through the earth.

She felt it before she saw it.

The sand began to sink inward.

A circular depression formed several yards away, and from its center emerged a column of crystalline water that rose toward the surface with impossible speed. Palm trees followed. Greenery spread outward across the surrounding dunes. Flowers unfolded among fresh leaves. Branches bent beneath the weight of fruit that had not existed a moment earlier.

Within moments, an oasis stood where only desert had been.

Galilhai laughed with delight and ran toward the nearest tree.

Sam remained seated.

The miracle did not surprise her.

Not anymore.

What captured her attention was the water.

Its surface remained perfectly still.

Not calm.

Still.

Like polished glass.

She approached slowly.

For a moment she saw only her reflection.

Then the image changed.

Another version of herself appeared beneath the surface.

Older.

Standing before a group of students.

The vision dissolved.

Another emerged.

A healer comforting someone in pain.

Then another.

A mother.

Then another.

A woman whose life had never crossed paths with Pyramid Lake.

Each possibility lingered only briefly before disappearing into the depths.

Sam watched without speaking.

The oasis offered no explanation.

It did not reveal a destiny.

It revealed possibilities.

Lives that might have been.

Lives that still existed somewhere within her.

When the final reflection faded, only her own face remained upon the water.

The surface trembled gently.

The visions vanished.

"Sam?"

She looked up.

Galilhai sat beneath a palm tree holding a piece of fruit in both hands.

The child tilted her head.

"What did you see?"

Sam considered the question.

Her gaze drifted once more toward the still water.

Then she smiled.

"I think I saw how many people can live inside a single person."

Galilhai seemed satisfied by the answer.

Together they rested beneath the oasis for a time, eating fruit and drinking from the spring while the stars continued their silent journey overhead.

When they finally resumed their walk, the desert no longer felt quite as empty.

Ahead, beyond the final dunes and beneath the hidden earth of the Hollow Beyond Wono, destiny waited.

The dunes gradually surrendered to stone.

As Sam and Galilhai crossed the final ridge, the desert opened before them and revealed the destination that had guided their journey across the Other World.

The Hollow Beyond Wono stood beneath the luminous heavens like a wound carved into the earth by an age long forgotten. Massive walls of weathered stone curved inward around a cavern entrance so vast that it seemed less constructed by nature than uncovered from beneath it. Shadows gathered within its depths, concealing whatever secrets lay hidden beyond the reach of moonlight and memory.

Both girls stopped and stood silently before the cavern entrance, allowing the immense presence of the place to settle around them.

The place possessed a presence unlike anything they had encountered during their journey. It was not the threatening sensation of a predator waiting in the darkness, nor the unease that often accompanied the unknown. Rather, it felt ancient. The kind of age that could no longer be measured by generations or centuries. Countless lives had crossed this threshold. Countless stories had begun or ended somewhere beneath those silent stones.

The wind moved softly across the desert.

Only then did Sam notice the figures.

Dark Shadows occupied the surrounding landscape in astonishing numbers. They stood upon ridges overlooking the entrance, gathered among distant rock formations, and lingered beside narrow passages leading deeper into the desert. Some appeared alone. Others stood in groups. Yet despite their numbers, the scene felt strangely empty.

None spoke, interacted, or even appeared aware of one another.

Their motionless forms resembled fractures within the world itself, places where reality had thinned and darkness had seeped through.

A subtle chill passed through Sam.

The sight disturbed her far more than any army would have.

Armies carried traces of life within them. They shifted their weight. They exchanged glances. They breathed. Even violence possessed a certain humanity when viewed from a distance.

These beings felt detached from life altogether.

The desert appeared to recognize the difference.

No animals ventured near them. The wind that moved freely across the dunes seemed to weaken as it approached their positions. Even the silence surrounding them felt unnatural, as though sound itself hesitated to linger in their presence.

Galilhai moved closer.

"They've been here for a long time," she whispered.

Sam nodded.

The realization settled heavily within her.

This was not a recently established defense.

The Dark Shadows had not discovered the caves by accident. They were guarding something beneath the earth, something important enough to station hundreds of their kind around a forgotten entrance hidden beyond the reach of ordinary worlds.

As the thought formed, another presence entered her awareness.

Esa.

His voice arrived without sound, emerging directly within her understanding.

Wait.

Sam lifted her eyes toward the sky.

For what?

The answer came gently.

For the moment they fear.

The words lingered.

Above them, the immense moon continued its slow passage across the heavens, its silver radiance spilling across the desert in waves of pale light. Only then did Sam notice another celestial body approaching from the distance, darker and smaller, moving steadily toward the greater moon's luminous face.

The eclipse had begun. At first the change was almost imperceptible as a small shadow touched the moon's edge and slowly expanded across its luminous surface.

Gradually the brilliant sphere became divided between light and darkness, and as the celestial bodies aligned, the atmosphere of the entire desert began to change.

The stars appeared to slow their migration while the wind weakened and even the dunes seemed to settle into stillness beneath an immense silence descending upon the landscape.

Sam felt it immediately. The change was not occurring around the Dark Shadows but within them.

For the first time since arriving, movement spread through their ranks.

Several lifted their heads toward the heavens. Others shifted uneasily where they stood. The rigid certainty that had defined them moments earlier began to unravel beneath the growing shadow of the eclipse.

A ripple passed through the gathering as one figure stumbled and another recoiled.

The darkness composing their forms seemed suddenly unstable, as though something hidden beneath its surface had begun struggling against confinement.

Sam stared as brief distortions moved through their bodies like images seen beneath disturbed water. For an instant, she thought she saw a face emerging from within one of them, then a hand, then another shape entirely before the darkness swallowed it once more.

The glimpses vanished almost immediately.

Yet they had been real.

Something existed beneath the darkness, something buried so deeply that even memory itself appeared unable to reach it.

A deep sadness entered Esa's presence.

For a very long time, they have survived by refusing to remember.

The words settled over her like falling ash.

Around the caves, the unrest continued to spread.

The eclipse deepened.

Light and darkness occupied the same celestial space, neither capable of fully concealing the other. The duality radiating across the heavens seemed to force a similar confrontation within the Dark Shadows themselves, exposing fractures they could no longer hide and truths they could no longer escape.

For the first time since Sam had encountered them, fear became visible. It was not fear of battle or death, but the deeper fear that accompanies recognition, the fear of seeing something one has spent an eternity avoiding.

As the eclipse approached its fullness, the path leading toward the Hollow Beyond Wono gradually opened before them.

Sam looked toward the ancient entrance.

Somewhere beneath those stones rested the Destiny Dice. Somewhere beneath those stones waited answers that had shaped generations long before her birth. Somewhere beneath those stones, the future of both worlds had already begun unfolding.

She exchanged a glance with Galilhai.

The child nodded.

Together they stepped from behind the rocks and began walking toward the cavern entrance while the eclipse darkened the heavens above them and the Dark Shadows struggled against the terrible burden of seeing themselves at last.

The eclipse continued its slow passage across the heavens.

Above the desert, light and shadow occupied the same celestial space, neither capable of fully concealing the other. The silver radiance of the greater moon remained visible around the encroaching darkness, creating a luminous ring that stretched across the landscape and painted the dunes in shades of blue, gold, and silver.

The Hollow Beyond Wono stood waiting beneath that strange light.

Around its entrance, the unrest among the Dark Shadows continued to spread. Their forms trembled and shifted as though some forgotten truth had begun stirring beneath the darkness that concealed them. The certainty that had defined them for so long appeared fractured now, replaced by something unfamiliar.

Something closer to memory.

Sam watched them quietly.

For the first time since arriving in the Other World, she felt neither fear nor confusion. What settled within her was not understanding exactly, but the quiet recognition that the struggle unfolding before her was larger than war, larger than survival, and larger even than the fate of either world.

Beside her, Galilhai gazed toward the cavern entrance.

Neither spoke.

Words felt unnecessary.

The path stretched before them.

Behind them lay everything they had known.

Ahead waited everything they did not.

Far away, beyond deserts, mountains, lakes, and worlds, Noah, Maia, Alejandra, Shilah, Wovoka, Pamahas, and Esa continued moving toward a future none of them could yet see.

They were threads of a single story, each drawn steadily toward a destination none of them yet fully understood.

The eclipse reached its fullness.

For one perfect moment, the heavens became a union of opposites. Light and darkness. Seen and unseen. Beginning and ending.

Sam lifted her eyes toward the sky.

Then she took a step forward.

Galilhai followed.

Together they crossed the threshold of the Hollow Beyond Wono and disappeared into the ancient silence beneath the earth.

Behind them, the desert remained still.

Above them, the stars continued their eternal journey.

And somewhere beyond sight, beyond memory, and beyond the boundaries of both worlds, destiny awakened.

to be
continued

A PYRAMID LAKE STORY
ABOVE THE SURFACE

The pine forest burned beneath a scarlet sky. Fire moved through the mountainside with relentless purpose, consuming entire crowns of pine while white smoke drifted between the trunks in slow, ghostlike currents that transformed the familiar landscape into something ancient and unrecognizable. Embers floated through the air like fragments of dying stars, settling briefly upon the forest floor before disappearing beneath layers of ash, and every gust of wind carried another wave of heat across Sam's face as she ran toward the shoreline with her heart pounding against her ribs.

Behind her, another tree surrendered to the blaze.

The crack of splitting wood echoed across the mountains before vanishing beneath the roar of the inferno, yet Sam barely noticed. Her attention remained fixed on the figure emerging through the haze ahead.

For a brief moment, relief washed over her.

Then she saw the way Noah moved.

His steps lacked their usual certainty, and his silhouette seemed to sway against the shifting curtain of smoke as he pushed forward through the burning forest with one arm pressed tightly against his chest. Beyond him, the shoreline had finally appeared, and the small boat remained tied to the dock exactly where they had left it, waiting in defiance of the destruction unfolding around it.

"Noah!"

He lifted his head at the sound of her voice.

Even from a distance she could see exhaustion carved into his features.

The remaining space between them disappeared quickly. Noah stumbled once before recovering his balance, and when he finally reached her side, Sam instinctively grabbed his arm to steady him.

"Do you have it?" she asked.

Noah nodded.

Slowly, he opened his hands.

The miniature Wono rested within his palms.

Its golden surface reflected the surrounding firelight, but another radiance seemed to pulse beneath the metal itself, faint and rhythmic, as though some hidden force had awakened within the artifact and begun answering a call only it could hear. For a moment Sam found herself unable to look away. The miniature pyramid felt strangely alive, not in the ordinary sense of movement or breath, but in the way certain places and objects sometimes carried a presence larger than themselves.

"I do," Noah said quietly. "Let's go."

Together they hurried toward the dock.

Only then did Sam notice the blood.

A dark stain spread across Noah's shoulder, partially hidden beneath soot and ash, and as she reached toward him her stomach tightened with a fear she could not immediately explain. The wound itself appeared small, yet the skin surrounding it had begun to change. Beneath the surface, subtle veins of blue extended outward in delicate branching patterns that resembled mineral deposits trapped within stone, spreading slowly across his shoulder and disappearing beneath his clothing.

"Noah, you're bleeding."

He glanced briefly at the wound before looking away.

"I'll be fine."

The words carried little conviction.

Even Noah seemed uncertain.

"Don't worry about me," he said. "We're almost there."

The boat rocked gently against the dock as they climbed aboard. For several unbearable seconds the engine refused to answer, and Sam felt panic rising within her chest while the fire continued advancing through the forest behind them. Then, at last, the motor responded, and the vessel pulled away from shore, carrying them steadily across the dark waters of Pyramid Lake while the mountainside continued burning beneath the crimson glow of the sky.

The farther they traveled from land, the quieter the world became.

The roar of the inferno gradually diminished. The wind softened. The flames that had seemed enormous only moments earlier began to shrink against the horizon until they resembled a distant line of flickering light beneath an ocean of smoke. Yet the silence that replaced them felt no less unsettling.

Pyramid Lake remained calm.

Its surface reflected the fire and the sky with uncanny stillness, preserving both within its depths as though the lake were observing the destruction without judgment, waiting patiently for events whose meaning extended far beyond the reach of ordinary understanding.

Eventually they reached the deeper waters near the center of the lake.

Noah's strength gave out without warning.

His eyes closed.

His body collapsed heavily against the deck.

Sam caught him before he struck the floorboards and pulled him close, feeling the warmth of his skin beneath her trembling hands. Tears gathered silently in her eyes as she brushed a strand of hair away from his forehead and pressed a gentle kiss against it. Neither of them spoke. There were no words capable of carrying everything she felt in that moment.

Their bodies lay intertwined within the small boat while the waters of Pyramid Lake carried them away from one inferno and toward another.

ABOUT THE AUTHOR

Ricardo L. Ogdon is a writer driven by an enduring fascination with the mysteries that shape human experience. His interests range from mythology, philosophy, and spirituality to history, symbolism, and the relationship between people and the landscapes they inhabit.

The idea for A Pyramid Lake Story emerged from years of curiosity about Pyramid Lake and Lake Tahoe, two places whose beauty and mystery left a lasting impression on him. What began as an exploration of history and folklore gradually evolved into an original mythological universe where ancient traditions, unseen worlds, and destiny intertwine.

A Pyramid Lake Story: Below the Surface is the opening volume of the *A Pyramid Lake Story* series. The journey continues in *A Pyramid Lake Story: Above the Surface.*

To learn more about Ricardo and his projects, visit www.piramidedorada.com

ABOUT THE AUTHOR

PIRAMIDE DORADA
PUBLICATIONS

Where stories awaken.